The Heir of Venus

The Heir of Venus

❨ *A Novel* ❩

Laura Shepperson

alcove
press

Copyright © 2024 by Laura Shepperson

Published in the United States by Alcove Press, an imprint of The Quick Brown Fox & Company LLC.

Alcove Press and its logo are trademarks of The Quick Brown Fox & Company LLC.

Library of Congress Catalog-in-Publication data available upon request.

ISBN (hardcover): 978-1-63910-843-5
ISBN (ebook): 978-1-63910-844-2

Cover design by Katie Ponder

Printed in the United States.

www.alcovepress.com

Alcove Press
34 West 27th St., 10th Floor
New York, NY 10001

First Edition: August 2024

10 9 8 7 6 5 4 3 2 1

For Lucian

The Gods

A **note to the reader:** Although we think of the Greek gods and the Roman gods as the same gods under different identities (or worse, that the Roman gods are copies of the Greek gods), what is more likely is that as Greek culture spread across the Mediterranean, the Greek gods were "mapped" onto local gods who had certain similarities to their Greek counterparts. I have used the Greek names of gods in the sections set in Troy and Carthage, and the Roman names in the sections set in Latium.

Description of God	Greek Name	Roman Name
Goddess of love	Aphrodite	Venus
King of the gods	Zeus	Jupiter/Jove
Queen of the gods	Hera	Juno
God of war	Ares	Mars
God of the forge and Venus's immortal husband	Hephaistos	Vulcan
God of love, sometimes said to be Venus's son	Eros	Cupid
Goddess of agriculture	Demeter	Ceres
Messenger of the gods	Hermes	Mercury

Description of God	Greek Name	Roman Name
God of music	Apollo	Apollo
Goddess of wisdom	Athene	Minerva
Goddess of the hunt	Artemis	Diana
God of the sun	Helios	Sol

Prologue

Beautiful Venus, sometimes known as Aphrodite, made her way into her husband's forge. She was not tired, despite having worked hard that day, influencing the war and protecting her favourites among mortals. Gods did not become tired in the same way that mortals did, just as they did not eat or drink like mortals. But she was weary. Some of the gods said that she had chosen this war; even held her, Venus, personally responsible for the Trojan War. But she was not one for thinking through the consequences of her actions. Assist a man to steal another man's wife, and suddenly there is war among nations? Astonishing.

She watched her husband, Vulcan, as at home among the fires and soot of the forge as she was in a bedchamber. His broken foot forgotten, he sped from bellows to coal, to keep the temperature of the flames high, and once the metal was ready, plucked it out with a pair of tongs too heavy for any mortal to lift, then placed it on the bench, ready to hammer it into subjugation. If he had just once looked at her the way he looked at that piece of metal, she may have been more loyal to him.

He raised a smoke-stained arm to wipe sweat from his forehead, leaving a grimy mark behind, and was suddenly aware of her presence. He carefully placed his hammer in the rest and turned to her.

"Venus, to what do I owe this honour?" he asked, his tone courteous enough. "Have you come to find out what I am making?"

She allowed a smile to curl up her perfectly proportioned lips. "I know what you are making," she said. "It is armour for that nymph Thetis's son, is it not?"

"The warrior, Achilleus," he concurred. "It won't save him, as I'm sure you know, but it will allow him to wreak a lot of destruction before he dies."

She nodded, although she didn't know—not exactly. Achilleus was neither one of her favourites, nor did she bear him a particular grudge. Let others follow his fate.

"It is strange, is it not, that you will make armour for a common nymph's son, while your own wife's boy goes unprotected?" she asked.

Vulcan smirked. "So that's what you're after? Armour for Aeneas. I knew there had to be a reason you were paying me a visit."

"Not for this war," she said quickly. "He's not destined to die in this war. But there are certain events to follow, and I'd feel better knowing that he wore the choicest armour and carried the most impenetrable shield."

Vulcan laughed. "Funny that you are so concerned now, when you never make any effort to see the boy. Tell the truth—this is because Themis has persuaded me to make her son a suit of armour, and you don't want to appear second-rate compared to a water nymph. No particular concern for your boy at all."

Venus was blessed with the sort of face that did not show what she was thinking, so she continued to allow the smile to play at her mouth, confident that her bright blue eyes betrayed none of the anger that threatened to burn her up. *He understands nothing,* she told herself. If he thought that her absence from Aeneas meant a lack of love for her mortal child, he understood nothing. And that was why she had taken care never to conceive a child with him.

She was alone among the Olympian goddesses in having given birth to a mortal child. Of course all of the gods, except perhaps Vulcan, had sired mortal children, but they did not need to show their offspring in their bellies and then suffer the ignominy of everyone knowing they had undergone the pain and misery of labour to push them out, like a common nymph, or worse, a human. It had never occurred to her that cavorting with beautiful Prince Anchises, whom she found looking after his family's flocks on a lonely mountain, would result in a half-human child. Demigods, such beings were called, although their mortal nature meant the name was a half-truth at best; they were always more human than god. But she had given birth to Aeneas, and he was her son.

Bored by her lack of response, Vulcan shrugged. "Of course I will make your son the armour he needs. You are my wife, and I love you, as we all must, goddess of love. I wish you sometimes showed a little more of the emotion you are best known for. I could not make the armour for this war, even for you, because Jupiter has forbidden me to arm the Trojans. But I am under no instructions as to what may take place in the next war."

Venus bowed her head in thanks. She would have kissed her husband, but she feared coming too close to the forge and singeing her dress. Instead, she looked her husband full in the face and treated him to the smile she had never been able to show Anchises, for fear its radiant power would kill a mortal. He raised a hand in response, then returned to his work, shaking his head.

BOOK ONE

LAVINIA

I sing of arms and the man who of old from the coasts of Troy came, an exile of fate, to Italy and the shore of Lavinium; hard driven on land and on the deep by the violence of heaven, for cruel Juno's unforgetful anger, and hard bestead in war also, ere he might found a city and carry his gods into Latium; from whom is the Latin race, the lords of Alba, and the stately city Rome.

—Virgil, *Aeneid, Book One*
(trans. by J. W. Mackail, 1885)

Lavinia, princess of Laurentum, masked the nervous feeling in her stomach with a vaguely interested expression on her face. She held her mother's arm as they stepped carefully through the camp Aeneas had set up on the shore, intended, he had informed them earnestly, to house the Trojans until such time as proper accommodation could be made for them, both within the city of Laurentum and outside its walls, when those Trojans who had originally been farmers were finally able to return to their calling. Her father, King Latinus, had nodded approvingly.

"You see, Lavinia. Aeneas has a proper plan. He's not here to invade Latium. He's here to support us."

Lavinia smiled weakly at her father and tightened her hold on her mother's arm. The campsite was crawling with people, like ants over a heap. She felt her mother, Queen Amata, twitch slightly as she looked around. Why had her father insisted on bringing her mother? There was no need for her to see these Trojan refugees, squatting in the field where Lavinia had once learned to ride a horse. Lavinia felt her jaw tighten and forced herself to relax the muscles. Soon this visit would be over, and she could take her mother back to their palace in Laurentum.

Looking around, she conceded to herself that the camp was well organised, consisting as it did of a series of rings. The outer wooden huts contained shared facilities: schooling, cooking, and washing areas. A group of huts was designated as living areas. Smaller huts housed little families, while larger huts were used as "men's areas" and "women's areas." There were far more men than women, Lavinia noted.

In the centre was a structure that Aeneas had briefly described as the "strategy tent," and the units where weapons were stored. He had taken the inspiration from the Greeks, he'd said, who'd constructed such temporary buildings on the shores of Troy. A shadow had passed over his face when he mentioned Troy, and he had quickly moved on to show them his own hut, perhaps the starkest of all.

Their tour completed, Aeneas took them to one of the small wooden huts that had been designated as a dining hall. Gallantly, he pulled out chairs for Lavinia and her mother. He and her father sat with them. The other men, both the Latin advisers who had accompanied her father, and the Trojan soldiers who flocked about Aeneas, continued to stand. Aeneas's son, a boy of about ten or eleven years, came to join them, and after hugging his father tight, he sat quietly at the end of the table, smiling shyly when Aeneas said, "You remember Ascanius."

A Trojan woman hurried over with a tray of small cakes. Lavinia tasted one carefully. It was good: delicate pastry flavoured with honey and almonds. She motioned to her mother to try one too.

"This is delicious, Prince Aeneas," she said, using the Greek language they both shared, and yet that sounded so different when spoken by a Trojan or Laurentine. "Your servants do well to cook such appetising food in the middle of the field."

"Thank you, Princess, but alas, all our servants remained in Troy. What you see before you are Trojan citizens, proud men and women who have had to work together to survive the tragedy that befell us."

Lavinia cast her eyes down in a show of sympathy. Her mother ignored her cake and spoke to Aeneas.

"Where is your wife, Prince Aeneas? Is she not here to greet us?"

Lavinia could have sworn she saw the Trojans flinch, although no one moved a muscle.

"My wife . . ." Aeneas said slowly. "Alas, she was not able to leave Troy. Only my son, Ascanius, my father, Anchises, and I escaped the burning city. My wife was left behind."

"What was her name?" Amata continued. Now Lavinia was sure she saw Aeneas's hands clench.

Lavinia looked at her father, widening her eyes. Lavinia had carried out the state engagements for her mother for so long that she was not sure her mother would see the signs. A diplomatic hostess would move on quickly, but Amata was not diplomatic, not even on her good days.

"Creusa," Aeneas said. "Princess Creusa. She was a daughter of Priam, King of Troy." He closed his eyes, no doubt remembering his lost wife.

"But Troy fell more than seven years ago," Amata said. "Have there been no other women since then?"

"Mother," Lavinia interjected as her father began to cough helplessly. "Prince Aeneas is our guest here. We do not need to interrogate him."

"We have been swept over the oceans and across the islands for seven years," Aeneas replied, his face stony. "It is not a life that gives itself to marriage. Now, of course, we hope to be settled in a peaceful area, where we can try to resume some of the normality of our lives before the treacherous Greeks invaded our city." He looked not at Amata, but at Latinus as he spoke, and Lavinia's father nodded.

"Of course, Aeneas. Perhaps you could tell me more about the men you have brought with you, and we can consider how

Laurentum can best use their skills." Aeneas nodded. He had not seemed perturbed, and yet Lavinia thought she saw him relax as he moved on to more comfortable topics of conversation. Lavinia, too, breathed a sigh of relief, although she would not completely relax—not yet.

Lavinia's mother picked up her honey cake and bit into it at last. Lavinia saw the small smile playing at the corners of her mouth, and wondered again why her father had thought it necessary to bring her.

☽

Their cakes finished, Aeneas escorted them back to the royal chariot. Lavinia waited for her mother to embark, then used Aeneas's proffered hand to pull herself into her seat. She settled back, but she couldn't help noticing from her vantage point the balding spot in the middle of his curly, grizzled hair. She smiled slightly; on arrival he had told them all that his mother was a goddess whom he named Aphrodite, the goddess of love. He had described her as being one of the most beautiful of the goddesses, but in Latium, they knew her as Venus, and she was usually displayed as being short and squat, her wide hips suitable for the childbirth she served as patron for. Her son was certainly built in her mould.

Lavinia was so busy chuckling to herself, relieved that the visit was almost over and her mother had not suffered one of her outbursts, that she almost missed Aeneas's final words to her father.

"Then if we are agreed, you will tell her soon?"

"Of course," her father muttered in response. "There is no issue here. She is my only daughter, and I want to do it properly."

Aeneas nodded. "I would want the same for my son," he allowed. The two men embraced, her father wincing slightly as he stooped down. Then Aeneas stood back and allowed her father's slaves to assist him into the chariot.

That was tactful, Lavinia thought. He hadn't wanted to show the older man up. But what did her father have to tell her? She wanted to question him as soon as the chariot pulled away, leaving the small Trojan camp dwindling behind them, but she was aware of her mother's presence, and she thought it best to wait.

Her father, however, did not. He turned to his wife and daughter and took a deep breath.

"What did you think of Aeneas?" he asked.

Her mother sniffed. "Not much," she said.

"He had nice manners," Lavinia said gently.

Her mother raised her eyebrows. "Nice manners! Is that what the girls want these days? Let me tell you, when I married your father, it was not because of his nice manners."

"Mother," Lavinia protested. "We do not need to marry Prince Aeneas. We are only granting him sanctuary in Laurentum." She turned to her father for support. "Isn't that so, father?"

He didn't meet her eyes.

A queasy feeling began somewhere deep in Lavinia's stomach. "Father?" she asked uncertainly. Her hands started to tremble. Finally he looked at her. His mouth, so like her own, tightened.

"I have some good news, Lavinia. I have agreed with Prince Aeneas that he will marry you. It is a good alliance. I think he will look after you well."

Lavinia felt as though her words had been ripped away from her. Her mother exploded first. "But what about Prince Turnus?"

There was silence. Latinus looked away, his face red. Lavinia was still struggling to find the words that expressed how she felt.

Her mother repeated herself. "Lavinia is to marry Turnus. It has been agreed since they were infants." As neither her husband nor her daughter said anything, she continued, her voice wavering now. "His mother was one of my dearest friends. Why would your father want you to marry this stranger when you could marry lovely Turnus, whom I once dandled on my own knee? Turnus, whose palace we know as intimately as we know our own? Ah, it is cruel, so cruel of your father, to rip you away from your family like this."

"I have agreed that she will marry Aeneas, and there is nothing more to say," Latinus said.

Finally, Lavinia found her voice. "What if I do not consent?"

Latinus looked upon her. He said nothing. Lavinia refused to be like her mother, repeating herself until he deigned to answer her. She stared back at him defiantly.

"You do not have the choice," he said at last.

Beside her, her mother started wailing. She clutched at Lavinia's arm, and Lavinia resisted the urge to pull away. Why could her father not have told her alone? That was as much a betrayal as the news. For so long she and her father had worked alongside each other, a pair, but now he behaved as though she were any other daughter, and Amata was a normal queen. Lavinia stared out of the chariot at the woodlands that sped past them. So familiar, and yet now so different. Everything was changed.

$$\mathrm{)}$$

When they returned to the palace, maids were waiting for them. Her mother was escorted, still sobbing, to her chambers. Her father looked as though he were about to say something to Lavinia, but she turned and walked off. *Let him manage his own affairs,* she thought. Let him play his own comforting music, share his ideas with his servants, plan his engagements by himself.

As she lay in her warm bed that night, her skin rosy from her bath, she thought briefly of Aeneas, lying on his austere pallet in his wooden hut. He had seemed proud of his frugal provisions, she thought, and instead of pitying him, she felt annoyed. If, as he and her father had agreed, he was to marry her, surely he could have moved into the palace. Let others sleep in the cold. She dismissed her thoughts of him irritably.

For all her mother's wailing, Prince Turnus was not even a consideration to her. They had played together as children, it was true, and a marriage between them would unite their kingdoms, but when she looked at Turnus, she still saw a small boy.

The person who proved impossible to dismiss, whose name was on her lips even as she fell asleep, was someone she had never met. What had happened to Aeneas's first wife, Creusa? Bards sang stories of the sacking of Troy, and she had heard of the murders and massacres of the people behind the Trojan walls when the walls fell. Especially the women. No wonder Aeneas did not wish to think of her demise. But that was no reason why she, Lavinia, should have to marry him. Marriage had not been her father's intention, or so she had thought. She wondered what had changed his mind.

☽

She was still seething when she woke up the next morning, but a messenger brought welcome news: King Metabus of the Volsci had arrived and brought with him his daughter, Camilla. A visit from Camilla never failed to lift Lavinia's spirits.

Lavinia performed her duties to King Metabus perfunctorily, checking that he had drink and comfortable cushions for his chair. Her mother, she noted bitterly, was once again indisposed, and her father simply assumed that his daughter would take over her role. And why not? She had done it for years, hadn't she?

As soon as the two kings were settled, Lavinia gave a deep bow, then swept Camilla away to the little courtyard which had been designated for her own use. She laughed to see her friend looking around eagerly as they entered the courtyard, and motioned to one of her attendants to bring the breads and oils she kept on hand for visitors. Her friend was as slim as a cypress tree, so active she never seemed to finish eating.

Camilla wolfed down the bread, but she couldn't stay silent for long. "We heard the news. You must be devastated."

"Devastated?" Lavinia asked, stretching out her legs in the sunshine.

"Isn't Aeneas so old? And what about poor Turnus? We thought you were going to marry him. My mother had already planned her dress for the wedding."

"I think that was a little premature," Lavinia remarked acidly. Camilla looked surprised, then chastened at her response.

"I'm sorry, Lavinia. I don't mean to make light of it. Just that Turnus was always so devoted to you. He had such big puppy-dog eyes that followed you round the room. Perhaps you could elope? That would be romantic."

In response, Lavinia threw an unripe fig at Camilla. Camilla put her hand up and caught it easily. They both laughed.

"Your training's paying off," Lavinia remarked, changing the topic. It worked; as she had expected, Camilla launched into a long description of her new training programme, designed to increase her speed: running through water so quickly she barely got wet. Lavinia stifled a yawn and changed the topic again as soon as Camilla paused for breath.

All too soon, it was time for Camilla to return home. The two girls embraced as though they were being parted forever, although they knew they would be seeing each other again in a couple of days, when the Volsci and the Laurentines together were to visit the Trojan camp.

When Camilla had left, Lavinia sat by herself in the now dusky courtyard. She remembered the first time her father had shown her the area, remodelled especially for her. The fig trees, which now skimmed the top of her head, had barely reached to her knees. She had exclaimed over the way the sun lit up the small pool of water in the centre, the delicate scalloping on the tiles, and the abundance of cushions scattered about the chairs.

"It is fit for a princess!" she had cried.

"It is fit for a queen," her father corrected her, and she felt her heart swell. He had paused, then said, "Lavinia, you know your mother is sometimes unwell."

She nodded; how could she not know? Her mother's temperament had governed her life. Sometimes she raged at the world, and sometimes she sobbed uncontrollably. Lavinia was never the direct recipient of her anger, and yet she felt that she had to tiptoe around her mother for fear the slightest misdeed might cause her to erupt. There never seemed to be a cause that Lavinia could see, but she had understood from a young age that she was never to let anyone know that her mother was unwell. But the queen's hysterics had been occurring more and more often.

"I think it is best that we allow your mother to rest more," her father said, his hands resting on Lavinia's shoulders. "I thought perhaps you might like to take over some of her duties."

"Yes, please," she had said, her eyes glowing.

"Excellent," he'd replied, patting her shoulders, then dropping his hands, and preparing to leave. He paused at the door and, almost as an afterthought, with an air that Lavinia could only describe as considered nonchalance, he had said, "I know your mother has spoken of you marrying young Turnus of the

Rutuli. Marrying a Latin prince is not the fate I have in mind for you."

He had turned again and left, leaving Lavinia thrilling to think what fate he did have in mind for her.

And so she had begun to assist her father, serving drinks to his guests and acting as the hostess while her mother kept to her own suite of rooms, distracted by her attendants. She took her responsibilities seriously, even though at first her father's guests chuckled to see her small, chubby hands passing around trays of delicacies. Her father discussed matters of state with her and even invited her opinion.

She had been cautious at first, but gradually grew in confidence, able to discern which of the visiting guests was a threat and which offer of trade was worth reviewing further. And the more she pondered her father's words, the clearer his meaning became to her. She was not to marry Turnus, or any other Latin prince, because she was to remain unmarried. She was her father's only child, and now she was to be his heir. Despite the cries of Camilla, Turnus, and her other friends, she'd ceased to play childish games with them and dedicated herself to her father's work. She had always resembled him in the face, and now she chose to dress in similar colours, dark reds and purples as befitted the monarch. She paid close attention to everything he said, sat in the law courts with him, and watched as he bestowed kingly justice or benevolence. One day, these obligations would be hers, and she was desperate to ensure she was worthy of them.

Now, sitting in this courtyard only a few years later, she felt as though she had been betrayed. Her father had never intended her to become his heir. He'd only wanted to wait, to make sure she married the right person. The person he chose. The person he thought had the most to offer—not to her, perhaps not even to Laurentum. The person who had the most to offer Latinus himself.

Lavinia tossed a stone into the little pond and watched it sink to the bottom, where it continued to fracture the light and cause the little pond to appear asymmetrical and imperfect. Truly, she had been a fool. No more. She clenched her fists with determination and resolve.

☽

A few days later, she and her father returned to the Trojan camp. Her mother was not to accompany them; her distress at the forthcoming wedding had brought on what Lavinia had long learned to call a "headache," and her mother would not leave her rooms.

Lavinia wished she could tell her mother that she was determined to ensure there was no wedding, but she knew it would make no difference; once her mother had made up her mind to give herself over to one of her vicious moods, there was no return until she had exhausted herself. Her attendants were chosen with care, both for their sensitivity and, more importantly, their devotion to silence.

Lavinia contemplated refusing to go too, but she saw that her father was accompanied by two of his burliest guards. She didn't think that he would order them to toss her into the chariot like a sack of olives, but she did not wish to risk it. So instead she climbed into the chariot and then fumed, her arms crossed and her brow furrowed. Her father could be in no doubt that she was displeased.

Her father, however, made no acknowledgement of her displeasure, and instead he informed her as they travelled that they were going to meet with the other Latin kings: King Metabus and Evander, king of Pallantium. Together, the kings would decide the best way to carve out land for Aeneas and the Trojans, at least until he inherited Laurentum from Latinus himself. Latinus said nothing about the fourth Latin king, Turnus, the boy-king of the Rutuli. He was an adult, not really a boy-king, but the others insisted on treating him as such, given that his father had died only recently, and he was the first of Lavinia's generation to inherit the throne. She had heard no rumours about his congress as king, and she wondered how he enjoyed it. Not at all, she suspected. Turnus had been a kind boy with a weak chin, more interested in spending time with Camilla and Lavinia than at his lessons, and he would have been woefully unprepared as a result.

She decided that she would not give her father the satisfaction of showing that she was interested in what he was saying, and so she did not ask him whether Turnus had been invited but had chosen not to come, or whether he had not been invited at all. As it was, if Metabus and Evander brought their children, two of her old playmates, Camilla and Evander's son Pallas, would be present.

The fifth member of their childhood group was unlikely to be present, and she was not disappointed by his absence. Many years ago, the northern Etruscans had exiled their king, Mezentius, reportedly for acts of unspeakable cruelty. Lavinia and Camilla had speculated on what such acts might entail, but unsurprisingly, they could never find anyone to tell them. Mezentius had made himself part of Turnus's father's court, more as a poisonous leech than in any useful role, and from then on, where Turnus had gone, Mezentius's son Lausus had followed. Compared to his father, Lausus had been positively pleasant, but Lavinia had always felt as though even his hands were cold and clammy; the warm blood that should pump through his veins was missing somehow.

Lavinia and Latinus were the first to arrive. Aeneas was prompt in greeting them and assisting Lavinia to disembark from the chariot.

"She knows, Aeneas," Latinus said bluntly.

Aeneas took half a step back, and he looked at Lavinia. She looked back awkwardly. Neither of them seemed to know what to say or do. After what seemed like a lifetime, he leaned forward and kissed her on the cheek. Lavinia pulled her cloak more tightly around her body and looked away. Latinus coughed gruffly in the background.

Lavinia sought for something to say, but before she could open her mouth, they were almost knocked off their feet by a horseman who careered through the camp, sending supplies flying as he passed. He rode between Aeneas and Lavinia, causing them both to recoil. Lavinia put her hands up to guard her head. The horseman wheeled about, holding onto the reins with one hand as his horse stretched its hooves to the sky.

"Prince Turnus," her father shouted furiously, "what are you doing?"

"Oh, you will see me now, will you, Latinus? It's *King* Turnus, you know, not Prince. I hear the princess Lavinia is to marry the Trojan invader?"

"Aeneas," her father said. He stepped to Aeneas's side and folded his arms.

"Ah, so at least now you can tell me to my face? It did not occur to you to do so before you announced it to the world, though? Lavinia is betrothed to me."

"I never agreed to that, Turnus," her father said, his tone a warning. A low whinny from behind her made Lavinia look around, and she realised that Turnus had not come alone; she recognised several members of his guard, all fully armed, and

Lausus, who had one hand on his sword while the other held his horse's reins.

"You didn't? I was certainly under that impression, and so was my father before he died. Well, no matter. I do intend to marry Lavinia, and I do not intend to allow the Trojan to take any more of our land—or our women."

"Let's discuss this like civilised men. There's no need for all this spectacle." It was Aeneas, not her father, who answered. Although he spoke Greek as well as any of them, his accent marked him as a foreigner.

Lavinia tried not to stare at him, suddenly interested in this man everyone thought she was to marry. He was grizzled, of course; his face lined and suntanned, not like Turnus's own clear and unmarked face. His arms were strong and muscular, and she imagined those arms wrapped around her or carrying her to their bed. She grimaced; a strong man to carry her to bed was all very well, but she had seen where that led. Childbearing, a lack of power, and the ability to influence only through nagging. Her mother's fate, written in Lavinia's stars.

"The time for discussion is over. You declared war when you landed your ships on my shore," Turnus replied, his voice sounding young and almost high pitched in comparison to Aeneas's.

"Not your shore, Turnus," her father retorted. "The Trojans landed on Laurentine land, not Rutuli."

Turnus grinned, the smile stretching his face in two, a humourless expression that made Lavinia shudder. He looked deranged, so unlike the laughing boy she had grown up with. "When I'm done, it will all be Rutuli land, Latinus, unless you withdraw your support for the foreigner."

Trojans were running towards them now, and Lavinia could see flashes of swords and spears. Unlike Turnus's face, theirs were composed and expressionless, the faces of men who had fought many wars before, and did not expect to settle in comfort without one more fight.

Turnus looked towards the men nervously, then back at Aeneas. "Call your men off," he said hurriedly. "This is a declaration of war. The fighting has not yet started."

Aeneas shook his head. "Do you think that war is fought like a boys' game, with strict rules of conduct? Believe me, you do not want this fight. Let us discuss matters." He held up his hand, and as one, the Trojans slowed down and lowered their weapons. Still, none of them spoke.

"I am not a child," Turnus exploded. "Do not treat me like one. Latinus, I declare war on the Trojans, and I intend to defeat them so soundly that not one man, woman, or child, will be able to settle in this land. If you remain allied with that itinerant and do not allow me to marry Lavinia, as is my right, I will fight Laurentum too. But it does not have to be this way."

He gave his horse a sudden kick in the flanks, so it ceased wheeling and instead cantered out of the camp. The guards followed. Lausus nodded half-heartedly at Lavinia as he passed her.

Lavinia looked down and saw her hands were trembling, although her rational mind was telling her that it was only Turnus, her childhood friend, and she had nothing to fear. She looked to her father and Aeneas and was dismayed to see Aeneas biting his lip, and her father stroking his beard, a gesture he used often when he was concerned. Lavinia stared at her father in consternation, but again, it was not her father who spoke.

"So we are at war again," Aeneas said, and sighed.

BOOK TWO

CREUSA

Aeneas stood discovered in sheen of brilliant light, like a god in face and shoulders; for his mother's self had shed on her son the grace of clustered locks, the radiant light of youth, and the lustre of joyous eyes; as when ivory takes beauty under the artist's hand, or when silver or Parian stone is inlaid in gold.

—Virgil, *Aeneid*, Book One

When her mother was laid in bed with one of her many confinements (Hipponous, she thought, based on her own age at the time, although then again, it may have been Iliona; those two were very close in age), Creusa had slipped out of the royal chambers and into the city to listen to one of the travelling storytellers.

Her actions were not, in themselves, prohibited; the royal children had the run of Troy because no one would hurt them inside the city, and the sturdy walls prevented any intruders from entering unchecked. But she still had the sense of freedom that only comes from being somewhere other than where everyone expects you to be.

The story the bard was telling was one she had never heard before, and judging from the nervous titters and nudges she saw in the crowd, one that contravened what was acceptable in some way. She slipped through the gaps in the crowd, jostled by elbows at first, then less so as people inevitably realised who she was and made space for her.

"The fox," said the storyteller, "had a litter of cubs, as many as six or seven. And the lioness also gave birth, but she only gave birth to one cub. The fox was very proud of her cubs and paraded them around happily. But when she said to the lioness, with pity dripping from her tongue, how sorry she was that the lioness only had one cub, the lioness was not upset. Instead she replied, 'Yes, I have only one cub. But my cub is a lion.'"

Creusa did not understand why so many in the crowd glanced at her nervously; no one could mistake her for a lioness. But as she got older and her resentment grew, so too did her understanding. She never held a grudge against the storyteller or his story, though. In fact, she wished she could find a storyteller to tell her the story again. Every time she asked one, the bard in front of her would look about cautiously and say he did not know the story she was referring to. They would try to distract her with other stories; the slow tortoise who beat the speedy hare at a race was always considered suitable, and sometimes the fox who could not reach the grapes, so told everyone they were sour, was a good choice, as it allowed the teller to act out the fox's motions, very amusing for a childish audience.

Her resentment was reserved for her parents. She hated being one of eighteen children, never seeing her mother without half a dozen younger siblings clamouring for her attention. As she grew older still, she begrudged her father the most. She overheard rumours, mostly told by the slaves who attended them at court, or by the stable hands in the legendary Trojan stables, and understood that all the shadow children who hovered on the edges of the royal court, joining the king's guard if they were boys, were also her half siblings. She found out that her father was famed for having no fewer than fifty children. And yet she did not believe he even knew her name—or any of his children's names other than his beloved Hektor, her oldest brother.

Creusa held that story of the lioness close inside her heart, a little secret she clutched to her chest and examined from time to time, and she swore to herself that when she married, she would not have many children—not six or seven, like the fox; not eighteen, like her mother; and certainly not fifty, like her father. She would have one child, and he would be a lion.

☽

Aeneas had first arrived in Troy when he and Creusa were both twelve years old. She was fascinated by him: a royal child like herself, and yet one whose family could not be more different to her own. His father clearly doted upon him. No siblings, no vying for attention. Anchises never looked at Aeneas with that searching look she saw her father use when he saw her, trying to remember which of his many children she was. *"Creusa,"* she wanted to shout. *"I am Creusa. The forgettable one,"* she would add, honest even in her own imagination. Not Cassandra, who is mad. Not Polyxena, whom everyone adores. Not one of the boys, strong Hektor or funny Polydorus or capable Helenus. Creusa, who is just there. Creusa who will one day presumably be married to a foreign king, to create a fortunate alliance for Troy. And for one day only there will be much rejoicing, and the name *Creusa* will be on everyone's lips.

Anchises was her father's cousin, and yet he had not, as her father had, sired enough children to repopulate Troy single-handedly. He'd had another son, Lyrus, who had died at the same time as his wife, Eriopis, and that was partly why he and Aeneas had come to Troy, for a change of scenery away from their home in Dardania, where Anchises's elderly father remained on the throne.

This fascinated all of them; their own father seemed elderly enough, but Anchises's father, Capys, was Priam's uncle, so how aged and decrepit must he be? Anchises, too, was not a young man, although he was less prone than Priam to complain about his backaches and ungrateful children. Even Creusa

knew, though, that Anchises was not in Troy because he found
Dardania too upsetting after his wife's and child's deaths, but
because of the rumours that the Hellenes, those nations to the
west of Troy, were spoiling for a fight, and they saw Troy, with
its vast coffers and peaceful people, as a suitable target. To have
Anchises in Troy was a sign that not only Troy's soldiers, but also
Dardania's, could be rallied quickly against any invaders.

In the meantime, Aeneas, along with his father, was a guest
in their court. Creusa studied him intently. He had dark hair,
the colour of driftwood, and dark eyes that lit up when he was
attentive. He was on the short side, and her oldest brother, Hektor,
towered over him. He was stocky, though, and determined. He'd
thrown himself into a couple of fights when he'd first arrived
in Troy, and soon gained the reputation, among the younger boys
at least, for being a brave fighter, someone who didn't cow easily,
and on that basis, a good fellow and one to be accepted.

The girls did not warm as quickly; he was not unattractive,
but he would certainly never be described as a beautiful man,
nor did he have the kind of body that a sculptor would be looking to carve in stone, with his stocky arms and his creased brow.
The girls decided he was too young for them to pay any attention
to, at twelve—a child rather than a man—and they returned to
cataloguing the princes of other courts.

Creusa continued to watch Aeneas.

A few disgruntled arguments made it obvious to everyone
very quickly that Anchises and Priam could not bear to be in
very close contact, so Anchises and Aeneas were provided with
their own home. But Aeneas joined Priam's children for lessons
at the palace, and he trained with the princes too.

Creusa listened to him speaking confidently from the other
side of their classroom, and she started spending her spare time

at the training grounds, perched, with her lunch to eat, on a wall nearby. Not for the first time, Creusa wished that her family did not swarm about her like bees, but that she might be able to fly freely and speak with whomever she wanted without it becoming the subject of discussion and interrogation. Still, although none of her family had ever noticed, Creusa was determined in her own quiet way, and when she wanted something, she would not let anyone stop her from getting it. She wanted to know for herself what it was like to be an only child who could command someone's full attention. How many mountains could she scale if someone looked at her as though she were the only person in the world? She resolved to find an excuse to speak with Prince Aeneas.

$$\mathbb{D}$$

Creusa hadn't been close enough to hear what the big boys said, but she saw that they taunted him with words, not fists—then ran off. One of the boys was her brother Deiphobus; the other she did not know, although, as was so often drummed into her, he might be her brother all the same.

Aeneas remained where the boys left him, his face red and his hands balled into fists. His lip quivered slightly, although he did not cry.

He looked up as she walked towards him, and with some surprise, she realised he was a little shorter than she was. He had never seemed small, from a distance, and it didn't bother her in the slightest.

"What do you want?" he asked ungraciously. She said nothing. "Are you here to taunt me and laugh at me too? Because I won't have it. Not even from a girl."

"Why are they taunting you?" she asked, her curiosity piqued. "Is it because you are small?"

"I am not small," he thundered, and she laughed. He glared, then a glimmer of a smile twitched at his mouth. "If you must know, they are taunting me because I don't have a mother—here in Troy, I mean."

She stepped closer to him, close enough to smell his musky skin. "I am sorry, Prince Aeneas. It was unkind of my brother to mock you because your mother is dead. I will tell my mother, and she will put a stop to it."

"My mother is not dead," he retorted loudly, and she stepped back again.

"My father said—"

"My mother is the goddess Aphrodite. She will smite your brother for his cruel words."

Creusa nodded cautiously. She did not know what else to say. No one had mentioned Aeneas being the son of a goddess before. She worshipped the gods, including Aphrodite, faithfully, but she had never met anyone who claimed to be descended from a god before, much less to have been birthed from one. But clearly Aeneas believed what he was saying with his whole heart.

"Is she as beautiful as they say?" she ventured at last.

"Of course," Aeneas replied, his chest puffed out with pride. "More so, even. Dazzling. Mere mortals cannot look upon her."

"Then how did . . .?" Creusa paused. She had assisted her mother in many of her confinements, but she had never had to speak directly of the act that created them before. Fortunately, Aeneas understood her meaning.

"She saw my father tending sheep one day and thought he was so handsome, she couldn't resist being close to him. She appeared to my father in disguise, dressed as a Phrygian princess, but he always knew she was a goddess. He didn't realise she was Aphrodite, though, until she told him she was with child. With me."

Anyone other than Creusa might have sniggered by now, looking at Aeneas's own blunt nose and heavy brow. But Creusa had long since set in her mind that Aeneas was by far the most handsome boy she had ever met, and she just nodded seriously.

"Why did my father tell us that your mother was dead?" she asked. "Was he jealous?"

"I don't know," Aeneas replied, frowning. "I expect it is more likely that he thought my father's wife was my mother. She died when I was five. She was kind to me, but she was not my mother."

Creusa nodded, her studious face concealing the flicker of excitement that was sparking inside her. She had thought Aeneas was interesting before, but now she knew he was the son of a goddess.

"Do you ever see your mother?" she asked.

"Sometimes, in visions," Aeneas said. "She's not in disguise, but she can't reveal herself fully, even to me, in case she burns me up. But she watches me, she knows what I've been doing, she gives me guidance. Just like any mother."

Creusa thought of Hekuba, currently with child again and unable to see what any of her children were doing at present, as her ankles had swollen badly this time, and the doctor had ordered bed rest. She wondered what guidance Hekuba would give her if she could see her right now. Feeling a pang of something she couldn't identify, she stepped a little closer to Aeneas again.

"Will she take you to live on Olympus one day when your time on earth is done?"

"Oh no," Aeneas answered, with the easy self-assurance she had already started to love about him. "I asked when I was younger, and she said no, and I cried, but then she explained that the Fates had a different plan for me. I am to found"—and for the first time he looked sheepish—"a new city, far from here. She calls it the new Troy, and it is going to last forever."

"Isn't Troy going to last forever?" Creusa asked, and they both stared at each other in horror as the implications of Aphrodite's prophecy dawned upon them.

☽

Creusa didn't know when she first became aware of her dead brother, the one who should have followed Hektor. She seemed to have always been aware that she should have had one more brother, in the same way that she knew that her father was the king and Troy was the wealthiest nation in the world. His name was Paris, and her mother prayed to the gods to keep him safe in Elysium every night. Her father never mentioned him. So she was shocked when she overheard two of the maids gossiping about him as they changed the bed linen in the room she shared with her sister Cassandra, unaware that Creusa was crouched under a cabinet telling herself the stories she had heard from the various bards.

"It was wicked what they did to that baby, the king and queen. Their own child too." A new maid, one Creusa hadn't heard before, spoke first.

"Aye, but if they hadn't, we might all be dead. That's what the priest said, you know. Troy would be doomed if the baby didn't die." She recognised the second voice, Arachne, an older woman who had served the family for many years. She tolerated the children, not seeking them out for attention, but never snitching to their mother about them either.

"But he was just a baby! You couldn't have done it, could you? Look me in the eyes and tell me you could have had your own baby killed just because of some prophecy? Poor little baby Paris. No wonder she prays all the time—" The woman broke off, and Creusa felt her eyes upon her.

"Please don't say anything, little miss," she begged, but Creusa jumped to her feet and ran for the door.

She never said anything about the gossipy maid, but either Arachne did, or the maid had been just as indiscreet in front of other people, because the next time Creusa saw the women changing the sheets, a different maid accompanied Arachne, and she never saw the younger maid again.

Creusa also kept quiet about the secret the maid had revealed. It broke her heart, thinking of the little baby who had been put to death because of something a priest said. It made her miserable to realise her mother kept returning again and again in her mind to the little boy who hadn't lived, while ignoring so many children who had.

Her younger sister Cassandra was not so tactful. She had always had a dramatic bent, but when she reached puberty, she had claimed that the god Apollo had spat in her mouth and given her the gift of prophecy. Creusa always tried to give her brothers and sisters the benefit of the doubt, but it was hard to fathom a god behaving in such an undignified manner. Cassandra would have been more likely to be believed, Creusa thought, if she had claimed the god raped her.

At first Cassandra remained in the confines of the palace. She was moved into her own room, and Creusa missed her company but was quietly relieved when she heard her ranting and raging at night from across the hallway.

One bright sunny morning, though, when Priam was visiting the children in the classroom to inspect their progress, Cassandra burst through the doors and pointed her finger at her father.

"Murderer! You have murdered all of Troy, you and my mother. Cowards! You should have checked yourself that the baby was dead. Now all your suffering will be for nothing because he will return and bring Troy's downfall with him!"

Priam's face turned white with anger. Creusa had never seen her father so furious, and she cowered away. Priam turned and marched out, and a few moments later the guards poured into the room. Cassandra was dragged away, one guard seizing her under her armpits, another pulling her by her hair. She screamed as she left, "This is what will happen to you, Father! You, too, will be dragged to your death!" Her shouts became fainter the farther away the guards pulled her.

"What was *that* all about?" Helenus, Creusa's brother, asked. None of the siblings knew except for Creusa, but she didn't tell them. She felt sick to her stomach and wished they would all stop talking about it, as though it had been the latest performance at the theatre.

Her father did not have Cassandra killed, at least. She was moved to the Temple of Apollo to serve as a priestess for the god she claimed to have defiled her. Creusa could not decide whether her father had been merciful or not.

$$☽$$

Nothing was ever said, but gradually, it became accepted that Creusa and Aeneas were usually to be found together. She would sit quietly and watch as he tussled with the other boys or attended the many fighting practices that Priam had instigated. It gave her a strange sense of pride to watch him hold his own, despite being one of the smaller boys. Aeneas, too, came to accept her as his silent shadow, and she was pleased to see him look about and then nod when she arrived. He never mistook one of her many sisters for her, and he showed no interest in any of them either.

She was sitting on her usual wall, her ignored embroidery in her lap, watching the boys practise sword fighting. It was a taught practice, not a free-for-all, so the boys had been lined up by an elderly tutor who, it was rumoured, had fought beside Priam when the Greek Herakles had besieged Troy long before they were born.

Each boy held a wooden sword and took turns stepping forward to try to best his opponent. The swords thudded as they knocked against each other, a very different sound to the scrape of metal she would have expected from a real duel. To Creusa's disappointment, Aeneas was the farthest away from her, fighting against Helenus. She looked up and smiled as Cassandra came and sat down next to her. It was the first time she had seen her sister since her outburst in the schoolroom.

"Cassandra, I haven't seen you in a while. How are you?"

Cassandra pushed her crown of laurel leaves back on her forehead and nodded at her sister. Her eyes were bright and bloodshot, and she had scratches on her hand. She was thinner than Creusa remembered, her collarbones protruding sharply from the top of her chiton. Since becoming a priestess of Apollo, she had slept in the temple rather than the palace. Creusa did not think the change suited her.

"I come bearing a warning, Creusa, a warning about that boy Aeneas, although you will not listen and you will not believe me." Cassandra shuffled on the wall, her fingers twitching and her feet tapping. Creusa did not think Cassandra was even aware of the motions. At least her voice was quiet enough that none of the training boys would overhear her.

"I will listen," Creusa said. It was hard for a daughter of Priam to stand out, she thought. Cassandra had chosen her own path to do so.

Cassandra blinked, surprised, before launching into her prophecy.

"You must stay away from him. That boy, that Aeneas, he will be the death of you, Creusa. I have seen it. You will burn, burn, burn, and he will leave you behind. He will take your child, and he will leave you behind." She rose to her feet, paused, then jumped off the wall, lifting her arms in the air. Creusa cringed, seeing boys start to glance over at them.

"Sit down, Cassandra," she muttered. "I don't want Aeneas to hear this."

"He cannot save you both," her sister continued. "He cannot save you all. Troy is going to fall, and Aeneas is going to run like a little coward, like the worm that he is. He has room for his father, and he has room for his son, but he has no room for you, no room for Creusa, and you will fall with Troy, and you will burn, burn, burn."

Her laurel crown fell from her forehead as she brushed her unruly curls back. Sweat poured down her cheeks. Creusa looked up at the blue sky with the odd cloud drifting across, the pleasant day completely at odds with her sister's wild words. Cassandra's skin was reddening now, and Creusa wondered whether her sister could see those flames, whether she was feeling the burn on her pale skin even while she spoke.

In the distance Creusa could hear girls laughing, and she could see her brothers jostling and teasing one another. The line of would-be soldiers was starting to disintegrate, intrigued by wild-haired Cassandra, and the tutor issued a sharp admonishment to recall them. In the distance, their city was embraced by its strong walls. It seemed utterly impossible that the things Cassandra spoke of could come to pass. Troy, fall? She might as well say that the sky was going to fall in.

But then Creusa looked at the wooden swords the boys were using for training, sharper than they had been a week ago, and she thought how Priam had invited Anchises to stay with them and was even now visiting the Amazonian queen on a state visit intended to strengthen the bonds between their nations. She thought of the prophecy of Aeneas's mother, Aphrodite: the new Troy that he was going to found.

"See?" Cassandra said as she slumped back down onto the wall. "You don't believe me. I knew it."

"Oh no," Creusa said, using her hand to shield her gaze from the sun as she looked at Aeneas, the only one of the boys whose practice had been uninterrupted by her sister's performance. He continued to wield his sword, practising positions, even while his opponent gawked at Cassandra. "I do believe you, Cassandra. I just don't care."

She felt light, as though she could rise off the wall and fly like a bird. Until that point, she hadn't dared think that Aeneas, Prince Aeneas, the son of Aphrodite, might ever be more than her fond cousin. But Cassandra had said they would have a child together. She had implied that she, Creusa, might actually marry Aeneas. She knew what the airy feeling was, she thought. It was hope.

BOOK THREE

LAVINIA

Many wooed her from wide Latium and all Ausonia. Fairest and foremost of all is Turnus, of long and lordly ancestry; but boding signs from heaven, many and terrible, bar the way.

—Virgil, *Aeneid, Book Seven*

With Turnus gone, Aeneas looked to the Trojans. His face was serious and his tone, stern. "Butes, Ilioneus, come with me. King Latinus, will you join us? We have much to plan."

Lavinia's father looked towards her, but she sharply turned her head, so he left without her. Lavinia tried and failed to understand what she had just seen. Turnus was king only because his father had died; were it not for that unfortunate event, he would still be a prince, barely any older than her. How could he have the power to plunge them all into conflict? Surely Aeneas's serious demeanour was premature, an overreaction. He was used to dealing with soldiers, and he had mistaken Turnus for one. No doubt her father would speak to Turnus, and it would all be resolved peacefully. There would be no war. Was this how Creusa had felt? she thought suddenly, when the Greeks had first threatened to come to Troy? But that had been a real war, fought between legendary warriors, sons of gods. Not boys she had seen cry when they fell from their pony.

She wondered what she should do next, left alone to her own devices. It was not a feeling she was used to; at home there were so many tasks that needed to be done to keep the palace running smoothly. She didn't have to wait long, though, before the Volsci delegation arrived. She directed Camilla's father to Aeneas's strategy tent. Then she turned to her friend. When they had embraced once more, she settled down on a grassy hillock to update Camilla. She wished she had not; the act of describing

43

Turnus's declaration to another person seemed to waft away the veils of denial she had tried to put up.

"I barely recognised Turnus," she mused. "Today he was so angry, so aggressive. When we were young, he was a sweet little boy."

Camilla nodded. "Your little puppy dog. Have you seen Pallas or Lausus?" she asked, referring to the other princes who had made up their little group.

Lavinia frowned. "King Evander and Pallas are expected, but they are not here yet. But Lausus . . ." She tailed off.

Camilla nodded. "His father was close to Turnus's father, wasn't he?" The two girls stared at each other, realising what this meant.

"We will be at war, and we aren't even on the same side," Lavinia said softly. She reached to Camilla, and they squeezed hands. Lavinia felt a chill as she thought what would happen to her old playmates if the war was not brought to a halt quickly.

"Do you think we should be worried about Turnus?" Camilla asked. "As his friends?"

Lavinia paused. She wanted to give a different answer but found she could not. "I am," she said. "That kind of bellicosity isn't good for anyone."

They sat in silence for a while. Lavinia was interrupted in her reverie by a shadow looming over her and a voice saying, "Your Highness, your father wishes to speak to you."

"Then he can come and find me," she snapped, "rather than sending his lackey to do the job."

"I do not think I am your father's lackey," the voice said, amused, and she looked up in horror to see Aeneas himself standing over her.

She scrambled up, hating that she was on the defensive. "Where is my father?" she asked, keeping her words and tone curt to disguise her mortification.

"He is in my strategy tent," Aeneas replied. He offered her his arm, but she pretended not to see it, and they walked to the tent in silence.

"Lavinia," her father greeted her as they arrived at the tent. Aeneas squeezed himself into the small space left behind her.

"I need to tell you something, Lavinia," her father said. "You understand that Turnus has declared war on the Trojans, and by extension on Laurentum? We have decided that, as a show of our loyalty to Prince Aeneas, you and I will remain in this camp until the matter is resolved."

Lavinia gaped at her father.

"That is all," he said impatiently, and waved his hand.

"Father, could we have a word in private?" she asked.

Her father looked about him, but although at their palace such a request would have been enough to have the various advisers standing and bowing, ready to leave at his nod, here no one moved. Lavinia narrowed her eyes. She would not let the Trojans or the Latins witness a brawling match between Lavinia and Latinus.

She gritted her teeth, then remembered his choice of words.

"Just you and I?" she asked.

"Your friend, Princess Camilla, is to remain as well, to attend you," he said. Out of the corner of her eye, she saw Camilla's father, a large, stern man of whom she had always been a little frightened, nod. But Camilla was not her concern.

"What about Mother?" Unthinkable that her mother would be required to remain here, she thought. Impossible that they would be able to keep her frequent hysterical outbursts quiet in the enclosed atmosphere of a war camp.

Her father had clearly had the same thought, because he looked closely at her. "I think at your mother's age, it is best that she remains at the palace."

That was something at least, Lavinia thought. But as for the rest of it . . . She had been outmanoeuvred, she thought, and she only had herself to blame. Her pride and her stubbornness. The decision had been made without her present. She needed to make sure her absence could never be used against her again. And that meant staying here, in the camp, the very decision she had been left out of. The irony was not lost on her.

"Very well," she said to her father. "If you think it is best we remain, so be it."

Her father looked shocked—and suspicious—but she smiled sweetly. He glanced at the Trojans, and she knew that he, too, wanted to avoid a family argument in public, so he nodded.

"Thank you for understanding, Lavinia."

"Shall I show you to your quarters, Your Highness?" Aeneas asked from behind her, his voice clear and polite despite his strong accent.

"I'm sure I can find them," Lavinia said, and strode past him out of the tent.

☽

When Lavinia left the tent, she was approached by a Trojan woman.

"Your Highness," the woman said, nodding to her.

Lavinia dipped her head politely in return and continued walking, but the woman caught her arm. "Madam, I need to explain to you your place in the roster."

Lavinia thought she must have misunderstood.

"My place in the roster? Whatever do you mean?"

"The cleaning roster, Your Highness."

Lavinia raised her eyebrows so high that they were in danger of shooting off her head. "I think you have mistaken me for someone else."

"Madam, it is Aeneas's orders. Everyone must take a turn. A clean camp keeps disease at bay."

"We will see about that," Lavinia muttered, and she turned and marched straight back into the tent.

"Prince Aeneas, please tell your servants that I am not here to clean for them." She could see by the look on his face that he knew exactly what she was talking about.

"Princess Lavinia, I have told you before, we do not have servants in our camp. Only Trojan citizens, and now Latin citizens, live here, and we must all take our turn at the chores."

"Must we? Do you wash dishes and clean clothes, then?" His skin reddened, and he rubbed at his neck with one finger nervously. "I didn't think so. Then why should I?"

"I have other duties," he protested. But Lavinia turned on one foot and left the tent again.

Behind her, she could hear her father remonstrating with Aeneas, and the words "She is a princess" floated back to her. The Trojan woman, who had been loitering outside, took a step in Lavinia's direction, but Lavinia flung up one hand, and the woman fled.

☽

Lavinia began to regret her decision over the next few days. She had nothing to do. At first she attended strategy meetings with Aeneas and her father, from which she learned that the war hinged on the support of King Evander. He was still travelling to the Trojan camp, and until Aeneas and Latinus knew his intentions, they were reluctant to commence hostilities. Instead, they invited Turnus to negotiate with them, to redraw the boundary lines so the Trojans would not encroach on Rutuli land. Despite her pleas, Lavinia was not allowed to attend those meetings.

"If you are taken hostage, it will put us in the worst position of all," Aeneas said severely. "And besides, you will distract Turnus, and it is hard enough to keep his attention as it is."

Lavinia looked to her father, but he said nothing. *Isn't he the king?* she thought. *Why is Aeneas taking charge?* But she never had the chance to speak to her father alone in order to find out.

When Latinus and Aeneas left to see Turnus, the camp felt unsettled. No one could predict the outcome of the negotiations, and it was as though a god or goddess had descended from above and dropped a giant fishing net over everyone. They were suspended in motion, unable to act or move or even think.

Lavinia didn't even have Camilla to keep her company. Camilla's father had ridden away to muster his own troops, and she began to wonder if Camilla had gone with him. Lavinia had hoped that she could persuade Camilla to share the small cabin she had found, after much searching, with her own bags and clothes inside. She should have taken Aeneas up on his offer of assistance, her stubbornness betraying her once more.

The cabin was hers alone, and she had to lie awake at night, listening to the noises outside and not feeling entirely safe despite the wooden walls. She had no idea where Camilla slept. Perhaps even now Camilla was safe in her own palace, sleeping on a proper bed, with her maids assisting her in washing and dressing her hair befittingly. But it wasn't like Camilla to leave without saying goodbye.

Eventually, Lavinia found her friend, practising her sword work in a small copse by herself. Lavinia stayed back and watched, Camilla's movements easy yet precise, every step deliberate and graceful. The muscles in her arms and thighs rippled as she pointed her sword, and yet she never looked tense or nervous. She could have been dancing, Lavinia thought. And the metaphor felt right too, because dancing, like fighting, was an activity that required a partner. Alone, Camilla's movements were sterile and unchallenged.

When Lavinia saw Camilla pause to wipe her brow and tighten the ribbon that held back her hair, she stepped forward. She didn't want to be caught spying on her friend, like a common knave. Camilla saw her and waved.

"Have you been avoiding me?" Lavinia called. "I haven't seen you in days."

Camilla's eyebrows rose. "Avoiding you? Lavinia, that's very melodramatic of you. Why would I be avoiding you?" And she went back to practising her moves with such studied elegance that Lavinia knew she was hiding something. Still, she purposefully sat down on the grass beside the copse, and after a few more feints, Camilla gave up and came to sit beside her. Neither of them spoke for a while.

Camilla caved first. "Do you have any news on the war effort?"

Lavinia shook her head. "No. The fighting hasn't started in earnest. No one has died yet." And she sucked in her breath at the sound of that word *yet* and what it implied.

"I envy them, the soldiers," Camilla said, her thoughts clearly on another path. "At least they are able to defend themselves and their country. We can only wait."

"I suppose," Lavinia said. She pulled a strand of grass out of the earth beside her and inspected its stem. She wanted to be queen, but she had no desire to lead an army. Leave the fighting to those who cared the most about it.

"I mean, look at Turnus," Camilla said, sneaking a sideways glance at Lavinia.

Lavinia felt her face start to heat up.

"He always seemed so . . . useless before now. Making cow eyes at you and trying to compose his songs."

"Turnus composed songs?" Lavinia was surprised despite herself. "I never knew."

Camilla sighed loudly. "It was terrible. They were always about you, and he could never get the rhythm right. I had to pretend to enjoy them, but then also not encourage him so much that he would make a fool of himself by reading them to you. Anyway," she said, clearly not interested in discussing Turnus's song-writing prowess, "now he is focused on the war effort, and he is actually interesting for a change. So dynamic, so brave. So strong."

"You really think so? I thought he had lost his mind. I've never seen him so aggressive or antagonistic. Such foolish bravado. I've seen toddlers with more decorum."

"I think we will have to agree to differ," Camilla said sadly.

A small cough interrupted them. They looked up to see Aeneas. Both of them scrambled to their feet, and Lavinia tried to brush out the leaves that seemed to be forever tangling themselves up in her hair.

"Princesses," Aeneas greeted them. "Please, no need to move on my account. We have a small interlude in our discussions, and I thought that I would come and spend some time with you both."

"That is most kind of you, sir," Lavinia replied automatically. She couldn't meet Camilla's eyes. At first she wondered what was wrong with her; hadn't she met hundreds of dignitaries over the years with her father? Foreign princes; emirs; high priests; demigods; and, she suspected, even gods in disguise. Why did this interaction make her feel disorientated, dizzy almost? Was it the incongruity of the setting? Or perhaps it was the fact that she was supposed to marry Aeneas. She still could not comprehend it.

"I wanted to talk to you myself, Princess Lavinia, about our forthcoming nuptials," Aeneas said, his tone formal and his back stiff.

"Would you like me to leave?" Camilla asked, looking at Lavinia, not Aeneas.

"I don't think that would be appropriate," Lavinia said hastily, leaving Aeneas no choice but to nod.

"All I wished to say," he told her quickly, "was that, in the circumstances, I have informed your father that we should continue to be affianced until an appropriate time. War is all-consuming, and it makes travel dangerous. You deserve a proper wedding, one fit for the queen of the realm, with guests arriving from near and far."

Lavinia nodded. She was certainly in no desire to hurry the wedding along.

Aeneas looked about him, ill at ease now that his message had been delivered.

"Are you looking forward to the wedding?" he asked. "Weddings are a most special time for Latin girls, I hear?"

Lavinia swallowed, unsure how to answer the question.

Camilla came to her aid. "Lavinia has not had long to accustom herself to the idea of this particular wedding. Give her time."

Aeneas nodded. "Perhaps you would be a bridesmaid, Princess Camilla? It is not a Trojan tradition, but I understand that having young women accompany the bride is an important ritual in Latin culture."

"Indeed, but the bride normally asks her own attendants," Camilla responded. Her tone was mild, but Aeneas accepted it as the rebuke it was intended to be. He nodded.

"I will leave you young ladies to enjoy your afternoon," he said, and walked away. Lavinia and Camilla exchanged a glance as they waited for him to move out of earshot. The balding patch on his head glistened in the sunlight.

Camilla made a face. "Oh, Lavinia, I am so sorry for you. Even the old poetry-singing Turnus was preferable to him."

Lavinia nodded miserably. Aeneas seemed to be so stiff and formal. So *old*. What would they ever have to talk about?

"And the new Turnus is a vast improvement," Camilla continued. "I had better return to my training, all the same," she added, leaving Lavinia feeling more alone than ever.

They embraced, and Lavinia walked away. It wasn't until later that night that she remembered Camilla had not been present the day Turnus arrived in the camp to declare war.

☽

Lavinia took to walking down by the beach during the day. She knew that once the fighting commenced, she would be refused permission to stray this far alone, so she made the most of the opportunity and enjoyed the tang of salt in the air and the feel of her long, dark curls blowing about her face in the wind. Strange, she thought, how she had so much more freedom now, when she was effectively a prisoner in this camp.

At the palace there had always been nurses, then tutors, then advisors to her father, all eager to tell her what to do and keep her confined. Here, no one even noticed her. The tide was out, and small gentle waves lapped at the sands.

Her thoughts were interrupted by a scuffle. The Trojans' tall ships were docked on the shore, their sails fluttering gently in the breeze. She could see several guards clustered around a small body curled up on the beach as though he had washed in with the tide. It was an interesting distraction from her own problems, and she decided to investigate.

"What have you there?" she called out to the guard who seemed to be in charge, who was currently poking the boy with the hilt of his sword, to see if he would move. The man, a Trojan, didn't hear her, or at least pretended not to. She sighed and spoke louder.

"I said, 'What have you there?' Oh!" she exclaimed, startled, because the figure sat up, and she realised it wasn't a boy at all. It was a woman, several years older than Lavinia, with long reddish hair cascading over her shoulders, tanned skin, and bright eyes the colour of the leafy forest behind them, tempered with glimpses of brownish bark. She was beautiful, Lavinia thought with a pang, something no one other than her father had ever called Lavinia.

"Let her be," she said sharply to the guard, and this time he listened and ceased his prodding. Once left to herself, the woman was able to bring her knees up to her chest, then stand up in a graceful move. She remained standing despite her pale face and a slight sway to her stance. Her clothes, shabby and designed to withstand the elements, contradicted her natural elegance, which would have had her at home in any palace across the land. She pulled a shawl tightly around her body and bowed slightly to Lavinia. The sea wind whipped her hair about her face.

"What is your name?" Lavinia asked.

The woman answered her in Greek that was at least passable. "I am a traveller, madam, a storyteller."

"Indeed." Lavinia nodded. "But I asked for your name."

The woman paused. "Anna."

It meant nothing to Lavinia. It wasn't even a name she had come across, although since the Trojans had arrived, she was learning new names all the time.

"I have never heard of a woman storyteller," she said.

The woman shrugged. "I have journeyed far and have many stories to tell. Why should it matter that I am not a man?"

"I suppose not," Lavinia said, surprised. She was intrigued; all the storytellers she had ever listened to had been men. Would the story be different, told by a woman? There was only one way to find out.

"Come with me," she said. "I would like to hear your stories. I can pay," she added a little awkwardly as the woman made no effort to move. Of course, Lavinia herself must look quite a sight, away from the palace and the maids who normally groomed her, with sea salt in her hair.

The woman nodded and picked up her bag. The guards glanced at one another and then at Lavinia, who waved her hand at them in dismissal. They departed, although one glanced back over his shoulder, as though he were reconsidering. Lavinia tossed her head. "We are only visiting this camp," she said. "Soon we will return to the palace, and I will find space for you in my suite."

"I have slept in palaces, and I have slept under the stars," the woman said. "One cannot be too fastidious in my line of work. Are you the queen?"

Lavinia flushed, but she prided herself on her honesty, so she said, "No, I am the Princess Lavinia. My mother, Amata, is the queen, and my father, Latinus, is the king. I work by his side," she added, although she did not know whether that was true any longer, and besides, she did not know why she cared so much that a travelling storyteller should understand that she was more than just a princess.

Anna allowed herself to be pulled along by Lavinia, and they continued past the sparse gorse bushes, making their way to Lavinia's small cabin. Lavinia was relieved to see the other woman pull bedding out of her bag and make a bed up on one side of the room; at least she wouldn't be alone that night, as the wolves howled and soldiers gathered to march against them.

When Anna had finished setting up her bedding, she pushed aside her himation and began to rewrap the cloths that covered her lower arms and hands. Lavinia tried not to gape at the scarred and misshapen hands beneath the cloths, especially as Anna saw

Lavinia watching her, and pushed her hands away beneath her skirts in response.

☽

The following morning, Lavinia barely had time to dress, shake the leaves from her hair, and wipe away the grass that seemed overnight to find its own way into her hut, when the Trojan messenger, Ilioneus, came calling for her. She wished that she'd had time to eat some breakfast, but then she supposed that her father required her assistance, and no doubt there would be food to eat with his guests—better food, even, than anything that might be served to common soldiers and women alike. She waved goodbye to Anna and told her to find the mess tent where she could get her own breakfast.

Lavinia followed Ilioneus through the camp, ducking under ropes and jumping over rocks to keep up, although she had to admit that Aeneas kept a tidy camp. He must have had lots of practice at it, she supposed, in the seven years he had been travelling since leaving Troy. She wondered again about Creusa, the wife Aeneas had left behind in Troy, and what she might have thought to know her husband was betrothed to another. Of course, she was a princess too, she thought. She had probably had as much say in her marriage as Lavinia had now.

Marry Turnus, marry Aeneas, marry . . . this log that someone has hung some washing on, she thought, nimbly skirting around a bedsheet. It was all the same to her.

She watched Ilioneus in front of her, his movements more elegant than her own despite his extra height. She still felt fond of Ilioneus. She remembered when he had come to visit her father in his temple, dressed in his finery to receive the Trojans he had heard were pouring onto their shores.

At first, Latinus had mistaken Ilioneus for Aeneas and had poured him the finest wine and draped the most luxurious cloths around his shoulders. But Ilioneus, blushing, had told her father that he was only Aeneas's messenger and that the Trojan prince waited for him on the beach. And soon the misunderstanding was forgotten by everyone except, presumably, Ilioneus himself, as Prince Aeneas, despite his snub nose and short stature, was commanding everyone's attention with his tales of the adventures of the Trojans en route from Troy to Latium.

Would she be happier if Ilioneus had been Aeneas? She remembered, although she would not have said anything to anyone, a warm feeling inside as she gazed on his tall, lean limbs; his face, bronzed from months at sea; his muscles, strong and well developed. He was a similar age to Turnus, but unlike Turnus, he hadn't been raised alongside her. She had never seen Ilioneus cry because he could not master his lessons, nor was his head grizzled like Aeneas's, his heart and hand given once in marriage before. As she almost tripped over a rope that someone had left lying about, she dismissed her own thoughts impatiently. She had no business thinking of marriage as something acceptable, or to be desired. She had determined that the wedding was not going to proceed, and therefore she needed a plan to prevent it. Lavinia had no desire to run away and give up the comfortable life she had enjoyed to date in the palace. She would need to work on her father, she thought, to persuade him that marriage to Aeneas—or to anyone—was a terrible idea. If only she could separate him from Aeneas and speak to him alone.

When she reached the clearing to which Ilioneus brought her, she looked about, surprised. She had expected to be taken back to the strategy room. Instead, they were in an open space, surrounded by trees. It was the most peaceful place in the camp, she thought. Aeneas and his generals stood to the front, and her mother and father stood to one side. *What is she doing here?* Lavinia thought in a panic, and then her stomach lurched painfully. This was it, she thought. They were going to marry her to Aeneas now. She had to stop this, and she didn't know how.

"We cannot be married now," she said quickly. "There are no bridesmaids here, and the evil spirits will seek me out."

Out of the corner of her eye, she saw her mother nod approvingly. But before she could say any more, Aeneas cleared his throat.

"Lavinia, we are not here for the marriage. We thought it best to make an offering to the gods and goddesses of this area, to ask them for their blessing in the war and in our forthcoming nuptials."

"We want to make sure that the gods want you to choose Aeneas, and not Turnus," her mother interrupted, her tone as harsh as her words were rude. Lavinia looked to her father, but for once he made no effort to contain her mother. Instead, he looked surprisingly relaxed.

A makeshift altar was set up in front of Aeneas. Her mother pushed Lavinia beside him, and she stood there, uncertain where to look or what to do. Aeneas muttered some words over the altar. *Is he praying to his mother?* she wondered. Right now she was unsure whether a divine mother would be a blessing or a curse. If divinity were to be bestowed upon her own mother right now, she did not believe she would be any better off.

"I, at least, am in no doubt as to the result of this test," her father chose that moment to announce to no one in particular. One of Aeneas's men brought Aeneas a lit branch, which he held to the altar in order to light the offering. Her mother scowled. Her father continued. "When Lavinia was only a baby, and it became clear that we would not have any more children, I saw the importance to our nation of the man that she would marry. I consulted an oracle then, to see which of the local men she should marry."

Lavinia whipped around. She had never heard this story before.

"The oracle told me," her father continued, unaware of any unease his words might be stirring up in his only daughter, "that if I marry my daughter to a local suitor, my line will cease to exist. Such a marriage would produce no offspring. However, a man will come from the seas, and that is the man who should marry my daughter. So when Aeneas's ships docked in our harbour, bearing not only the riches that could be saved from the besieged city of Troy, but also a prince, one who had lost his own wife and needed a mother to care for his little son, I knew that the man my daughter would marry had arrived."

Lavinia turned back again to stare at Aeneas, still involved with his offering. Was it true that the gods had ordained she should marry this man? She knew her father well enough to recognise the oratory in his words, the emphasis on Troy's riches to show Aeneas was no upstart seeking to benefit from the Laurentine wealth. Before she could think further, though, her mother cried out, "Lavinia, your hair!"

She put a hand up to her head and felt the heat emanating from it at the same time as she smelt the burning. She screamed, sure that she was going to die. She couldn't see the flames, but she knew they were flickering closer to her head as she started to feel pinpricks of pain, then small angry bites at her head. She couldn't hear anyone else anymore, couldn't see her mother or her father. Aeneas turned to her. The horror in his face mirrored the dread in her heart. For a moment they stood, frozen together in their fear, united for the first time.

Aeneas moved first. He pulled his himation over his head and wrapped the cloak around Lavinia's hair. When he pulled the cloak away, the fire had been put out, but long strands of her hair peeled away with the himation. To her relief, her scalp seemed to be intact, although she could feel a terrible headache starting up behind her eyes. She put a finger out to gently poke the singed ends of hair. It seemed foolish and vain to grieve the loss of her hair when a moment ago she had thought she was going to die, but she felt it anyway.

"A sign," her father roared, ignoring Aeneas, who had stumbled away from them all and stood clutching his cloak. His chiton beneath had partly come untied. "The god of the sun has blessed this marriage, bestowing light upon our golden daughter! The wedding must proceed without delay."

Lavinia could think of nothing to say. Surely her father was the only person there who thought this was a positive sign? And yet Aeneas's advisers and friends were nodding their heads sagely, agreeing with her father's bold words. She looked at her mother, who frowned, then turned away.

"Not today," Aeneas returned to them, his bare chest heaving. "I am not properly dressed, and the bride probably wishes to rest after her ordeal. The wedding will proceed, Latinus, as we agreed," he said, holding up his hand as Lavinia's father opened his mouth to protest. "But not today." And he turned and walked away, saying under his breath, "I am plagued by ghosts wherever I go. Will fire follow me my entire life?" Lavinia wished she were a man so she could walk off too, instead of standing gaping after him.

☽

Lavinia returned to her quarters to find Anna waiting for her. Lavinia felt exhausted and overwhelmed, her head aching and her eyes itching. Her mother had announced that she was returning to the palace, and Lavinia had hoped that she might accompany her, but her father, euphoric about what he had begun referring to as the "crown of fire," had forbidden it.

Her mother had muttered as she left, "I will ensure that my hairdresser is sent to assist you," and Lavinia supposed she should be grateful for that at least. Otherwise, no one had given any indication that the incident had been anything less than a blessing for Lavinia. Aeneas had refused to speak to any of them.

Accordingly, she was both relieved and gratified to hear the gasp of horror escape Anna's lips and to find herself being ushered into her hut with soothing noises alternating with a request to hear the full story, but only when she was ready, of course.

Anna took a bucket of water and a cloth, and Lavinia allowed her to begin dabbing at the singed edges around her face while she sank back onto her bed and closed her eyes. Anna worked quickly and quietly, and eventually, Lavinia told her about the ritual, the offering, and the resulting fire.

Anna responded as Lavinia would have hoped, with sympathy and kindness, and she did not intimate that such a result might be a blessing. Instead, when she had thoroughly cleaned Lavinia's face and hands, she fetched her some wine and bade her drink before she tried to fix her hair.

"We could leave it, of course," Anna remarked. "But I think the smell will bother you. Better to cut it away. You are young—it won't take long to grow back."

Lavinia had never been especially vain about her hair, but she did allow herself a few self-pitying sniffs at the thought of her exposed scalp, sensitive to the elements. She hoped that some of her hair could be saved, even though she had seen the thick tendrils that had come away. Anna chatted casually as she chopped off locks of hair with a small knife, and then she bundled the whole lot out of sight and away from the quarters.

Lavinia sipped her wine and realised that, although she might look a fright, she did feel better without the acrid scent clogging up her nostrils, and when Anna returned, she brought a small mirror that she held up. Lavinia took one look at her head, burnt to a crisp, small knots of stubbly hair poking out all over it, and she burst into tears.

Anna rubbed her back and made soothing noises, and gradually Lavinia's feelings of general unhappiness crystallised on one man, the man she held responsible. The man who had disrupted her entire life and now ruined her appearance too.

"I have been set alight for the vainglory of Prince Aeneas," she exploded. "My own father has offered me up as the burnt offering for his success."

She intended to continue, but she was stopped by the stricken expression on the other woman's face.

"Prince Aeneas? Do you mean the Trojan?" Anna asked.

"Yes. Do you know him?" Lavinia asked, puzzled.

Anna quickly shook her head. "I have . . . heard of his reputation. Do you want to marry this Aeneas?" Anna asked. She pronounced his name in the Trojan way, Lavinia noted.

Lavinia knew that she did not, but Anna's strange behaviour, and her hands, almost shaking, had put her on her guard. She had already said too much to a woman she didn't know. "He is a prince and I am a princess. It's a suitable marriage. Are you married?"

"No," Anna said. "No, I lived with my sister when I was younger. And when she died, I left our city and became a travelling storyteller. I've never been married."

"That sounds wonderful," Lavinia said before she could help herself. "Travelling where you like, making your own decisions. Not tied down by husband and children."

Anna smiled, a dry, humourless curl of the mouth. "My life is nothing to envy, I can assure you. Many's the time I've longed for male protection, especially when I've caught the attention of the wrong man. Or worse than that, his wife. Still, it makes for a good story."

"I will look forward to listening to your stories," Lavinia said. She frowned, gingerly feeling her head again and already thinking once more of her own dilemma. It had been disagreeable to think of marrying Aeneas before now. Now it was simply impossible.

Anna, noticing, reached out her hand and gently caressed one of the stumps of hair on Lavinia's head. "Oh, Lavinia," she said, "you do remind me so much of my sister. Would you like to hear about her?"

Lavinia nodded, suddenly drained. She lay back on her bed, and Anna pulled the cover over her. "What was your sister's name?" she asked.

"Dido," Anna answered. "Have you heard of her?"

"No," Lavinia said, then added, "I'm sorry. Should I have?"

"She was a queen," Anna said proudly. Her face glowed.

Lavinia felt the embarrassment welling up in her throat, the heat of the blush that she knew was staining her neck and cheeks. "Your sister was a queen? But that means you are . . ."

"I *was* a princess." Anna laughed. "Don't worry, Lavinia. I have left that life behind me. Now I'm just Anna, the travelling storyteller. But my sister was a queen, and what is more, she ruled with no king beside her."

Lavinia bit her lip. She recognised the fate she had always imagined her father had in store for her when he prevaricated and dissembled and never said outright to Turnus's father, Turnus, or any of the elders that he would approve the marriage. And all the time, he had put his faith in a prophecy of a stranger from over the sea, a prophecy he had chosen not to share with her. Why had he never told her? She wondered. Had he thought she would rebel or run away? Worse, had he thought she'd respond like her mother, with hysterics and feigned illnesses? Or perhaps, until Aeneas had actually arrived, widowed and in search of a kingdom, he simply had not had enough faith in the prophecy.

For whatever reason, he had kept her in ignorance at the very time she had thought he was lifting her up to eminence. Ah, how foolish she had been.

"She was brave," Anna was saying. "She was brave and determined and independent." And Lavinia heard no more as she drifted off to sleep.

☽

Lavinia slept deeply for hours. When she next awoke, the sun was bright in the sky, and Anna had disappeared. She also realised that she had not eaten the day before, and she was starving. She gave her shorn hair a rueful glance, then left for the mess room.

A Trojan woman pushed a bowl of unidentifiable slop towards her, after giving her the most curious of looks. Lavinia tossed her head back and ignored her. Hair would grow, she thought. She was still a princess.

She ate her meal quickly, avoiding eye contact with anyone who came near.

When she had finished, she pushed the bowl away and stood up. She felt her mouth purse as she strode through the camp, looking for her father, and she tried to compose herself.

She found Latinus in a makeshift shelter that was clearly intended to function as his own strategy room, although its wooden slats and makeshift chairs were a far cry from his comfortable rooms in the palace, and indeed, this room wasn't even as big as Aeneas's.

"Lavinia," her father greeted her, waving her towards a chair. "How lovely to see you, my dear. What do you think of this room Aeneas has given me? It has a better view than the main strategy room, doesn't it? And nicer chairs." A small frown appeared on his forehead, even as he waved his daughter towards one of those chairs.

"Why did you never tell me about the prophecy?" Lavinia asked, ignoring social niceties and continuing to stand. "Didn't you think I had a right to know?"

Her father raised his eyebrows. "Right? What right could you possibly have? You are my daughter."

"I thought we had an understanding," Lavinia said unhappily. "Haven't I always assisted you, played hostess for your meetings, kept your secrets for you? I've been a good daughter to you. You could have told me about the prophecy."

"Are you worried about marrying? Aeneas is a good man," he said, his tone soothing.

"I've only just met him! *You've* only just met him! How can you possibly know if he's a good man?" Lavinia exploded.

"Lavinia, please, calm yourself," her father said, raising his hands. "You are starting to sound just like your mother."

Lavinia shut her mouth with a snap. How could he? All her life, she and her father had worked together to keep the court from knowing the extent of her mother's erratic moods and delusions. They had both spent long hours trying to soothe her after one of her fits and made excuses to visiting dignitaries, claiming headaches, women's problems—anything rather than telling the world that the queen of Laurentum was prone to rages and mania. Lavinia was nothing like her mother.

"I just wish I had known about this prophecy," she said, keeping her tone even and hoping that her father couldn't hear the small shake that betrayed how upset she was. "I would have had time to prepare. You could have done that for me, at least."

Her father stood up. "My beloved daughter," he said slowly, "all I do, I do for you and for our family. You believe me, don't you?"

Lavinia looked into his warm brown eyes, so like hers she could have been looking into a mirror. She searched for an answer, but she found none. "I believe you," she said, although she did not know whether she did or not. She blinked away her tears, and with them, the final vestiges of the delusion that her father may ever have intended her to inherit his throne. "I don't want to marry Aeneas, though."

"It is not for me to decide," he said firmly. "The gods have spoken."

Before Lavinia could respond, a messenger knocked on the door.

"Your Majesty, Your Highness, your presence is required," he said.

"By whom?" her father asked, raising his chin imperiously.

"His Majesty King Evander and his son the Prince Pallas have arrived," the messenger said.

Latinus nodded. "Send them to us."

The messenger flushed. He was a little too old, surely, to colour so easily, Lavinia thought.

"Your Majesty, they are in the strategy tent with Prince Aeneas. It was thought better that you joined them there."

For a moment it seemed as though they all—Lavinia, the messenger, and the king—held their breath. But then Latinus said, "Very well. We will do so."

"I suppose it has more space," Lavinia said as they walked together to the tent. She may as well have kept silent; her father said nothing.

When she walked into the strategy tent, King Evander embraced her immediately, and she could not help but smile. He had always been her favourite of the local kings, an ally of her father who had always had a piece of honeycomb in his pocket for the children. In fact, she was surprised that he did not produce one for her now. And his son, Pallas, was the little brother Lavinia would have loved to have had, sweet-natured and full of fun, his little legs never tiring from running after the older children. When Evander released her, he held her at arms' length but said nothing about her hair.

"Princess Lavinia, you have clearly inherited your mother's beautiful looks and your father's sharp mind. Lucky you didn't get those confused!" His booming laughter rang out, and she could see even her father relax a little.

"Welcome, King Evander. It is so lovely to see you," she said in return.

He rubbed her shoulder, then moved on to briefly clasp her father. She could see King Evander's twinkling blue eyes looking about him all the time, missing nothing. What did he make of it all? she wondered. She had no time to ask him, though, because she felt a tap on her shoulder, then another hug.

"Pallas," she said, delighted. "I'm so happy to see you! You know that Camilla is here too?"

Pallas beamed at her. She was surprised to realise that he had outgrown her, her head barely reaching the top of his shoulder. His cheeks were still chubby, though, with only the barest hint of downy fluff covering his upper lip.

"Let us go and find her at once," he said. "They won't miss us." She looked at the elders, but they were already deep in discussion. Aeneas had not even noticed her hair, she thought, then wondered why she cared. She thought she heard the name of Ascanius, Aeneas's son, mentioned, and saw Evander pat Aeneas on the shoulder.

"Come on," she said, and they slipped out of the tent.

"Stuffy old men," Pallas breathed when they were outside. Then he looked at Lavinia, his face stricken. "I'm so sorry, Lavinia—I didn't mean it."

For a brief moment, lulled into a false sense of normality by the arrival of two dear old friends, Lavinia had no idea what

Pallas was talking about. But then she remembered. She was to marry one of those "stuffy old men."

"Don't mention it," she said. "I mean it, Pallas. Not another word. And don't dare say anything about my hair either."

His eyes grew very wide. "I wouldn't dream of it."

She sniffed. "Do you know why you and your father are here?"

"Oh yes," he said, cheering up again quickly. "We are here so my father can decide whether our army will fight for Aeneas or not. And if we do, I am to join the troops. I have the most beautiful new armour to wear. Our smiths created it especially for me. Can you imagine it? Me, in a real battle! And my father is to offer to take Ascanius back to our palace, to keep him safe."

"You, fight in the battle?" a cool voice interrupted them, and they turned to see Camilla. Pallas turned bright red.

"Yes, it is true."

Camilla shook her head. "But you are a mere child."

"Camilla, don't be rude," Lavinia said. Pallas's face creased, as it had when they had run away from him as children, but Lavinia knew from experience that he wouldn't cry, and he would never tell their parents about any of the teasing they had subjected him to.

Camilla shook her head and raised her eyebrows, but she said nothing more, even when Pallas began to enthusiastically describe the specifications of the shining new armour his father had already commissioned for him.

When he took a breath, Camilla turned to Lavinia.

"Your hair looks awful, even worse than I imagined. Does your head hurt?"

"I thought you weren't interested in appearances," Lavinia grumbled, half under her breath, although she had noticed before that Camilla's own hair was always very shiny, for someone who claimed to spend no time on it.

"I don't see any point in primping myself for hours, but neither do I go about setting my hair on fire. And who cut it afterwards? A blind priest? I thought your mother had better hairdressers than that." Camilla shook her own fair locks as she was speaking.

Lavinia scowled. "Anna did it, actually. I think she did a fine job, considering."

"Oh, you mean the travelling storyteller," Camilla said.

"You've met her?" Lavinia asked, surprised.

"Of course. She came for breakfast. She's very exotic, isn't she?"

"What do you mean by that?" Lavinia asked coldly. Pallas looked from one to the other of them, his eyes again wide.

"Only that she has travelled far. I do admire a woman who does what she wants. But what do you know about her, Lavinia? Have you told Aeneas she is here?"

"I'm sure one woman could not be that much of a danger to us all," Lavinia said defensively. Of course, she should have told Aeneas or her father of the new arrival. "And Aeneas's guards were the ones who found her first. They know she's here."

Camilla's mouth creased in a small smile. "Where has she come from? Maybe she's a Greek."

Lavinia mused on this thought. Camilla was, it was kindest to say, known more for her prowess on the battlefield than in her lessons, but sometimes she did surprise everyone with an instinctual insight. Could Anna be a Greek, one displaced from her home because of the war?

"Have you seen her hands?" Camilla was asking. "She keeps them wrapped up, but I saw her replacing the bandages and they're all shrivelled up, as though she has been burned in a fire."

"I'm sure she is no danger," Lavinia said. "We'd better go back to the strategy tent. Camilla, why don't you come with us? Your father is there."

"No, thanks," she said. "I'd rather train. I suggest you train too, Pallas."

Pallas and Lavinia snuck back into the tent and retook their places towards the back. Their subterfuge was unnecessary; no one even seemed to notice they had gone. They exchanged conspiratorial glances, then turned and faced the front. Lavinia was still thinking about what Camilla had said. Of course she should have told someone that Anna had arrived; she could be a spy. But Lavinia did not think this was true.

"It is a kind offer," Aeneas was saying. "But it worries me, Evander. You are a father too. You can see my concern."

Evander looked about him before speaking, then nodded to Pallas and Lavinia. Lavinia smiled brightly, hoping this was the first time he had looked for them. "Yes, but my son is a little older than yours. If he were the age of your son, I would want him somewhere safe."

"But where is safe?" Aeneas asked. "Queen Hekuba and King Priam thought they were keeping their youngest son safe. They sent him with money and gifts to King Polymestor of Thrace. When we fled Troy we found his body, killed by that so-called friend for a few paltry gifts."

"The difference here is that you won't be sending him with money," Evander said, and Aeneas laughed politely. "Look," continued Evander, "It's your choice, man—of course it is. But I would want my child to be out of harm's way, not on the periphery of a battlefield. I make you this offer in good faith, with as open a heart as I offer my troops, led by my own pride and joy, my son Pallas. Not all Latins wish to be at war with the Trojans."

Aeneas stepped forward and held Evander by the shoulders. "You speak sense, King Evander. Thank you for your support. May I take care of your boy as well as I know you will take care of mine."

Lavinia was surprised to feel Pallas quivering with excitement beside her. She reached out and squeezed his arm. He turned and beamed at her.

"I'm sure your new armour will be magnificent," she whispered.

☽

When Evander and Pallas left, Lavinia returned to her room. Anna was there, laying out, on the ground, flowers that Lavinia knew could only be found in a grove on the outskirts of the camp.

"You shouldn't leave the camp," Lavinia said, sitting down on her makeshift bed. Anna still preferred to unroll her packed mattress each night and roll it up again in the morning. "It's not safe. What if Turnus's men carry out a surprise raid?"

Anna grimaced. "I'm probably safer out there than I am in the camp."

Lavinia leaned forward. "Why do you say that?"

Anna looked away.

"Are you a spy?" Lavinia asked sharply, grabbing Anna's wrist. "Perhaps I should take you to my father and to Prince Aeneas. They will know how best to deal with spies."

"Please, don't!" Anna exclaimed quickly. "I promise you, I am not a spy. I did not intend to come to this place. I am just a traveller." Her eyes were wide and innocent. Lavinia relaxed her grip.

For a few moments, Anna continued to lay out her flowers while Lavinia watched. A beam of sunlight pierced the hut through the open door. They had an unspoken understanding that the door was left open whenever the sun was shining, as it was the only chance they had to allow any light into their dank temporary home.

"What are the flowers for?" Lavinia asked eventually.

"I will dry them, and they will be useful," Anna said, her tone evasive. "One never knows when natural remedies—or toxins—will be needed."

"For a storyteller?" Lavinia asked. "I've never known a bard to carry treatments."

Anna smiled. "The needs of a female storyteller can be a little different," she said. "Travelling as a woman can be fraught with danger. It can also provide opportunities to help people. I don't like to miss out on those, for the want of a few plants."

"I wish I could travel," Lavinia said wistfully. "Aeneas told us all about his adventures before he arrived here. He saw Scylla and Charybdis—imagine! I wish I could go on adventures like that."

"Do you really?" Anna asked, her tone amused. "I had the impression that you were eager to return to the palace as quickly as possible."

"Well, yes," Lavinia admitted. "But that's because it's always cold and damp here, and no matter how much I try, I can't stop the leaves from getting into the hut, which means I always wake up with leaves in my hair."

"A floral crown for a lovely princess," Anna said, and smiled. "On adventures it gets uncomfortable too. It isn't all dashing exploits and beautiful strangers. A lot of the time it is sleeping out in the open, where it can be cold and damp. I am used to warmer climates, and I am—forgive me—a little older than you, so I do feel the cold in my bones."

"Latium is warmer in the summer," Lavinia said. "And it should be warmer here. Aeneas just chose to set up his camp, with the sea at his back, in the middle of a forest grove that blocks off all the sun."

"I imagine he didn't have a lot of choice about the location," Anna said, although the words were stretched, and her mouth curled up as she said them.

"Why do you say that? Do you know Aeneas? Do you dislike him?" Lavinia said, her suspicions aroused again. "Are you a Greek?"

"I am not," Anna answered, stung. "I am a Phoenician, and I made my home in Carthage, with my sister, the queen. If Aeneas told your father of his travels, surely he did not omit Carthage's generosity and bounty? I think Aeneas would not be here today without the assistance Carthage provided him."

Lavinia frowned. "No," she said slowly. "No, he has never mentioned Carthage."

"Perhaps he discussed it when you were not present." Anna turned back to her flowers.

"Perhaps," Lavinia said softly.

"Ask him about Dido," Anna said, her voice muffled as she pressed her flowers to her nose. "Ask him about my sister. See what he says."

"Tell me about your sister," Lavinia said. "Why wouldn't Aeneas want to remember her?"

Anna looked at Lavinia carefully, weighing something up, although Lavinia was not sure what she held in the balance. For a moment, all was still, other than the winds howling outside. Then Anna spoke.

BOOK FOUR

DIDO

In the heart of the town was a grove deep with luxuriant shade, wherein first the Phoenicians, buffeted by wave and whirlwind, dug up the token Queen Juno had appointed, the head of a war horse: thereby was their race to be through all ages illustrious in war and opulent in living. Here to Juno was Sidonian Dido founding a vast temple, rich with offerings and the sanctity of her godhead: brazen steps rose on the threshold, brass clamped the pilasters, doors of brass swung on grating hinges.

—Virgil, *Aeneid, Book One*

Dido dispatched a messenger to her brother, and then she acted quickly. She ordered her maids and menservants to pack up her palace. She felt a small twinge when she looked at some of her beautiful furniture, like the carved dining set for more intimate parties that had been passed down from her mother. She had not allowed herself the indulgence of grief when her beloved husband, Acerbas, died, though, so she certainly would not wallow in it over some chairs and a table. Ostensibly, the furniture was accompanying her. The message to her brother had stated that she would close up her own palace and move into his, for her protection. She could almost imagine him rubbing his hands in glee at the thought of the wealth he would acquire along with control of his sister.

Dido and her staff were not alone; several of the new palace guard—rough, skulking men hired by her brother, Pygmalion—were watching them closely. She quietly told her maids to sweep up twice as much dust, and throw about the rugs ten times as often as was needed, so it was impossible for anyone to follow closely what she was doing. Even so, it was obvious to everyone, or so they thought, that the gold was being placed into large hemp bags.

Eventually, the palace was packed, aside from the bare essentials that would be needed for the night. The palace guards retreated. All of Tyre was still.

Dido looked out over the dark night. All her life, she thought, Pygmalion had underestimated her. Most men did, never seeing past her big green eyes and her coiffed hair. But her father, King Belus, had known better. He had arranged for her to marry Acerbas, a priest of the new cult of Herakles. While she would be the first to admit that her relationship with Acerbas had been more familial than romantic, she had loved him all the same. He had been kind to her, and her father had groomed him to be his successor.

For two happy years after her father had died, Dido and Acerbas had ruled Tyre together. But now Acerbas was dead, and Dido was not safe.

She gave herself a little shake. There would be time enough to reflect on her grief when they were all safely away from Tyre. Her most loyal maids and men stood waiting for her. She took them through to the kitchen and showed them the bags of flour and jars of honey, simple domestic vessels that hid the real gold. The men hoisted them onto their shoulders, staggering under the unexpected weight. She awoke Anna, her younger sister, and led her, half asleep, blinking and stumbling, to the boat that she had arranged in the harbour. She bedded the child down in blankets and pillows and left her to sleep, guarded by the men and women she trusted the most. Then she returned to the palace and waited until the morning.

Day broke, sun streaming through her windows. She took her last steps through the palace where she and Acerbas had been so blissfully happy for such a short time. Bereft of furniture, her footsteps echoed hollowly, and she could see the dust motes preparing to take ownership.

What would Pygmalion do with it? she wondered. He wouldn't live here, for all that it was a more aesthetically pleasing building, with a view of the harbour. He preferred her father's palace, large, flashy and loud. She could have thought of many uses for the property, from housing visiting dignitaries to forming a new school for the children of the aristocracy, but she expected that Pygmalion would simply let it fall into disrepair. So be it.

She had asked Pygmalion to meet her on the steps to the marina, and until she arrived, she could not have been certain that her plan would have worked. But there he was, waiting for her, his arms stretched wide, the picture of munificence. Nearby, her attendants stood in front of the decoy bags of gold, and she saw Pygmalion glance in their direction every so often, licking his lips avariciously. "Easy to be munificent," she muttered, "when it's my gold he will be receiving."

"Did you say something, my dear sister?" he called to her, his voice almost whipped away by the winds.

She smiled. "Yes, dear brother," she called back. "The god, Herakles, visited me in the night. He told me that none of us will have quiet slumbers unless we offer Acerbas's gold to the depths of the sea." She raised her hands, and at the prearranged signal, her attendants emptied the bags into the sea.

It was comical, almost, to watch Pygmalion's face turn pale. She saw him wring his hands, wondering, no doubt, whether he should jump in and save the gold immediately or whether he could save some face by trusting it would be heavy enough to sink to the bottom so he could retrieve it later. She did not have time to see which choice he made. She marched to her boat and leapt in. Her trusted attendants followed her, as planned. They cast anchor and sailed away without looking back.

Once they had sailed a reasonable distance from Tyre, with no signs that they were being followed (and why would Pygmalion come after her? It was the gold he wanted, and he believed she had emptied that into the ocean), she gave the signal that allowed Anna to come up onto the deck of the ship.

The child raced up as quickly as she could on unsteady legs; she had been awake for many hours, of course. Dido smiled as she watched her sister exclaim with surprise at their watery surroundings. Anna was on the cusp of puberty, and it wouldn't be many more moons before she thought herself too old for such childish enthusiasm. *She resembles me,* Dido thought, looking at her sister's deep green eyes and the cheekbones that were starting to protrude as her baby fat diminished. *We are fighters.*

It pained her to think of how Acerbas had been found bludgeoned to death in the temple. If she had let it, that detail alone could have reduced her to a pool of tears. He had been betrayed when worshipping the god to whom he had devoted his life. He had been attacked violently, Acerbas, who had been such a gentle man. He had been attacked from behind, so at least, she hoped, it had been sudden, and he had not had time to be frightened. If he had known, she suspected that he would have offered up a prayer for his attackers, rather than any recrimination. That was the sort of man Acerbas had been.

She had not seen the body herself. When he hadn't returned home late one night, she had sent her servants to check the temple, and it was they who had reported back to her. The body had been found soaked in blood. Some jewels were missing from the temple, and so it was thought that he had been attacked by brigands. She knew better, though. Pygmalion had never forgiven Acerbas for winning her father's trust, even though Acerbas had not been underhanded. And although she had tried to rule by herself, she was limited by being a woman.

She looked around the court one day and realised that of the palace guard, she recognised perhaps ten men who had been hired by Acerbas. The rest were newly hired by Pygmalion. She tried not to allow anyone to see her shaking hands or her pale face, and she excused herself and her personal guard from the court. She had come up with her plan alone because she had no one with whom to confer, and she had ordered her staff to execute it. It had worked, which was more than she had dared to allow herself to hope for. She smiled at Anna and opened her arms for an embrace.

☽

Their party travelled slowly, stopping off at Cypress along the way. Dido had listened to travellers before she had left Tyre, and she understood that there were plentiful lands to be had to the south. They sailed as far as they could, then continued on foot. The party grew as they journeyed, picking up disenfranchised and disaffected people along the route. Ex-prostitutes, runaway slaves, and itinerant ne'er-do-wells: all were welcome within Dido's company, and yet somehow, none of the quarrels, troubles, or strife that such characters normally brought with them visited their group.

Dido noticed as they journeyed that Anna was growing into a beautiful woman. This did not gladden her heart as once it would have done; she knew only too well how vulnerable a lone, attractive woman could be. She would need to arrange a marriage for Anna before long.

Dido wondered sometimes if she had become some sort of lifeless automaton, a plaything of the gods, not a person at all. She still had not grieved for Acerbas. There never seemed to be the right moment to sit and think of him, to wonder whether his chosen god had smoothed his path to the Underworld. To wonder whether he could see her now and if he would be proud that she was looking after herself, or dismayed that she had had to leave their kingdom, or some other emotion altogether that she couldn't imagine. But she knew that taking that time to sit would take more out of her than she had to spare, and she needed all her resources to keep her people safe.

☽

Finally, she reached her chosen destination, a small coastal inlet on the border of Numidia. She and her followers paused and surveyed the land. She had chosen well, she felt; there was fresh running water, space for boats to dock, and a place to build. But even though it fell just outside the boundary of Numidia, she would need to persuade the king, Iarbas, to allow her to settle there.

Taking only two of her oldest advisers, Mattan and Melqart, she made her way to his palace. She had been careful with her dress, choosing a modest and subdued outfit befitting a widow. She ensured that neither she nor her advisers were bedecked with outlandish jewels or other marks of wealth. She was not foolish; she knew that Iarbas would have been advised long before she reached his door as to who she was, how strong her numbers were, and how she seemed to have had no trouble purchasing the supplies she needed on her route, but she hoped that he would be generous all the same.

When she reached the palace, she gave her name to the guards and waited. She did not have to wait for long. Soon she was shown to a small yet exquisite room, and she and her advisers were provided with wine. She sipped it and noted with some surprise that it was the best wine she had drunk in some time, lighter than the wines she had drunk in Tyre, suggestive of a younger grape. She sipped her wine and felt a mellow mist descend.

The doors were thrown open, and the king stood smiling at her. Her first, alarmed thought was *He has too many teeth. He is like a hybrid of a shark and a man.* But she suppressed that reaction and stood up and greeted him politely. He continued to smile at her, his canines glinting as the sun caught them.

"My dear queen," he greeted her, "how honoured I am that you have chosen to visit our humble nation. You are most welcome here, most welcome indeed."

He ushered her to a seat, and she felt his eyes scurrying over her. She forced herself to smile.

"Thank you, that is most kind of you," she said. "It is a beautiful nation, ruled by a benign king whose reputation precedes him."

His smile widened. For a moment, neither of them spoke. Dido was thinking how to broach the subject of the small piece of land she wished to settle on. Iarbas's mind was clearly on other, more personal matters.

Iarbas broke the silence first. "I understand condolences are in order. Your husband is no longer with us?" His eyes lingered on her garb, although she was confident it was not the modesty of her dress, but the figure underneath it, that interested him most.

"Alas," she replied. "My husband died before we left Tyre. That is why we are here, my lord. We seek . . ."

"I have no wife," he broke in, and smiled again, a most inappropriate expression, she felt. "I can offer you sanctuary—"

"I could not accept any offer of marriage, with my husband so freshly buried," she replied quickly, and the smile flagged a little. "I seek only a small parcel of land on your borders."

"Then we would be neighbours?" he asked.

She tried to smile and managed a faint response to his toothy grin. "Indeed."

He stood up abruptly. "I will provide you with a temporary refuge. You may have as much land as you can enclose within an oxhide. Of course, should you prefer, my palace will always be open to you instead."

He turned and left. Dido and her advisers exchanged worried looks but said nothing until he was out of earshot.

"He will be a most dangerous neighbour," Mattan said.

Dido nodded.

"We will be at war instantly," Melqart replied. "How will we fit so many people within the shape of an oxhide? We should leave before morning instead."

The corners of Dido's mouth twitched. "As to that, I have an idea. But we will have to act fast. I suspect he will come to inspect our settlement before too much time has passed."

☽

When they returned to the place they intended to settle, Dido called for an oxhide to be brought to her. She worked through the night, flaying and stretching it. It was lucky that she did because it was the very next morning she found herself greeting Iarbas with fingers dripping with blood and eyes bleary from a lack of sleep.

"Queen Dido, what is the meaning of this?" he demanded, striding over to her. "I said that you may have land that can be enclosed within an oxhide. You have taken over the entire inlet."

Dido forbore to point out that the inlet was not, technically, within Numidia's borders. Instead, she silently took him to see the fine strips of hide, barely thicker than a baby's little finger, that encircled their encampment.

Iarbas said nothing at first, his dark eyes flashing dangerously. Then he broke into a loud laugh and patted her none too gently on the back.

"Congratulations, Queen. You are as wise as you are beautiful! When you are out of your period of mourning, you will make a fine wife."

He strode off. Dido waited until he had crossed beyond the small hills that marked the outskirts of her new land before sinking to her knees with exhaustion. But she allowed herself only a few moments before she stood up again. There was much to do. She intended to invest Acerbas's gold into making her new city the most impressive metropolis in North Africa. And then, in the known world.

$$\mathbb{D}$$

Under Dido's careful guidance, her city, which she called simply Qrt-hrst, or new city, flourished. She was never stingy with her wealth, never cheated traders or underpaid workmen, and as a result the city attracted the very best, and she could make her choice in all areas of city life. There was a small but steady flow of immigrants from her neighbours' borders, including Numidia, but it was subtle enough that Iarbas didn't notice, or at least pretended not to.

Dido supervised the digging of the foundations of the new city herself, so she was there when a workman called out in surprise, holding his spade aloft. She joined his comrades in bending over the hole in which he was digging, and she saw for herself the dark glint of an eye. She stumbled back, thinking of the body in the temple and the blood, so much blood, which she hadn't seen herself except in her dreams. A voice called out, "It's a horse!" The head was carefully excavated and brought above ground for all to examine.

"What good luck," a man standing close to Dido, his torso stripped bare and sweating in the sun, cried out. The cry was soon taken up. Dido was astonished; she had no idea that a horse's head was considered fortunate.

"I make a proclamation," she called out. "Henceforth, the horse's head will be a symbol of Qrt-hrst, and all will know our good fortune by our emblem!" The proclamation was popular; the cry was taken up, and there was much jostling to see and even touch the lucky horse's head.

Dido herself had no desire to do so. She lay awake that night, remembering the flash of light as the eye caught the sun, the glossy mane, and the seared culmination of the horse at its neck. But despite her offering several men a substantial bonus, no one had been able to find the horse's body. A decapitated head alone seemed destined to be the new symbol of her fledgling city.

☽

If she had hoped that Iarbas would forget her with the passing of time, she had been naive. If anything, his attentions increased as her city's fortunes grew.

When the city walls were complete and the inhabitants numbered in the thousands, he began to send her gifts. She consulted with her advisers, who threw up their hands in despair. To keep the gifts was to suggest that she might one day accept her benefactor, but to return them risked offending Iarbas, and that could result in war. And Carthage, as the city was now familiarly known, was too small still to win a war with anyone, let alone Numidia. She kept the gifts.

Anna, a child no longer, yet not quite as mature as she should be, found the gifts, ranging from enormous bouquets of flowers to lethal hunting knives, hilarious. And even Dido had to admit that some of them were amusing.

"Dido," Anna called to her one early morning, her face brimming with mirth, "you will not believe what Iarbas has sent you now."

Dido pulled on her robe and stumbled into the newly decorated drawing room of her private chambers, a place to greet guests that was not as formal as the throne room. At first she could not see what was causing Anna to hold her sides as she giggled, but then a mewling noise drew her attention to a cage in the middle of the room, and Melqart holding his robes fastidiously beside it.

"It's not a cat?" she gasped in disbelief, but Anna shook her head and pointed her shaking finger at the cage. Dido stepped closer to see a thin, wary leopard.

"Oh, this is too much," she said. "What am I supposed to do with this?"

"He probably intends you to hunt it," Melqart said, his voice dry as he gazed at Anna with disapproval.

Anna stopped laughing instantly, although it was Melqart's words, rather than his censure, that achieved his desired intent.

"Oh, Dido, you can't," she said. "It would be cruel."

"So is penning it up," Dido murmured. She held a finger up to the bar of the cage, then pulled it back quickly as the leopard's teeth flashed. "I think he's hungry."

The leopard was taken to the kitchens and provided with meat, and Dido discussed her options briefly with her advisers. She could not release it, in case it terrorised the local farmers. Like Anna, she did not want to see it hunted and killed. She hated to see it imprisoned, but she felt she had no choice. It was removed to a side hut in the grounds of the palace close to the kitchens, and the amount it was fed equalled that of three grown men. Eventually, it was a relief to everyone when it died of its own accord, although from time to time Dido would pass the hut and feel an unaccountable sadness at the thought of the cage, now left empty and bare.

As much as Dido hated the gifts, she hated it still more when the gifts became less frequent. In their place, Iarbas sent his guards to visit her city on flimsy pretences. Soon there were as many of Iarbas's guards walking the corridors as there were Dido's. Dido began to feel the same prickles down her spine that she had felt when she knew that Pygmalion was due to make his move, but this time, she didn't want to abscond in the night. She had built this city from nothing. She had seen every brick in the foundations laid. It was not Iarbas's city. It was hers. She wanted to keep it, to defend it, with her life, if necessary.

She said none of this to Anna, not wanting to frighten her. With her advisers, though, she was more open. They knew that her nerves were on edge as she waited for a proposal that she would have no choice but to accept. Her only hope was to present another suitor, but there was no one suitable to take that role. Iarbas would only accept defeat at the hands of another prince. Any lesser man would be deemed to be a peasant and in all likelihood put to death. At Mattan's urging, messengers were sent back to Phoenicia to appeal to all the royal houses. Dido could only pray that none of the messages reached her brother, as dangerous, if not more so, than Iarbas.

She stopped sleeping and ate little. The bards sang of the fate of the Greeks caught between Scylla and Charybdis, the sea monster and the whirlpool that sat each side of the Strait of Messina, and Dido felt herself there in the water with those unfortunate sailors.

And then Aeneas arrived. For months they had been hearing rumours of the diaspora of Trojans, and Greeks too, set adrift across land and sea in search of new homes or trying to recover old ones, but Aeneas and his small party were the first to reach Carthage.

Dido was upstairs in her palace when they arrived, contemplating the harbour and trying to decide what she would build next in Carthage. A theatre, or perhaps a dispensary. She saw the commotion and sent messengers down to the shore. They quickly established that this was Prince Aeneas of Troy, weary of his seven years of exile.

Dido instantly saw the possibilities. She called for her maid to assist her in choosing her finest jewels, brushing her face with subtle powders, and rouging her mouth. Finally, she snatched up the one luxurious piece of clothing she had managed to bring with her from Tyre, a large green shawl that set off her eyes perfectly. When Aeneas saw Dido for the first time, he would see only her innate beauty and would have no idea as to the amount of work that went into maintaining her natural advantages.

The gods smiled on her, because Aeneas chose to visit first the Temple of Juno that she was building. It was an elegant structure, reaching up to the sky, intended to show Carthage off in much the same way as Dido's own powder and rouge. But more than that, the master mason had been inspired by the stories of the Trojan War, which were, six years after its fall, as popular among the bards as ever.

When Dido first appeared in front of Aeneas, he gazed upon her through a mist of tears caused by the depiction of the destruction of his homeland. He fell to his knees and said, "Good Queen, I know that you will show mercy upon us, because you so clearly understand our tragedy."

Dido reached out a hand. Aeneas seemed like the answer to her prayers, and she could sympathise with someone in mourning for his home. She gently raised him to his feet and led him to the palace. Once guest rooms were found for the Trojan warriors, Iarbas's guards melted away. Dido expected that she would sleep soundly with such protection under her roof. Aeneas was even the son of a god. But instead, she found herself lying awake at night, remembering a pair of dark brown eyes, shining through tears.

BOOK FIVE

CREUSA

Creusa, alas! whether, torn by fate from her unhappy husband, she stood still, or did she mistake the way, or sink down outwearied?

—Virgil, *Aeneid, Book Two*

Two summers passed. Creusa had only one rival for Aeneas's affections, and it was not a rival she had expected. He had eyes for no girl or woman. But, like all the boys, his eyes were drawn whenever her oldest brother Hektor entered the room or the training ground or, above all, the stables.

Hekuba was fond of telling everyone that love grew with every child she birthed. It multiplied, she would say, spreading like the ivy that covered the castle walls. If this were true, Creusa wondered, then why did Hekuba love Hektor beyond all others, while Creusa wore passed-down chitons and played with her brothers' discarded toys? Creusa thought that love was like a fine wine, dropped into a flagon of water, growing weaker and more insipid the farther it travelled. And so Creusa would say that she loved her brother Hektor, but she would be hard-pressed to say what that love meant.

Aeneas, however, was full of talk about Hektor. When he and Creusa were alone together, he would ask her whether she had seen her brother that day, or if she thought her brother might like the new sword he had received, or if her brother would be available to spar with him later. She always answered these queries with an exasperated shrug, but it did not stop Aeneas from asking. Sometimes, when she looked at Hektor, she saw her own big brown eyes looking back, and she worried that Aeneas was spending time with her in lieu of Hektor, the way one might play with a wooden sword if a metal one was out of reach. Her feeling was buttressed by the fact that Aeneas behaved around her just as he did with any of the boys in the classroom, away from the sparring and physical training.

Still, the little place she had carved out for herself with Aeneas seemed so delicate, so fragile, that she said nothing, and instead watched Aeneas following her brother, trying to ingratiate himself with him or, the preferred option for some reason that made no sense to her, be chosen to spar with him.

She found herself watching Hektor too, measuring him up objectively, trying to decipher what it was that made all the other boys desperate for his approval. He was at least a head taller than Aeneas, but he was no broader across the shoulders. He had long arms and legs, though, which meant that his spear flew farther, and when sparring, he could keep his opponent at bay. He trained harder than most of the boys, she had to admit that. And watching him in this dispassionate way, she also had to admit he had a manner about him that could only be described as kingly. He was no more royal than many of the boys there; Creusa's other brothers were all princes too, and he wasn't the only boy destined to inherit a throne. Aeneas was still in line to inherit his grandfather's kingdom, although his father had made them a home in Troy. But when there was a conflict, it was Hektor who stepped forward to mediate. When a bear threatened their training grounds, it was Hektor who gave the chase. When someone suggested abandoning their gear after a furious horse race to go for a swim instead, it was Hektor who led the way in wiping down his horse and saddle and putting his kit away before leaping into the water with a loud whoop.

In the boys' eyes, Hektor could do no wrong, and grudgingly, Creusa had to admit that they might be right.

Hektor himself seemed completely unaware of the adoration that surrounded him, and he had certainly never chosen a best friend for himself, although he could have taken his pick. He trained with all the boys alike, and he spent most of his free time with his parents, learning statecraft from Priam or making himself useful with Hekuba, pregnant once again despite her grey hair. But that was all about to change.

Creusa had followed Aeneas back to his house one evening, as she usually did, and he, as always, had slowed down to allow her to catch up. Every time, Creusa held her breath as they walked, and checked for pebbles in her path, sure that stumbling once would be enough to convince Aeneas never to walk with her again.

They walked in silence; Aeneas had been trying to break a particularly difficult horse, and she could see his mind was still there, trying different options, different approaches. He might be defeated today, but tomorrow he would be better prepared. But then, out of nowhere, he said, "Some of us are going on an exploration tomorrow. Up into the hills, taking a picnic. Hektor is going. Will you come?"

"I'm sure I don't need to follow my brother around like a puppy dog," she surprised herself by responding, and saw his face turn red.

"I didn't mean that. I only meant that—well, that your mother and father would not object to you going if Hektor was there."

"Oh," she said, stunned. It had never occurred to her that her parents would object to her spending time with Aeneas. They never noticed what she was doing in order to object. But once he said it, she saw that of course there was a difference between watching the boys train behind the city walls, and travelling into the hills where only shepherds and nymphs could see them.

"Perhaps you don't wish to come. It doesn't matter," Aeneas said, a new awkwardness entering their interaction, and he stepped a little away from her so their arms could no longer touch occasionally as they walked.

"But I do," she said hastily, and he moved back into place again.

"I will call for you in the morning," he said. They continued walking in silence until Aeneas said slowly, as though he were finally puzzling something out, "Did you think I spend time with you because of who your brother is?"

Creusa thought her face must surely be on fire, she felt it burning so brightly. But she just said, "Don't you?" and closed her mouth very quickly, hoping that giving words to one of her greatest fears wouldn't make it come true.

Aeneas didn't reply. But when they reached the small house that Aeneas shared with Anchises, and before he went inside, he leaned over and kissed her on the cheek, something he had never done before. She closed her eyes and counted to ten, and when she opened them, he was still there, laughing at her.

"I spend my time with you for you, Princess Creusa," he said.

☽

The next day dawned, and Creusa felt nothing but excitement as she waited for Aeneas. Her excitement wasn't even dimmed by the realisation that several of her sisters had also been invited to join the party. After all, they hadn't been invited by Aeneas.

She sat next to her mother, winding hanks of embroidery cotton for the tapestries her mother never had time to work on, and she felt as though she were hiding a jewel in her lap. That she should have warned her mother that Aeneas was calling for her didn't occur to her.

But at the appointed time, she saw his curly brown head approaching, and she sucked in her breath. Her mother heard and looked at her appraisingly.

"Your Majesty," Aeneas said to her mother, inclining his head. "Your Highness, we are due to depart shortly."

"Where are you going, Creusa?" her mother asked, but her tone was gentle and amused, not the scathing tongue of the later months of her pregnancies, when she became large and uncomfortable.

"There's an expedition," she said uncomfortably, then added, "Hektor's going."

"Ah, I knew I was losing Hektor to this party, but I did not realise you were going as well. I will have to wind my own thread," Hekuba said. "Prince Aeneas, will you wait for my daughter outside? I wish to speak to her in private."

Aeneas nodded, then quickly made his escape. Creusa thought she saw relief in his eyes to have gotten off so lightly.

"So, Creusa, several of my children are going for a picnic today, but Prince Aeneas only called for one daughter. Is there something you wish to tell me?"

Creusa felt a blaze spread across her skin yet again. Would all this blushing mar her skin forever? She said nothing to her mother, but her mother smiled all the same.

"I like Aeneas, Creusa. He's got a good head on his shoulders, unlike that bombastic father of his. And goodness knows, there are enough of you children to worry about. I will speak to your father. Now don't keep the young man waiting."

☽

When Creusa finally joined him outside, Aeneas, who had been leaning against the wall, jumped to his feet.

"Will you be coming?"

"Yes," she answered.

"Good," he said, and smiled. He took her arm, and started to tell her about all the delicious luxuries that had been packed for the picnic, from slices of spit-roasted pork and mutton to honeyed cakes for dessert. She listened, beaming with joy, and didn't tell him that it wasn't only a picnic that her mother had given her permission for. Did Aeneas realise what he had set in motion, like a giant ship setting sail for foreign lands, never to turn back to its home shore? Perhaps, she would think later, he did.

☽

The weather was perfect for their picnic, and Creusa thought that Helios, the god of the sun, had seen their plan and smiled upon it. And why wouldn't he? For perhaps the first time in her life, Creusa thought that there was something to say for being part of a large family. Here, with her brothers and her sisters, she felt at home and safe. She enjoyed watching Aeneas interacting with them, seeing how easily he became one of them. Of course, he was a member of the family too. Anchises was her father's cousin, so that made Aeneas . . . a second cousin? She wasn't sure. But regardless of his heritage, he was certainly a Trojan prince. He made the right jokes and laughed in the right places. He understood Trojans, the rhythms and the cadences of their speech.

The only person who was a little stand-offish, his brow furrowed as though he bore the responsibility of the world, and not just this party, on his shoulders, was Hektor. She caught sight of him scanning the horizon, looking not back towards the city walls and gates, but out across the woods and hills that surrounded Troy.

"What are you looking for?" she asked. He jumped and turned to her. "Sorry, Creusa, I was lost in my own thoughts. Brigands, mostly—not that I think there are any," he hastened to reassure her. "Just that one hears rumours, and we are all so used to being locked behind the city gates, I'm not sure we know how to defend ourselves outside them."

He had a point. The walls of Troy were thick and high. They had been built many generations ago; not only Creusa, but her father, and his father before him, and *his* father before him, had never known a time when they didn't have strong walls to keep them safe. The gates stayed open, but there were sentries posted on them at all times. And although Troy sat on the shore, she had never set foot in a boat, and she didn't think many of her siblings had either.

But she said only: "We are not that far from the city. We could be home before any brigands realised who we are."

Hektor gave her a look that was almost amused. "I'm not sure brigands would care." But he relaxed a little and even went so far as to take his hand off his sword, although he did not remove the sword from his body as others had done.

"Did you know I am to be married?" he asked, changing the subject abruptly. Creusa shook her head.

"Her name is Andromache, and she is a princess from Cilician Thebe. Father has arranged everything. I am to go and collect her myself, bearing gifts for her family."

Creusa now understood the purpose of this picnic, whether Hektor realised it or not. A last chance for him to spend time with his brothers and sisters, to be one of them, before marriage and his impending role as king of Troy lifted him away from them all. She also understood that it was a futile exercise. Hektor had never just been one of them.

"What's she like?" she asked, feeling some response was called for.

"I don't know." Hektor laughed awkwardly, a red blush staining his cheeks. "I've never seen her. I hope she's kind."

Creusa smiled, but before she could say anything else, they were interrupted.

"Hektor, look to the south—quickly." It was Aeneas.

Hektor and Creusa both followed the direction in which Aeneas was pointing. Creusa expected to see brigands on the horizon, raising their swords and shouting barbarous calls as they approached the royal party. Instead, she saw a far more threatening sight, a herd of cattle thundering towards them. On closer look, she saw the herd were only three, but the three were bulls, their heavy hooves creating a dust storm as they approached.

"I have a plan," Aeneas said quickly. "I will distract them, make a commotion, flash my sword. I'll lead them to that gully over there. You can take everyone else behind that ridge. They'll be safe there."

Hektor whistled through his teeth. "It's a risk, Aeneas. I should be the runner. I'm taller than you."

"Yes, but I am the son of a goddess." And Aeneas grinned, a smile that transformed his face and made Creusa's heart sing. "You get everyone to safety. Especially . . ." And he looked at Creusa.

Hektor nodded grimly. "I hope your mother is watching you now," he said, then calmly mustered their party, most of whom had been oblivious to the impending crisis. Creusa and her sisters grabbed each other's hands and followed their oldest brother, flanked by the other male members of the party. The boys all held their swords in their hands like Aeneas, although what use would a sword be against a rampaging bull?

Behind them, Creusa heard Aeneas shouting at the bulls. She felt the ground beneath her feet tremble as the bulls thundered past them, and she coughed at the dust they raised, a storm that meant for a moment she couldn't see Aeneas at all. Then she heard a crash and a triumphant cry, and saw the bulls had fallen into a crevice while Aeneas stood on the ridge above, his sword raised now in victory.

She'd wanted to be the first one to reach him, but of course that would never be possible as her long-legged brother Hektor raced across to him, laughing and shouting, "It worked! It worked!" He pulled Aeneas into an embrace, and the two started to cheer and dance around while the angry bulls snorted below them.

As the rest of them caught up, Aeneas was the subject of many back pats and kisses, any vestigial traces of his outsider status gone forever. His face glowed with new authority. Creusa took advantage of the chaos to sneak her hand into his, and she was rewarded by feeling him squeeze it in return.

As the euphoria wore off, Aeneas looked at Hektor and said, "It's good that the plan worked, but it should never have been needed in the first place. Where is the cowherd who should have been minding these bulls?"

"You're right," Hektor said slowly, looking down at them. "I thought they were wild, but of course . . ."

As he trailed off, they saw a youth approaching them. Creusa gasped involuntarily when she saw him; she thought he might be the most beautiful person she had ever seen. He had long, dark eyelashes and fine cheekbones, and his skin glowed without blemish or scar. He had the type of looks more usually associated with a lovely woman or even a god. Ganymede, cupbearer to the gods, came to mind.

"You," Hektor called, "are these your bulls?"

"They are," the youth answered, and Creusa thought she saw a shiftiness in his eyes and an indolence in his limbs, which undermined her earlier impression. "Thank you for penning them so neatly for me."

'Take better care of them next time," Aeneas said. "Someone could have been hurt."

The youth half nodded, half shrugged. Aeneas glanced at Hektor, perhaps expecting him to support his position, but Hektor was mesmerised, staring at the boy. The boy stared back, and Creusa shivered. Despite the fact that the boy was younger than Hektor, lither, and of course exquisite to the eye, there was something about the two of them that resembled each other. But that was ridiculous. Why would her broad-shouldered, pleasant, if not exactly attractive brother look anything like this languid cattle herd?

She thought of all her half brothers, but they were all sturdy types, fathered on buxom maids and kitchen servants. And besides, she had never heard that her father had sought his comforts outside the city walls. And yet the boy was staring back at Hektor now, he and Hektor locked into something so tense you could cut the atmosphere with a sword.

"What is your name?" Hektor asked slowly.

"Alexandros," the boy replied. "Who are you?"

"Speak more civilly to the prince of Troy," Aeneas snapped, but Hektor just shook his head.

"Hektor," he replied. "Sorry, I thought you were someone else. Come on, Aeneas. I think we have had enough excitement for one day." And he led them all away, but as they went, Creusa felt Alexandros watching them, and she felt a distinct sense of unease, as though she had passed too close to her own ill destiny.

BOOK SIX

LAVINIA

Camilla rages, a quivered Amazon, with one side
stripped for battle, and now sends tough javelins show-
ering from her hand, now snatches the strong battle-axe
in her unwearying grasp; the golden bow, the armour of
Diana, clashes on her shoulders; and even when forced
backward in retreat, she turns in flight and aims darts
from her bow.

—Virgil, *Aeneid, Book Eleven*

With Evander's support ensured, Aeneas no longer held his forces back. Days, then weeks passed, and Lavinia and Camilla learned what it meant to be at war. They both chafed at the bit that had been forced upon them, but each in her own way.

Camilla trained almost constantly, despite Aeneas, Latinus, and her father all standing firm that she was not allowed to join the battle. Her arms, always slender, developed strong muscles from the heavy swords she wielded, fighting against the mercenaries, whom she paid, or the young Trojan boys, who were overawed by her. Her legs thickened as she swam and ran whenever she wasn't fighting, and her face lost the last residues of girlish cheek fat. Lavinia thought it was possible that for the first time, she looked almost as pretty as her friend, but she had no long mirrors in which to check, and there were few men around to compare the two of them anyway.

Lavinia worried about her friend almost as much as she worried about herself; they spent very little time together, and there were long swathes of time during which Camilla was not to be found in the camp, and Lavinia had no idea where she went.

Lavinia, in comparison, did not want to join the battle, but she wished she could return to her palace, her comfortable bed, and her mother. Her hair was growing out now. She checked the ends, but she could have used a full-length mirror and, she suspected, a professional hairdresser to cut and shape it for her.

She asked her father regularly for updates on the war, but she was never satisfied with the responses. He no longer asked her for advice, and Lavinia began to have her suspicions about his own involvement in the strategy of the battles, although he was not a warrior, she reminded herself, and he did not lead an army, but paid others to do that for him. She felt her mind dulling with no whetstone against which to test it.

The general understanding continued to be that a wedding could not possibly be arranged while the war was going on, and it was in Lavinia's interests not to test this theory.

She never saw Aeneas. She was his fiancée in name only, and sometimes she wondered about his wife, Creusa, and whether he was still so in love with her that he couldn't bear to see Lavinia, or whether it was the opposite, that theirs had been a political marriage, and Aeneas had no interest in women at all.

She began, unreasonably, to have arguments with Aeneas in her mind, holding him responsible for all her concerns about the war: her mother, Camilla, even the spiders that she sometimes found crawling over her pillow or tangled up in her hair.

The rainy season had begun, and the camp that had once seemed so neat and tidy now oozed mud from every nook and cranny. Lavinia imagined the mud rising up, a wet sticky mass that slowly resolved itself into a figure of a man, the man who had thought this was a good place to set up camp. She would tell him so with great joy, watching the mud monster try and fail to open his clay mouth and reduced instead to making groaning noises, acknowledging how right she was. Ultimately, though, these arguments were always unsatisfactory because the real Aeneas wasn't there to respond.

At night, Anna told her stories, sometimes about her own travels, but mostly about Dido. Dido in her youth ran faster than any other girl, and as she matured, had more suitors than any other woman. She was kind to animals and children, and while no one ever got the better of her, she was, in Anna's tales at least, never boastful or haughty. After the first night, Anna never again mentioned Aeneas, though, and Lavinia had begun to wonder whether she had misunderstood Anna, and her sister had never known Aeneas at all.

Lavinia was concerned for Anna. Anna now refused to leave the hut at all except to perform her ablutions, which she did furtively while the rest of the camp slept. Lavinia had to bring food back for her from the mess tent, and Anna ate it like a squirrel, a portion now and a portion stored away in her bag, as though she was storing it up against some future unnamed emergency, until Lavinia had to clear the bag out as the hut began smelling of rotting meat.

Camilla stopped by to visit Anna occasionally and listen to her stories while stretching her long limbs. Lavinia implored Anna to walk about the camp herself, trying to persuade her that Aeneas left the camp each morning to lead the Trojans into battle. But Anna just shook her head and shrank further back into the shadows.

Despite the casualties, Lavinia noticed that the Trojans remained optimistic. The women cleaned and sang constantly while the men were away fighting. Lavinia heard rumours that suggested the Laurentine army, made up of professional soldiers, was less hopeful. Her father rode out infrequently, and the gossip was that the numbers were dwindling as the Laurentine soldiers were deserting. Lavinia spent her days playing her kithara for her father, who stared into space or drummed his fingers to the music. They were seldom interrupted. Lavinia suggested they return to their palace, but her father insisted that they remain

close to the war effort. She had to take deep breaths before playing, lest the tension and frustration she felt in herself worked
its way through her fingers into the music. Sometimes she wondered whether she should send Aeneas a message, asking him
to involve her father more thoroughly, but she knew this would
only embarrass Latinus.

Lavinia had barely left her hut for her father's one morning
when she was interrupted by Aeneas. "Lavinia, I need you to
come with me, please. Don't argue," he added as she opened her
mouth. "This is important."

She followed Aeneas, who was walking so quickly he gave her
no time to question him. She increased her pace and thought of
the many items she needed to address with him, starting with his
disregard for her father and by extension for her. It felt strange to
have the flesh and blood man there; she had spent so long talking
to a mirage that she had almost forgotten that he was a person in
his own right, and not an automaton she had dreamed up.

Aeneas led her to his strategy room. Sitting on a chair in
the centre, his legs spread out and one arm slung casually over
the back of the chair, as though he were in a tavern rather than
an open-air hut, was Mezentius, father of one of her childhood
friends, and an ally of Turnus's. Standing behind him was his
son, Lausus, the fifth member of their little childhood group,
Lavinia remembered, and her heart ached for those simpler times.

"Lavinia, my dear," Mezentius said as soon as he saw her,
although he made no move to sit up. "I don't think this war is
suiting you. You are looking most unwell."

"I am quite well, thank you, King Mezentius, and I'm sure
the war will not last much longer," she replied.

"Then you do recognise this man," Aeneas said, his tone
calm. "He claims to be an ally of Prince Turnus."

She nodded. "This is Mezentius, once king of the Etruscans, and his son, Prince Lausus. Lausus and I were friends long ago." Lausus flushed, and she wondered whether she had overreached. They had been part of the same group, but she had never spent any time with him when Turnus was not present, and it felt strange to be here with him now.

"Why are you here?" she asked. She addressed Mezentius with her words, but she turned towards Aeneas, and it was he who answered her.

"Mezentius is here with an offer," he said. "A proposal, one that will put an end to the fighting. But he refused to tell us the terms unless you were here to hear them."

Lavinia scoffed. No one else in this war seemed to care what she thought. But Mezentius spoke anyway.

"Those were Turnus's terms, not mine. I am carrying out his will, and I have abided by his terms. Now that the princess"—he sneered as he referred to Lavinia—"is here, I will lay his offer out for you. He suggests a duel, a fight between the Trojan invader Aeneas and the rightful king, Turnus. The winner may rule peacefully in this land while the loser must exile himself immediately."

"An end to the bloodshed!" one of the Trojan elders exclaimed, but Aeneas held up his hand.

"Is that all?"

"No." Mezentius smirked. "The winner will marry the lovely Princess Lavinia."

"Turnus is most keen on this prize," Lausus added, the first words he had spoken. "He remains as inexplicably infatuated with you as ever."

There was silence. Lavinia easily set aside Lausus's insulting tone and thought instead about Turnus. Was he infatuated with her? Both Camilla and Lausus seemed to think so. She found it difficult to summon up any romantic enthusiasm about him, but then she supposed that was one of the qualities of infatuation. Whomever you were in love with did not need to love you back.

"Aeneas, we can end this war," one of his advisers said, breaking the silence.

Aeneas spun round, his eyes blazing. "We've heard that before, haven't we? That was what the fight between Menelaus and Paris was intended to achieve."

"And we also all know why it didn't achieve that," the Trojan replied. "Your mother spirited Paris away."

"Better he had died," Aeneas said softly, his rage spent as quickly as it had arisen. "He died anyway, didn't he? Better he had died at the hands of Menelaus, and we had allowed the Greeks to take that wretched woman home."

Lavinia's eyes widened as she heard Aeneas say those words. She had heard so much about Helen of Troy. The bards were forever singing of her beauty, her grace, her eloquence. Second only to the goddess Venus herself in beauty, Queen Helen was the prize everyone wanted. She had never thought to hear Aeneas describe her as a "wretched woman."

"Is that all the message you have for us?" Aeneas asked, turning back from the hurried conversation he had been having with his advisers.

"It is," Mezentius confirmed. Lavinia wondered whether he would ask to speak with her father, but he did not.

He continued to scowl, even as Aeneas said, "In that case, you had better return to Prince Turnus. Tell him we will consider his offer."

Mezentius sauntered out of the tent, looking as though he were merely taking fresh air rather than walking out of an enemy camp. Lausus accompanied him more cautiously, looking about himself nervously. Aeneas nodded to his guards, and they moved to a few steps behind the deposed king and prince, following them out of the camp. Mezentius quickened his pace. Lausus needed no further invitation to follow suit.

"Wouldn't do to have him making himself too familiar with the place," Aeneas said. He sat down on a chair and sighed. The advisers instantly started to debate the proposal that had just been offered up, but Aeneas took no part in the discussion. Lavinia studied him, trying to work out what he was thinking, but he was like a closed oracle to her.

"Of course, his mother may just spirit Aeneas away, and then what?" the words of one of the advisers floated over to them, and Aeneas grimaced. He stood up and offered a hand to Lavinia.

"Your Highness, will you walk with me?"

She nodded, and took his arm. They walked about the camp in silence. Aeneas seemed reluctant to say anything, and Lavinia had no idea where to start, so she looked about her at the sights, once so new, and now so familiar. They passed the mess tent, where Trojan women were already ladling out lunch to the returned soldiers, and the hospital tent, where a few wounded men sat together and laughed despite the fact that they only had two working arms between them.

She glanced across at Aeneas next to her, his brow furrowed in thought. He had fought in so many wars, and she could see the scars, some silvered, some fresh, where blades had cut his flesh. But he still had both arms. He was still alive. Would he survive a duel with Turnus, a man younger than he by about twenty years? She thought back to the Turnus she had known, always training, skilful with a sword, fast on his feet. And now he had a new fierce energy motivating his every move.

"They wish that Hektor were here instead of me," Aeneas said, startling her as his deep voice broke across her thoughts.

"Surely not," she murmured politely.

"Why not? Hektor was my brother-in-law and my cousin," Aeneas answered. "Hektor was my best friend. He was the best of us, best of all the Trojans, and better than any Greek, not that being better than those butchers would be difficult. He was a good man. And I know what you are thinking now because I think it every day: Why did Hektor die and Aeneas survive? Why indeed."

"No," Lavinia said, shaking her head. "I wasn't thinking anything like that at all—"

"I think it," Aeneas replied. "I know the answer too. Did I survive because I was braver or stronger or a better fighter? Did I survive because I am nobler or wiser or better at strategy in the heat of the battle? None of these things. I survived because Hektor is a mortal man, and I am the son of a goddess, and that goddess did not want her son slaughtered at Troy. That is all."

"Then I suppose your mother will not want you slaughtered at Latium either. It will be a quick duel," Lavinia retorted. Aeneas pulled his hands through his curly hair, drawing Lavinia's attention to the places where it was thinning.

"That boy, Lausus—he does not seem to like you very much," he said eventually. "Nor did his father for that matter." Lavinia smiled.

"Lausus, Turnus, Camilla, me—we all grew up together. Pallas too, although he was a little younger. Lausus always thought we girls should be weaving and playing music, and leaving the boys to their fighting and training. Turnus was not like that."

"No?" Aeneas asked.

Lavinia wrinkled up her forehead, thinking. "No. I do not understand why he has changed so much. Turnus, when I knew him, was a kind, gentle boy. When he came to declare war, he seemed so angry."

Aeneas swallowed. "War will change most men. The gods use the lesser men, manipulate them, to ensure that their favourites are protected. But in the end we are all just their playthings."

Lavinia looked at him in surprise. For the first time, she wondered whether they had made a mistake, identifying his mother, the goddess of love and beauty, with the rotund, amiable goddess the Laurentines knew as Venus. Aeneas seemed to be thinking of a far darker pantheon.

"I shall not take the duel," he announced suddenly. "I am no one's toy. Better to die an honest death on the battlefield. Sometimes I welcome such a fate. Sometimes I think I am going mad, seeing ghosts everywhere I walk."

They continued to walk. Aeneas glanced down at Lavinia. "You are easy to walk with, easy to talk to. I haven't known a woman with whom it has been so easy to simply co-exist since . . . well, since my wife."

"What was she like?" Lavinia asked reluctantly. She looked at her hands, then across the camp towards the river. Anywhere but at Aeneas.

"Strong," Aeneas said, and smiled. "Far stronger than me. I didn't realise how strong she was until I saw her give birth to our son. I've fought many battles, but I don't think I could allow myself to be torn asunder like that, and then immediately love the one responsible for the tearing." He laughed. "Of course, you have no children as of yet, Your Highness. You don't know what it's like, but somehow every woman seems to fall in love with the little warrior in her womb."

Lavinia shuddered. "I can't imagine," she said, hearing her voice sounding high and tight. Aeneas must think her a prig.

"She wouldn't have a wet nurse either," he continued, seemingly oblivious to her growing distress. "Suckled him all by herself. And a strapping boy he is now."

Lavinia thought of Ascanius, whom she had met only briefly before he had been sent away to keep him safe. It was hard to imagine the young boy, stocky and sturdy like his father, had once been a baby sucking at his mother's breasts. The thought made her feel slightly ill.

"To be frank with you, Lavinia, I find my memories of my wife and my son as a little boy to be most bittersweet. When we were travelling here, we passed through Buthrotum. Do you know it? It is the city ruled by Trojans, King Helenus and Queen Andromache. They made us welcome, but Queen Andromache cried to see Ascanius. Her own son, Scamandrius—or Astyanax as we called him—died, you see, in the aftermath of the war. I was worried at first that seeing Ascanius made her sad, but she said the same thing, that it was bittersweet to remember those days when she and my wife used to sit and suckle our babies together. Even though there was a war raging, even though her husband and I would go out to fight each day, we could still enjoy moments of happiness. And now we see Ascanius, and all we can think is that Creusa is gone, Astyanax is gone."

"But you survived, and her husband did too," Lavinia said, but Aeneas shook his head.

"No, Helenus was her second husband. Her third, I suppose, if you were to insist on counting the barbarous Greek who enslaved her. Thank the gods he died, and Helenus was able to marry her. But her first husband was Hektor, our champion."

To Lavinia's horror, Aeneas's voice cracked as he mentioned Hektor.

"Even so, Hektor did not survive, and you did. That must make you a better fighter," she said hastily.

Aeneas shook his head. "Better than Hektor? No. I am not. No one was. Achilleus was faster, true, and he had the advantage of the armour his mother made for him—he was the son of a goddess too, although a less powerful one. She couldn't guarantee him safety. My mother is an Olympian. Only Zeus is more powerful than she. Many of the male gods like to throw their weight around, but none of them could defeat her in battle."

"How nice to have such a powerful mother," Lavinia said drily. "I can't possibly imagine what it would be like."

"Perhaps our parents aren't so dissimilar," Aeneas said. "Your father is marrying you to me because of a prophecy. Your wishes don't come into it."

Lavinia flushed. It had been so long since anyone had mentioned their marriage that it had almost felt like it had been forgotten, but it continued to be the sword that hung over her head.

"I survived the Trojan War because my mother wanted to be the matriarch of the new Troy and all that would follow it," Aeneas said grimly. "I survived because she wanted this land, and she wanted her heirs to inherit it. A true mother sacrifices herself for her son; she doesn't expect her son to sacrifice himself in aid of her plans."

They had reached the mess tent, where Trojan women were offloading the supplies that had been sent by local farmers. Aeneas turned away from Lavinia and began to lift the heavy sacks, motioning to the women to sit down. They did so gratefully. It was a kind act, Lavinia thought. It gave her the courage to ask a question that had been playing on her mind.

"Aeneas, do you know of a woman named Dido?" she asked.

Aeneas put down the produce and turned to face her, his eyes dark and wary.

"Who gave you that name?"

"I don't know," she said, surprised by the vehemence of his response. "Who is she?"

"If I find out someone has been spreading rumours," he muttered, but then looked up and saw her face and tailed off. "I do not know anyone by that name."

He was lying. Even a child would see through him. But why? She pursed her lips as she considered her next question.

"By Zeus!" Aeneas exploded. She stepped back, shocked. "These figs are rotten. Why am I the only person who is working to take care of our people?" He threw the offending figs to one side, and stalked off.

Lavinia looked down, and saw her hands were shaking. She had never been so close to an angry man before. She felt small suddenly, small and soft. Her questions felt asinine, and yet also of keen importance. She thought of all the subjects she had refrained from discussing with him, all the arguments they had had in her mind. She should have raised her concerns, she saw now. She had been cowardly, and a simple question had caused him to erupt in rage regardless. She crept closer towards the figs spilled over the ground and gently picked one up. She was no expert, but the fig seemed perfectly fresh and edible to her.

☽

Anna was waiting for her when she walked back into the hut.

"Is it true?" she asked. "Has Aeneas been challenged to a duel?"

"It's true," Lavinia said. She sank down onto her mattress.

"That must be hard for you," Anna observed. "Your past suitor fighting your current one."

Lavinia closed her eyes. She thought Anna meant well, but she didn't want to talk about it. "It is nothing to do with me," she said. "They fight over the land. I am the means to securing it, that's all."

Anna leaned forward. "But what if you could be more than that? What if you could have control over your own life?"

"Like your sister?" Lavinia asked, and was surprised to see Anna frown in response.

"Let me tell you the rest of her story, and then you can be the judge of that," she said.

Before she could start, though, they were interrupted by Camilla, bursting through the door. "Has he really refused? Coward!" she spat at them.

Lavinia flushed. "Camilla, Anna is here too."

"So what? Is it true, Lavinia? The entire camp is saying Aeneas is too frightened to face Turnus."

"I don't know if it's because he's too frightened," Lavinia replied.

"What other reason could it be? He's brave enough when he has soldiers to hide behind. When he can use your father's army to fight his battles," Camilla said furiously.

Anna raised a hand, as though she wanted to try to calm Camilla, but she took one look at Camilla's face and dropped it again.

Camilla slammed her fist into her palm. "No more of this, Lavinia. I have reached my limits with this upstart. I don't understand why you are supporting him."

Lavinia stood up. "It's not that easy for me—" she began. But Camilla just turned away. Lavinia frowned. All their lives, she had been the leader. She had decided what game they were to play, which of the guards they might secretly find attractive, the matching dresses they would wear to the palace events. And now Aeneas had come, and her world was turned upside down. Camilla would never have dared to speak to her like this before.

And besides, Aeneas was the son of a god. Neither Anna nor Camilla had walked next to him and watched the muscles ripple in his arms. Neither of them had felt the air crackle with his power. She did not know why Aeneas would not fight, but she did not think it was because he was a coward.

"I've made a decision, Lavinia," Camilla said now. She took a deep breath, then expelled her words in a rush of air. "I'm going to join the fighting."

Lavinia stared at her friend in disbelief. She knew Camilla had been practising her skills, but she had never for a moment thought that she would join the men on the battlefield. The sun dropped behind a cloud, and the room became dark. For a few moments, neither of them spoke; then they both started at once.

"I'm as well-trained as most of the men—"

"Are you mad? This is not our fight—"

They both stopped again, their words sinking in.

"How is this not our fight?" Camilla asked. "Aeneas is taking our land."

Lavinia was silent for a moment. Then, realising what Camilla's words implied, she responded, "You will be fighting against us."

"I will be fighting for my land, against Aeneas, the usurper. I will be fighting with Turnus, our childhood friend and the man you thought you were to marry. I have spoken with Turnus, and he is at least prepared to allow me to take my place on the battle-field, even if my father is not."

"Turnus has declared war on Aeneas and all those who support him, and that includes Laurentum," Lavinia said. Anna, sitting beside them, said nothing, but Lavinia was conscious of her eyes, shining green in the semidarkness of the dank room. "Why do you have to go to war?" Lavinia asked. "Let Turnus and his soldiers fight. Let my father and Aeneas and the men who serve them fight. Not you, Camilla."

She wished she could make out the expression on her friend's face. Camilla's voice, soft and calm, sounded reasonable, but the words she was saying seemed to Lavinia to be anything but.

"I am a princess of Latium, and this is my land too. I told you, I am as good as any of the men out there. You know it's true. I've defeated Turnus himself many times in hand-to-hand combat. Even Pallas, a mere boy, is earning credit on the battlefield. I can defend my own land. Besides, I've heard about the Amazonian warrior women who fought at Troy. They are as revered as any man. Ask Aeneas if you don't believe me."

Lavinia turned her head away. She didn't want to ask Aeneas anything.

"I'm tired, Camilla," she said instead. "I'd rather go to sleep. Please, leave me."

Camilla said nothing, but she got up from the bed and left the hut. Lavinia thought she heard her sniff a little as she left, but she couldn't be sure. It was only after Camilla had gone that Lavinia thought to say that the Amazonian women had fought on the Trojan side. They had been defeated at Troy.

Out of the darkness came Anna's voice, eerie and disembodied. "Would you like me to tell you my story now, Lavinia?"

"No," Lavinia said curtly. And Anna was silent.

☽

Lavinia returned to see her father the next day. She felt some sense of normality in the small tent with him. She used to spend most of her days in the throne room, assisting her father. She had even heard court cases, much to the consternation of the petitioners. But her father had always assured her afterwards that her verdicts were sensible, even identical to those he would have chosen himself.

"Hello," she called as she came to the door. She breathed in sharply as she saw her father squint to see who was there; she knew he was struggling more with his eyesight lately.

"It's me, Lavinia," she added, and saw his face light up. Another sharp breath.

"Lavinia, how lovely to see you. I missed you yesterday. Come in, my dear."

She tiptoed into the small room, darker than she had expected, and sat down on the chair next to her father. "What are you doing? Can I help?"

He frowned. "I don't know that I need much help, Lavinia. Aeneas has everything very much in hand."

"There must be something that needs doing," Lavinia objected. "I can't remember you ever having so much as a spare moment."

"I have a spare moment now," he said, and smiled. "Were you spending time with Aeneas? It would be a good idea if you could, although he is very busy with the war."

Lavinia smiled weakly. When had her father become so doddery? She wanted to blame witchcraft or the work of the gods that accompanied the Trojans wherever they went, whether to support or destroy them. But deep down, she knew that it was something different and far more dangerous.

"Father, do you need to stay on the campsite?" she asked, choosing her words carefully. "Mother must miss you, at the palace by herself. Perhaps you should go to keep her company?"

"Why do you say that?' her father asked. Then he scowled. "Don't mollycoddle me, Lavinia. Our army is fighting a war. If I can't fight, at least I can be a visible figurehead. And I'm not in the grave yet, young lady."

His sharp tones sounded more like the monarch she remembered, but even so, Lavinia hesitated. They were interrupted, though, by two men shuffling up to the door of the tent. They were both hunched over, from which Lavinia deduced they were Trojan refugees, past fighting age. Any Laurentine men of the same age would be at home, other than her father.

"Can I help you?" her father called, and she heard that same note of uncertainty, the worry that came with being unable to assess a situation in a glance.

The two men entered the tent and kneeled in supplication. "I am Amicus and this is Clytius," the one who had entered first said. "We are Trojans, and we come to appeal to King Latinus."

Lavinia scrutinised the two men. They were, as she had first surmised, both elderly, and their beards were soft and white. Like all the Trojans, they looked as though they had not had a hot bath in some time. If she ran the camp, the first thing she would do would be to provide boiling water and order everyone to scald off the smell of defeat, she thought, then felt ashamed of herself. She forced herself to focus on what the man was saying.

"King Latinus, please, you must petition Aeneas to accept the duel."

"What duel?" her father asked, and she felt a strange combination of a pang of guilt that she hadn't updated him, coupled with annoyance at Aeneas for not keeping him informed. Aeneas would do well to remember whose army was doing the fighting, she thought, and resolved to remind him at the next opportunity.

The two Trojans exchanged looks, then Amicus said, "Prince Turnus has challenged Father Aeneas to a duel. Father Aeneas has said he will not fight."

"Father Aeneas?" Lavinia asked, her curiosity piqued. "Is that what you call him? You must both be several years older than him, if not old enough to be his father."

"Nevertheless, that is what we call him," Amicus replied, and Clytius nodded. "He led us out of the burning city of Troy and guided us across the ocean to this fertile land. He has cared for us almost as well as he has cared for his own son."

"He's going to found the new Troy and be the father of many generations of our children. We owe everything to him. Without Father Aeneas, the Greeks would have destroyed everything that is Trojan."

The two men stared at her earnestly without blinking. Lavinia didn't know what to say. She nodded.

"Would he not prefer Prince Aeneas? Or even King Aeneas?"

Clytius laughed. "Perhaps he would, but he is stuck with Father Aeneas now. No doubt your people have names for you too."

"I suspect I would not like to hear them," Lavinia said, and smiled to herself as her father shot her a glare. "But why, if he means so much to you, do you want him to fight this duel? Aren't you afraid that he will lose?"

"He will not lose," the two men said in unison. They exchanged glances and chuckled nervously. Clytius motioned to Amicus to continue.

"Aeneas is the son of a god, it's true, but it's more than that. Many a time we watched him from the walls of Troy. We have spent every day with the man since leaving Troy. He is a skilled fighter. Turnus has youth on his side, but nothing else."

Lavinia's father nodded before she could ask any more questions. "I have made up my mind. I will speak to Prince Aeneas. You will excuse me if I do not call him Father Aeneas, on account of my somewhat greyer beard," he added. "Please, send Prince Aeneas to me."

When the men had shuffled away, Lavinia's father stroked his beard and looked worried. "Of course I cannot make him fight. I'm hoping that he will come to see me of his own accord because I almost certainly can't make him come here."

"Father?" Lavinia asked, hearing her voice crack a little.

"I'm afraid I have no control over Aeneas now. Oh, I suppose that isn't exactly true. Most of his army is Laurentine; I could force his hand by withdrawing troops. But I'd rather not do that until I actually want to withdraw them and keep them from the fighting." He drummed his fingers on the table. Lavinia waited silently. She knew from experience that any questions he posed in this mood were hypothetical only, and he would not appreciate her attempts at an answer.

"Let us see what happens," he said eventually. "No need for rash decisions. Perhaps you will play for me?" He motioned casually towards the side of his tent, to her kithara, and she picked it up and began to strum. From time to time she glanced towards her father, but he seemed lost in his own thoughts, so she continued occasionally accompanying her playing with a burst of song, but more often allowing her instrument to sing for her.

"Is that a lyre?" she heard a voice at the door say. She glanced up, startled; she had forgotten that her father had asked Aeneas to visit him.

"A kithara," she said shyly. "I'm not very good, though."

"It sounded beautiful to me," Aeneas replied. He nodded conspiratorially at Lavinia, and she saw that he, too, would not mention their conversation of the day before to her father. He crossed the room, nodding to her father, and took the instrument from her.

"Similar concept to a lyre," he mused. "Strings here, and a chamber for echoes. But much more beautiful. The Greeks used to play the lyres at night," he explained. "I can't tell you how unsettling it can be to hear enchanting music swimming up from the beaches outside your city. And then knowing that the men making that beguiling music that pleases you so much desire nothing more than to kill you, to rip you open from head to toe and leave your body for the birds to feast on." He sighed. "The human nature is a complicated beast. King Latinus, I was told you wished to speak to me. I am sorry for my tardiness, not least because I wish to speak to you, too."

Her father cleared his throat. "Yes, indeed, Aeneas, we have perhaps both been a little remiss in communications. What is this I hear about a duel?"

A dark cloud passed over Aeneas's face, apparent even in the dimming light of the tent. "It is an irrelevance, Latinus. I won't fight it."

"The terms of the duel affect the terms on which my army engages in this war. Fight it or not, it is most certainly not an irrelevance, and I should have been informed." Latinus rose slowly to his feet, putting out an arm to steady himself.

Aeneas's mouth tightened, but he stepped back to give the older man space. "I apologise, Latinus. From now on I will give you a full briefing." The words were like small pebbles spat from his mouth. "Nevertheless, I will not fight the duel. I do not fight with puppies."

"You wouldn't hesitate to engage with him on the battlefield, though, would you? Why's this any different? Scared?" Her father snorted.

"The battlefield is different. Anyone who has ever fought on one knows that." Latinus glowered, and Aeneas waited a breath before adding, "Sir."

"But surely it is different because Turnus has called for the duel," Lavinia said, keeping her tone mild. "You cannot be to blame for that, and you could save so many lives."

"Rutuli lives," Aeneas said. "Our losses are minimal."

"The Rutuli are our neighbours," Lavinia said gently. "Until now, we have always maintained good relations. We attend each other's celebrations. We marry—" She stopped short. The Laurentine princess and the Rutuli prince were not going to marry each other after all. She was aware of her father's piercing eyes, watching her.

"If he doesn't want to fight, there's nothing we can do," her father said. He sank back down onto his chair. "You said you wanted to talk to me, Aeneas. What is it?"

It was Aeneas's turn to redden. He looked at Lavinia. "Perhaps this would be better said in private."

"Anything you can say to me, you can say in front of my daughter," Latinus declared.

"This concerns her mother," Aeneas said gently.

"It's her mother. She does not need to leave. Tell me, what has Amata done?"

Aeneas shuffled, then stared at the ceiling. His mouth was working, but no words came out.

"Just tell us, man," Latinus said.

"I am hearing reports that she is claiming to be possessed by the gods, and participating in certain mysteries. At night. She and some of her attendants are chasing about in the woods, dancing naked."

Lavinia felt her jaw drop. Why was no one attending to her mother? Her father shook his head.

"You say *claiming* to be possessed? Why do you think she is *not* possessed? Your own mother has been known to interfere with the free will of humans."

"That's a good point," Aeneas conceded. "But those who have seen her allege she seems a little too knowing. Recovers herself a little too hastily. And she's too swift to advise that such madness is a sure sign that we shouldn't be fighting this war."

Latinus nodded slowly. "I see. You know that she does not wish for you to succeed to my throne nor to marry her daughter."

"She has made that very clear," Aeneas said gruffly. "Even without such displays of madness."

"I will have her confined in the palace," Latinus decided. "This insubordination is impossible."

Aeneas nodded. "Thank you. What about Lavinia?"

Lavinia narrowed her eyes, but she said nothing. Further defiance would only anger her father.

"She can stay here, at least for now. It will destroy morale if I'm seen to remove all my family to safety."

Aeneas shrugged. "Very well. She is your daughter after all. I am due to travel for a few days, to visit King Evander and see my son."

"Ah, yes, I forgot Evander was taking care of your boy. Is he not old enough to fight for us now? Perhaps you will bring him back. It will boost spirits, I am sure."

Aeneas's flat nostrils flared. "My son is still a child." He glanced at Lavinia and frowned, then looked back at Latinus. "The troops' spirits will need to rely on the efforts of adults. I will not allow my family to be used as playing pieces in a ghastly game."

The two men glared at each other. "Are we both now fully informed?" Aeneas asked.

"I do hope so," Latinus said. Aeneas leaned forward to embrace the older man, their bodies both held stiffly apart as their arms touched. Then he nodded to Lavinia and turned to go. As she watched him walk away, Lavinia wondered whether she should have mentioned Camilla.

"I wonder," her father was saying, "I wonder if he was always so arrogant."

"Arrogant?" she turned to her father.

"Only one man can ever be the king," he said, and sighed. "He does not intend for it to be me."

☽

As Lavinia walked out of her father's tent, she found herself being pulled around roughly. She screamed in horror. Although it hadn't hurt, she did not think anyone had ever laid hands on her person in that way. The culprit, she saw, was Aeneas, but far from looking apologetic as she would have expected from his respectful demeanour to date, his eyes were blazing with fury. He leaned over her.

"Where is the Princess Camilla?" His chest rose and fell in indignation.

Her mouth dropped. "I am not Camilla's nursemaid," she retorted. "Ask her servants where she has gone. I am sure I am not one of them."

"You are her friend, though, are you not? Stop prevaricating and answer me." He squinted a little as he looked at her, and she wondered if he was really seeing her. But all the same, she did as he asked.

"She told me that she was going to join Turnus's army. If you can't find her, I expect she has done so."

Aeneas staggered back. "Her father entrusted her to me," he said, almost to himself.

"I think he entrusted her to my father," Lavinia replied. He ignored her.

"Women should not fight in battle," he said, addressing the air, it seemed. Lavinia wondered if he was speaking to the godly mother she had never seen.

"Camilla is a good fighter," she said loyally. "As good as the Amazon queen, I'm sure. She could defeat most, if not all, of the boys, even as a child-"

"This is not training," Aeneas exploded, smacking his fist into his open palm. "I saw the Amazon queen, Penthesilea, die—do you understand me? She was as close to me as you are now, and Achilleus butchered her as though she were of no more importance to him than a pig—less, in fact, because he would have taken the pig's carcass to prepare for his supper, whereas Penthesilea's body he discarded before it had even left his sword."

Lavinia opened her mouth, but Aeneas lifted his hand and carried on. "And before you say it, I've heard the nonsense the bards are prattling about. How he looked into her eyes and saw she was his true love, only for it to be too late. I was there, and I'm telling you, he never even saw her—not as a person, not as a woman. She was nothing more than another enemy to him, to be briskly dispatched."

Both of them were silent. Aeneas's chest rose and fell as though he had been running. Lavinia felt as though she had seen a Gorgon and been transformed to stone.

"But she is fighting against *us*," she said quietly, hearing her voice break. "She will not be just another enemy to you. To my people. We all know her."

"It will not matter," Aeneas said, his voice gentle. "War is ugly, and there is no time to reflect on past loyalties when someone is trying to kill you."

Lavinia sobbed, the sound catching in her throat. Aeneas put out his hand, but she ducked away. No one could comfort her now.

☽

That night, Lavinia was preparing for bed when she heard a noise outside her hut. She stepped outside, expecting that Aeneas had arrived to apologise for his behaviour. But it was not Aeneas who stood waiting for her. It was her father.

Wordlessly, Lavinia followed her father as he led her out of the camp, being careful not to make any unnecessary noise. Once she tried to ask him where they were going, but he pressed his finger to his lips, and so she carried on, hoping that he would reveal everything soon. She started when they crossed the boundary of the camp and she saw a pair of horses and her father's old groom waiting outside. But she obediently allowed the groom to assist her onto the horse. She wasn't the best rider, but she was capable, and she was relieved when her father waved his hand at the groom who was trying to mount the horse behind her. Instead, the groom crept behind a bush, presumably to wait for them to return, and she gave her horse a gentle kick to prompt him to follow behind her father's steed.

They rode at a steady pace. Her father stayed a little in front of her, staring into the night. It occurred to her that this might be what being kidnapped could feel like, but of course, her father could not kidnap her. She was an unmarried woman; her father could take her wherever he might.

She still felt a wave of relief, though, as she saw their palace looming up ahead in the distance. She was going home at last. She felt a sob catch in her throat and choked it back. She would return as a princess, composed. Perhaps her father had received

another omen, one that required him to upset her life all over
again. It didn't matter. She just hoped that he would allow them
to remain in the palace long enough for her to take a long bath
and scrub the smell of the camp from under her nails.

They crossed the gates into Laurentum and made their way
down the silent streets to the palace. She noticed that her father
had a cowl over his head; even had any of his people been about
to see him, they probably wouldn't have recognised him. And
when they went into the palace, they went through the servants'
entrance. But when they reached the stables, they were instantly
surrounded by a dozen grooms, strong, silent men who assisted
her down from the horse and led it away before she knew where
she was.

Finally, her father embraced her. "Come inside—your
mother is waiting," he said. "I'm sorry for all the secrecy, but it
is important that no word of this meeting reaches . . . well, you
will understand."

She didn't, yet, but she assumed that he meant Aeneas. Who
else would want her to remain in the camp? Her thoughts were
confirmed when her father led her into a small room in the royal
quarters, the private area of the palace reserved for the family.
And there, clasping the hands of her mother, sat Turnus.

"What are you doing here?" she asked.

Turnus and her mother both rose to their feet. Amata spoke
first. "Lavinia, Turnus has taken a great risk coming here. You
should listen to him."

"You didn't send Mezentius and Lausus this time?" she
scoffed.

"I wanted to see you," he said. "Mezentius told me he'd spoken with you."

"Did he tell you what he said?" she asked.

Turnus shook his head. Lavinia recoiled; she was hit by a strong smell of wine.

"It doesn't matter," she said, suddenly feeling exhausted. What was the point of dredging up his childish insults, in front of her parents too? They weren't children anymore.

"Lavinia, Turnus has arrived to make his suit," her mother said pointedly.

Turnus wasted no more time. He stood up and began to pace, punctuating his speech by punching his left hand with his right fist. "Please, Lavinia, you do not know this Aeneas. He has lost one wife already, through his carelessness and his own selfish need to found a nation. I love you. I have always loved you. I always thought we would marry, and the Rutuli and Laurentine nations would unite as one." Turnus stopped, his mouth slightly open, and she had a cruel thought of him and Mezentius practising this speech over and over until he could say it without a single mistake. She glanced at her father.

"Lavinia, you have heard my view," he said, his brow furrowed. "You have heard of the vision that I have had, the prophecy. I believe that our bloodline is doomed if you do not marry Aeneas. But you are my only daughter. I have not been blessed with sons to carry on my name. And I could never bear to see you unhappy. So if you would prefer to marry Turnus, so be it." He shuffled his feet. Lavinia wondered if he believed what he said; she certainly didn't.

"So this has nothing to do with Aeneas taking control of the army? Nothing to do with what you said about him intending to be king?" she asked sharply.

Turnus smirked and she glared at him. Her father raised his hands haplessly.

Lavinia looked from one to the other of them.

"What if I prefer to marry no one?" she asked eventually, exasperated. "Why do I have to marry anyone at all?"

"Lavinia," her mother gasped, but she was in full flow now.

"Turnus, are you here because you love me or because Aeneas has turned down your request for a duel? Are your troops not sufficient to beat him on the battlefield, so that you have to call for single combat against a man old enough to be your father?"

"Is that why he will not fight me? Because he knows that I will win?" Turnus shot back. His face had turned a mottled red, and the fumes of alcohol were almost overpowering now. It felt impossible that this ugly, aggressive man had ever been a friend of hers.

She shrugged. "I do not know, and I do not care. I tell you, I do not wish to marry either of you."

Her mother burst into tears.

"Oh, Lavinia," her father said sadly, "why do you say these things?"

Because they are true, she thought. Because the choice in front of her was unbearable. She was tired of Turnus, his posturing, his poor choice of friends. She had known him since he was a boy, and she did not want to be his wife. But was Aeneas, the man who had left his wife to burn in a fire, any better?

"She's just saying those words to hurt me," her mother said, sobbing, and she glared at Lavinia. "Please, Lavinia, tell Turnus you still love him, and there will be no need for you to return to that dreadful camp."

She shook her head. "I do not," she said, then added, "I do not know."

Turnus stood up and strode towards the door. He staggered slightly as he turned back and said, "Lavinia, that man is a cheat. But I promise you now: I will meet him on the battlefield, and he will bleed like any other man. We Rutuli have our weapons too, you know. And his mother will not be able to spirit him away before we get our chance to use them."

He lunged towards her with his sword, then pulled back again, laughing at the horrified expression on her face. The smell of wine was overpowering this time. Again she looked to her father, wishing that he would do something. He had started this war. He had invited Aeneas in, and he had alienated Turnus by announcing that she would marry Aeneas. And now he was abdicating his decisions to her? How could the crown sit on top of such a weak head? she asked herself, and felt a pang of disloyalty.

Amata was weeping. "Turnus, you are the one true hope of all Latins. Lavinia must marry you. Do not meet Aeneas in battle, because if you fall, we are all lost. Marry Lavinia and none of us need die. I, for one, do not want to live to be a captive, seeing my daughter married to that pretender, Aeneas."

Turnus crossed to her mother's side and took her hands in his as though she were his mother, and not Lavinia's. Lavinia wondered whether Turnus was as confident about his prowess on the battlefield as he seemed.

Her father sighed loudly and heavily. "I should not have met like this. I have given Aeneas my word, and although I am no longer entirely certain of his plans, I should not be retracting that word. Lavinia, I will take you back to Aeneas's camp. He must not know that we have met like this. But I tell you now, this is your choice. I will not force you to marry a man you do not desire."

"But you will force me to marry," she said, yet so quietly her father chose to pretend he hadn't heard her.

They left together, Turnus comforting her mother behind them. She hadn't even had her bath, Lavinia reflected sadly.

The ride back to the camp seemed faster, perhaps because the horses knew now where they were going. When they reached the camp, her father did not dismount.

She looked up at him. "Please Father," she said. "Why do I have to marry either of them? You know I am intelligent, and I have learned from you for many years now. Let me show you what I am capable of."

"Not this again," her father said. His voice, perhaps intended to sound sharp, merely sounded petulant, even reedy. He kneaded the reins between his hands, and Lavinia noticed how prominent his veins were and how his knuckles bulged out. *They are an old man's hands,* she thought, then felt the pang of perfidy once again.

"I cannot protect you," he said suddenly. "Perhaps once I could, but it is too late now. Aeneas already has a foothold in our land, and Turnus will beat down the door. They are too entrenched now to ever retreat, and one of them will succeed in making this kingdom his own. It will not matter how intelligent or capable you are, once you are a woman alone."

Lavinia remembered Anna's story of her sister trying to manage her little kingdom while Iarbas sent her unwelcome gifts.

"Then what should I do?" she asked. "You said it was my choice."

He shook his head sadly, and Lavinia felt angry. How could her father, who had been so strong throughout her life, be so weak now? How could he fail her when it mattered most?

"Good night, Father," she said. She stood and watched as he rode away. She sniffed a campfire on the breeze and remembered those other kinds of fire—a woman escaping a burning city, a girl with her hair caught alight. Was she destined to burn?

☽

Anna was full of questions when Lavinia returned to the camp. Where had she been? Had Aeneas been there? Did Aeneas know she had left? Lavinia answered no to the last question, although she did wonder if this was correct. After all, even though Aeneas had left to see Evander, the only reason her father had been brave enough to risk the journey, he had spies everywhere.

"If he had known he would not have let you leave," Anna said, as though she could read her thoughts. She nodded, chewing on her lip. "It's good to know that you can move without causing alarm, if necessary."

Lavinia frowned. "Are you really frightened of him, Anna?" she asked, thinking of Anna's continued reluctance to leave the hut when Aeneas was in camp.

Anna didn't answer her, but instead replied with a question of her own. "Would it be so bad to marry Turnus? He is your childhood friend, isn't he? And he would be able to protect you from Aeneas."

Lavinia shuddered, remembering Turnus's bloodshot eyes and the stench of alcohol that surrounded him. "I think I'd rather take my chances with Aeneas."

"Aeneas is not reliable, though," Anna said. She sat back on her haunches and reflected for a moment. Lavinia studied her face, those eyes, the colour of sea grass. They gave nothing away. Anna's face was passive, aside from a small muscle that twitched in her jaw. Then, just as Lavinia was growing impatient, Anna said:

"I will tell you about my sister and Aeneas now."

BOOK SEVEN

DIDO

Aeneas is come, born of Trojan blood; on him beautiful Dido thinks no shame to fling herself; now they
hold their winter, long-drawn through mutual caresses,
regardless of their realms and enthralled by passionate
dishonour.

—Virgil, *Aeneid, Book Four*

Although Dido was almost beside herself with curiosity to hear the Trojan prince's story, she allowed the Trojans the customary day or two to settle in, to eat and drink and recover from their ordeals without undue questioning.

On the second night, Aeneas and the Trojans joined Dido and her court for dinner. Aeneas presented Dido with gifts salvaged from the wreck of Troy: some funerary urns and a long Trojan sword, glinting in the firelight.

Dido sat at one end of the table, Aeneas at the other, and he smiled encouragingly at her. He knew what was expected of him, and he was not surprised when she said, "Prince Aeneas, you are most welcome here in Carthage. But please, tell us all how it is that you come to be here? How did you and your loved ones escape the fires of Troy?"

"Alas," he said, "this is a sorrowful story you ask me to tell. Because although I was able in the confusion to escape the city with my father, who has recently passed away, and my small son, my beloved wife did not escape. When I realised that she had not accompanied me, I returned to the burning city and searched the streets, being careful to avoid the marauding Greeks. But at last I heard a voice cry out to me: 'Aeneas, it is not to be. I am not to leave Troy, but you are to go and find a new Troy, as your mother, the goddess Aphrodite, always promised.'"

Aeneas looked at Dido, and she met his eyes directly. His curly hair was receding from his forehead. He was on the short side—stocky, even. But his eyes were dark and intelligent, and she thought she might lose herself in them.

Aeneas continued to describe his adventures, the travels the Trojans had undertaken, meeting famed Greeks and Trojans alike on the route, but Dido's mind was elsewhere. She didn't even notice when he described his voyage through the Strait of Messina, past the paired monsters that had taken up so much of her attention recently. She did notice, smiling inwardly, that Anna was rapt, her mouth parted slightly, wincing or sighing as the story called for it.

As soon as the meal was finished, Dido bade her guests to enjoy hot baths and comfortable beds once more, a command they agreed to with gusto. And once they had departed, she dismissed everyone except her most trusted advisers, Melqart and Mattan, and, on a whim, her sister. Perhaps it was time Anna became more involved in the state decisions that came so easily to her older sister, especially now that there might be more security in their realm.

Melqart spoke first, not standing on ceremony. "He claims to be the son of the goddess, but who is he really?"

Mattan was not slow to add his own thoughts. "And he claims his wife was so beloved, yet he left her behind. That story about her voice speaking to him was a little too pointed, in my view."

Dido was silent. They watched her, unblinking. They had known her for so long, since she was just a girl. It was natural for them to be protective.

"I thought he was telling the truth," Anna said. They all turned to her. Dido was surprised that her sister had spoken out. She suspected the old men had forgotten she was even there. "And," Anna added, "I thought he was most taken by you, Dido. Of course."

"Of course," Dido murmured. She thought again of those piercing eyes and of a man who needed to found a city—or find a new home. "It is late," she said briskly. "I don't know why I imagined we had anything to discuss tonight. Let us all go to bed."

☽

Aeneas and the Trojans stayed—for a week, then longer. Families were moved into houses, individuals found jobs within the palace. Aeneas spent most of his time with Dido. He paid a visit to Iarbas, one prince to another. Dido did not know what was discussed at that visit, but afterwards Iarbas's gifts stopped.

Melqart and Mattan continued to air their disapproval of Dido's behaviour whenever they met with her without Aeneas present. She was not paying enough attention to matters of state, they said. She was neglecting her duties for a foreigner. They had a point; she hadn't sat in the law courts since he'd arrived. But Iarbas had retreated, at least temporarily, and that was a reason to celebrate.

At first, Dido escorted Aeneas about Carthage, showing off the city she was so proud of. They discussed the difficulties in setting up a new nation, the task that Dido was in the process of completing and one that was still ahead of Aeneas. At first they walked apart, as befitted a monarch and her guest, but soon Dido found more reasons to put a hand on his shoulder or, more daring, to direct his gaze by brushing her hand against his cheek. She clasped her shawl, sometimes allowing it to slip and expose one lovely shoulder, and she saw that Aeneas always noticed but remained reserved, allowing her to replace it without fanfare. And before long, she had shown him all there was to be seen of her little queendom, so they moved their conversations to her small courtyard, where her servants would bring them wine, and they would laugh and enjoy the sunshine.

Ascanius would play in front of them, and they would marvel at how he thrived in the Carthaginian sunshine. Soon Dido arranged for a tutor so Ascanius could return to his lessons, and then Dido and Aeneas would discuss Ascanius's progress, or any other matters that crossed their minds, without the need to pay any attention to the child himself.

Dido found that she had less time to spare for Melqart and Mattan. She did not demote them. If anything, it was a promotion, as she delegated so many of the duties that had once been hers alone to them. But she spent most of her time with Aeneas, and if not with Aeneas, with Anna.

Dido was pleasantly surprised, then delighted to find that Anna had developed into an eighteen-year-old capable of being a confidante. After so many years alone, with only doddering Melqart and disapproving Mattan to confer with, to suddenly have both a male companion and a female best friend was more than she had dreamed of. Anna was excited and enthralled by the romantic potential of Aeneas, the suitor from over the sea.

Dido could talk to Anna about Aeneas, how wonderful he was, how alike their perceptions. It was Anna who first suggested that, given Aeneas was agreeable, and sensible besides, why would it not make sense for Dido to marry him? Dido and Aeneas could rule the kingdom together.

Dido thought her sister spoke good sense. She knew that Aeneas spoke of his destiny, the kingdom he intended to found, but why found a kingdom when he had one right there for the taking, in sore need of a king? He could manage the advisors. He could assist her with the dispensing of justice. In time, they would have a son who could ascend to the throne. By then Dido and Aeneas would be elderly, grateful of the opportunity to fade into the background. Aeneas would himself become an advisor to the new king, one with first-hand knowledge of ruling the kingdom. Carthage was a wealthy city, and with Aeneas's guidance it would only become wealthier, and so Dido and Aeneas could live out their days in comfort and luxury.

Dido acknowledged that Ascanius, Aeneas's son, marred the neat tapestry she had woven for their lives together, but she was sure that something would work out for him. He was young, after all, and there were many nations in need of a ruler.

The more Dido and Anna conferred, the more their plan seemed not only ideal but also pragmatic. While Anna had no romantic experience, Dido had only a little more, her marriage to the much older Acerbas. Where Acerbas had seemed to humour her, and treat her like a child, Aeneas welcomed her touch.

Encouraged by Anna, she dressed more daringly, casting off the large shawl in favour of the Greek style of chiton, and she saw him eye her body appreciatively and even lick his lips nervously when he thought she wasn't looking. Dido could think of nothing other than Aeneas, but Aeneas also made no move to continue on his travels.

Finally, one day when Ascanius had departed for his lessons and they were alone in the garden, Dido stumbled, or seemed to stumble, over a rock that lay in her path. Aeneas caught her arm to hold her upright, then pulled her close to him. His mouth closed over her own and he kissed her. Dido had never felt anything like it. She clung to him as though she were drowning, and he held her in return, cupping her in his hands. He kissed her everywhere, her arms, her hands, her breasts, and only pulled away, reluctantly, when the sun started to drop in the sky, and they knew that Ascanius would be looking for them after finishing class.

That night in Dido's chamber, Anna listened, wide-eyed, as Dido told her of their newfound passion. Dido was in ecstasy, consumed by the fires of her love. "But," she asked Anna, her eyes wide and pleading, "What will I do when he leaves, as he one day must?"

"Marry him," Anna said simply, her hands clutched to her chest as though her sister's story was a romance told by a travelling bard. She had every faith in a happy ending.

"I can't make him marry me," Dido said, rolling over on her bed in despair.

"You don't have to," Anna replied with relish. "We are in Carthage, remember?"

Dido sat up and stared at her sister, not understanding.

"The local custom," Anna said slowly, "provides that if a man and a woman spend a night together and awake together the next morning, in front of witnesses, it is the same as a marriage."

"But Aeneas is not Carthaginian," Dido objected. "Nor am I."

Anna shrugged. "It is the custom," she said.

Dido smiled at her sister, not wanting to put her off. Ah, if she could just spend a night with Aeneas, she thought. His strong arms, his gentle mouth, so very different to old Acerbas's. But out loud she said, "Even if I could persuade him to spend the night with me, how do I ensure he wakes with me in front of witnesses? Men are not always so eager to stay until the morning," she added, although in truth, her knowledge of the ways of men where sex, rather than politics and violence, was concerned, was no greater than her sister's.

She thought that was the end of it, and although she knew that she should, as a modest woman, dismiss Aeneas from her presence, she could not. Instead, she drank from him, like some intoxicating draught. She told the servants to make themselves scarce each day, and she and Aeneas spent the next few days alone together, fondling each other and communicating without words. He never mentioned, as he had done so often in the past, his need to found another city in a foreign land. Instead, she allowed him to discover her own hidden places.

Dido thought that stolen kisses in a hidden garden were all she could hope for, but she had underestimated her sister. After a few days, Anna came to her, brimming with excitement and outrage.

"Dido," she said, once more in her sister's private chamber, which Aeneas had never visited, "you can't let him take advantage of you like this. Why should this foreigner turn up at our door, bringing with him the refugees we have fed and housed? Why should he be allowed to take advantage of your good nature, committing the very deed that should determine you married, and then sneak away from you like a thief in the night, as no doubt he will when he has tired of Carthage?"

Dido looked at her sister, her mind full of Aeneas. "Of course I don't want him to do this anymore than you do," she said. "But what do you suggest we do?"

Anna outlined her plan. She could consult a sage who was expert in determining weather conditions. She would ask the sage to predict a sunny day that would change to thunderstorms. Such days were not unknown in Carthage. At Anna's suggestion, Dido and Aeneas would go hunting. When caught out by the resulting rain, they would be forced to take shelter together in a cave, where they would be discovered the next morning by a search party.

Anna had turned the plan inside out, checking for flaws, but she could see none. If the sage was wrong, well then, Dido and Aeneas would simply return home and no one would be any the wiser. But if the sage was right, Aeneas would not be able to resist Dido while cloistered in the cave together. He could not escape early because he lacked Dido's knowledge of the local terrain. And so they would be discovered together.

Dido, in her turn, considered the plan. She knew that it must have its flaws. If she took it to her advisers—she could not help but snort at the idea—they would tell her she had lost her mind. And yet, she could not look past the fact that if she allowed this plan to proceed, regardless of what might happen afterwards, she could spend an entire, precious night alone in a cave with Aeneas, and nothing would prevent them from enjoying each other in the ways that she most desired.

The sky was bright blue on the morning of the hunt. Dido looked at it anxiously, hoping that the promised clouds would appear. She saddled her horse and rode off with Aeneas, having promised him the hunting for which Carthage was famous. Aeneas, of course, did not know that Dido herself never hunted, that she thought it cruel and unnecessary. Never mind. The storm would come soon, and she would not even have to string the bow hanging uselessly by her side.

As they rode, the clouds built up until they could no longer withstand the pressure, and the rain lashed down from the sky. Aeneas looked about in alarm, shouting at Dido to take his cloak, but she ignored him, confidently leading her horse to the cave she and her sister had determined on in advance.

They tied up the horses. Dido sneaked a glance at Aeneas, engaged in lighting a fire, his wet chiton clinging to his chest.

"You will catch cold," she said, her voice husky with anticipation. "You should take off your wet clothes."

She had thought he might protest, might adhere to the limits they had so far set for themselves, the respectability that might be expected of a queen and a visiting prince caught alone in an unexpected downpour. But he was, she supposed, his mother's son. As soon as the fire was blazing, he pulled his chiton over his head, then pulled her towards him, kissed her roughly, and pulled off hers too.

She stared at his chest, the strapping muscles that had been honed through the years of travel at sea, and the outdoor tan that seemed to make his skin glow even in the dark cave, and she paused only to whisper, "Can you be human?"

"I—no," Aeneas replied, sounding confused. "I'm a demigod—I've told you that before." But then he kissed her again, and she could think of nothing beyond the cave.

☽

Dido awoke the following morning to find the fire still slumbering, and Aeneas's brawny arms wrapped around her. At some point in the night, she had rolled her cloak into a pillow, and Aeneas's larger cloak was covering both of them as a blanket. She closed her eyes and basked in the glow. Acerbas had slept by her side every night of their marriage, but she had never felt as intimate with him as she did now with Aeneas. She pulled back and looked at him, his long eyelashes hiding those dark eyes, his warrior's torso tense even in sleep.

If only this moment could last forever, she wished, even as she heard the calls from the search party outside the cave.

"Dido," she heard loudest, a light, girlish voice. Anna had found them. She supposed that she should try to cover up, or at least feel ashamed of their nakedness. Next to her, Aeneas sat up, woken by the cries. He stretched and yawned, and turned to her as though he would say something. She never discovered what it was. At that moment Anna ran into the cave and embraced her, congratulating her loudly on her marriage. Dido looked at Aeneas and saw his dark eyes flash with anger. He understood everything, she thought, panicked. But he said nothing.

BOOK EIGHT

CREUSA

For hither borne, two Chiefs, bravest of all
The Trojans, Hector and Aeneas rush
Right through the battle

—Homer, *Iliad, Book Seventeen*
(trans. by William Cowper, 1791)

Creusa was sitting with her youngest sister, Polyxena, when Aeneas burst in. Polyxena was nearing two now, and thankfully her mother showed no signs of becoming pregnant again. This new age of life did not suit her, and strangely she seemed grumpier than she had done when she was lumbering around with a baby inside her womb. But even she agreed that Polyxena was an absolute delight of a child with which to end her birthing years, and besides, with an oldest son due to return with his own bride any day now, Hekuba was looking at becoming a grandmother next, not a mother again.

"Call your father," Aeneas said, grinning so widely that even Polyxena began to laugh, although she had no idea what was happening. "They're here—they've returned."

Creusa wasted no time. She dispatched the nearest servant to find her mother and father, then she grabbed her cloak and Polyxena's hand and raced to the window. "We'll never see them from here. Aeneas, will you take us to the shore?"

"Gladly," he said, hopping from one leg to the other in his desire to be off. He waited a moment for Creusa to wrap her cloak around herself, then swung Polyxena onto his shoulders, and together they chased down the corridors, out of the palace, and towards the harbour.

The large city gates stood wide open as citizens and slaves alike came to see the return of the beloved Prince Hektor. There was a pleasant buzz in the air as the crowd realised that the

moment they had been waiting and talking about for weeks, the
first sighting of the woman who was to become Hektor's bride,
and one day their queen, Andromache from Cilician Thebe,
was almost upon them. And no one could be more excited than
Aeneas himself.

Since the day almost an entire year ago when he and Hektor
had worked together to divert the bulls, they had been almost
inseparable. They had trained together, sparred together, and
broken horses together. And that meant that Creusa, too, now
officially betrothed to Aeneas, had spent more time than she had
ever imagined with her oldest brother. She knew that he only
tolerated her because of Aeneas, but at the same time, she saw
that his attention made Aeneas light up, and for that reason,
she forgave him. And besides, she reasoned, what older brother
ever wanted his little sister with him at all times? Hektor and
Aeneas had petitioned for Aeneas to join Hektor on the trip to
Cilician Thebe to bring home Andromache, but old Anchises,
Aeneas's father, had intervened and told Aeneas in no uncertain
terms that he was to stay home. He did not want his son running errands for Priam's. Creusa was not unhappy about this; she
supposed that she could have been allowed to join them, under
Hektor's care as her brother, but she hadn't wanted to travel to
Cilician Thebe. She did not have the head—or the stomach—for
sea travel.

A group of girls started a song, and soon all the women were
singing, a holy song devoted to the goddess Artemis, their protector. Creusa raised her voice too. Nearby a boy joined in with a
flute, and other instruments, kitharas and castanets, were added
to the chorus. it was a hymn to Hektor and Andromache, and
even though Creusa knew that her brother was only a mortal,
she still felt as though she might be welcoming home a pair of

gods. The young women's song died away, to be replaced by a more raucous one, and this time Aeneas, next to her, was singing lustily, laughing and chanting in the same breath.

Now she saw her father approaching the shore, riding in a chariot. The smells of incense, myrrh, and frankincense were in the air. Aeneas leaned over to her and shouted in her ear, trying to be heard above the din: "I wish I could give you this sort of reception, Creusa."

She shook her head; it didn't matter to her. She was enjoying the pomp of the day, she couldn't deny it, but she enjoyed it far more as a participant in the crowd. She didn't know how it would feel to be lonely Andromache, away from all her family and friends, brought to a strange place where she knew nobody and so much was expected of her. But Aeneas was still talking: "One day, one day I will take you home to Dardania, and you will be welcomed as a queen."

Dardania, Anchises and Aeneas's home. She was so used to them living in Troy, Anchises consulting with her father on the running of his kingdom, that she had forgotten they had their own home, their own kingdom to inherit. Anchises visited regularly, she knew, and was consulted by his own father, surely in his dotage by now, but Aeneas never left Troy. Would it still feel like home to him? And would she be happy living outside Troy? A small voice inside her told her that it was not something she needed to worry about, and so she didn't. She concentrated instead on the sunshine, the scents, the people jostling her. And then the ship was docked.

First, they unloaded the dowry that Andromache had brought with her. The crowd gasped to see it, the crates of gold bracelets, of perfumed purple cloths, painted toys of a kind she had never seen before, and silver cups and ivory cutlery, all exquisitely

beautiful. Cilician Thebe was a holy city, she knew; had Andromache's dowry been compiled from the offerings brought by travellers to the temples and shrines? The crowd oohed and aahed,
but soon their gasps of adoration died to a quiet hush as Prince
Hektor himself stepped out of the boat. Had her brother grown?
Surely not, and yet he seemed taller, statelier than ever before.
Aeneas next to her was the son of a goddess, but Hektor seemed
to emit a glow, his tall, plumed helmet blowing in the breeze. He
turned and offered a hand to the slight woman behind him, and
she, too, stepped out, holding her betrothed's hand for support.

First one old man, then a few more, then everyone, Creusa
and Aeneas too, dropped to their knees before the now slightly
embarrassed-looking Hektor and Andromache. Creusa dropped
her eyes, but not before she saw her father seeming highly satisfied before he pulled himself out of the chariot and went to
embrace his oldest, and almost certainly favourite, son. His
hands trembling a little, he handed Hektor a sparkling piece
of jewellery, and even Creusa gasped as she realised it was the
shimmering diadem that had once formed the centrepiece of her
grandmother's collection. As a little girl, she had once asked her
mother whether she might inherit it, but her mother had told
her, her tone brisk but kind, that this diadem was reserved for
the next queen of Troy, the one who would inherit the throne
when Priam passed away.

Hektor's wife, Andromache, would be the next queen of
Troy. Creusa watched as her brother's large, bearlike hands gently placed the diadem on his new wife's head. Despite his care,
he must have misplaced it, as she immediately put her hands up
to adjust it, and they smiled at each other, enclosed in their own
private Arcadia. Then they turned back and waved at the crowd
again, who cheered even more wildly at this tender display.

The young couple joined Priam in a chariot to be driven back to the palace, and the crowd dispersed. Aeneas swung Polyxena back down to the ground, the little girl still giggling excitedly. Creusa remained thoughtful, her hand resting on Aeneas's arm. It really had felt divine, a pair of gods bestowing their presence on mortals like a precious gift. And yet something about it sent a shiver down her spine. It wasn't wise to call the gods' attention to yourself.

$$)$$

Creusa, always watchful, had seen him first. It was only a single moon after Hektor and Andromache's wedding, which was as beautiful and joyous an occasion as everyone had anticipated. Creusa had worn a new dress, with flowers strewn through her hair. Until today, she had not spent much time with Andromache, who had been cloistered with her mother since she had arrived in Troy. But now she was watching Hektor and Aeneas breaking a new horse, using the uniquely Trojan method that was gentle but firm. They talked to the horse, walked it around, showed it the field in which it would live and the grains it could eat for supper.

Creusa had seen foreigners break their horses almost literally, thrashing them until they had no choice but to follow their new owners' commands. But they never achieved the centaur-like unison of man and horse that Trojans did, and as a result their horses were slower and more likely to shy when faced with new obstacles.

Beside her sat her new sister-in-law, her hands folded in her lap, and Creusa thought that she should probably make some conversation, like asking her how she was finding Troy, but Andromache seemed reluctant to chat, and if Creusa was honest with herself, she wasn't that keen either. And so she'd allowed herself to sit in silence, taking in the two men in front of them, and the lovely cool air early in the morning, and she had seen the man standing across from them, staring at Hektor.

"Who's that?" she asked, unwilling to point and nodding her head in his direction instead.

"I don't know," Andromache said, her lovely voice lilting like a melody. "I'm afraid I don't know many Trojans yet, though."

Creusa frowned. "You haven't seen him here before?" she asked. "He looks familiar, and he seems very intent on Hektor."

"Everyone is always watching Hektor," Andromache said happily. "He's going to be king one day. It's understandable."

Creusa gritted her teeth, annoyed not by the fact that Hektor was to be king, and by extension, Andromache queen—after all, Creusa herself would marry Aeneas, who was himself a prince, and in Creusa's mind far more interesting than Hektor would ever be, but because Andromache expected her to be jealous. But then she shook her head, not allowing herself to be distracted by such trivialities, and looked again at the stranger. And then she exclaimed, "But it's the cowherd!"

Hektor and Aeneas both looked up, startled by her cry, and she flushed. She hadn't meant to say anything at all, but she had been so surprised to recognise him, the words had burst out of her. Of course, she hadn't identified him at first, because she remembered him as a boy, and he had clearly done some growing in the moons since they had seen him. But now that she did know him, she couldn't mistake him for anyone else.

He was still beautiful beyond compare, as elegant as a woman with his high cheekbones and lustrous hair, still as beautiful as Ganymede, cupbearer to the gods, with his green eyes and slender limbs. And yet there was something else there, something in the shape of his head, or was it the way he held his shoulders, that called to mind her brother Hektor. Could he be one of her reputed half brothers? she wondered again. Perhaps one her father wasn't aware of, meaning his mother hadn't been paid off like all the others?

Hektor followed her gaze and, seeing the cowherd, he, too, frowned. He leaned over to Aeneas and whispered something. Creusa didn't hear what he said, but Hektor and Aeneas were soon on their feet, binding the horse so it couldn't run, and making their way over to the cowherd.

"Alexandros, isn't it?" Hektor called, his voice loud and cheerful, although Creusa could see he felt anything but. "What are you doing in the city, man? Tell me you haven't left your bulls to run rampant again."

"Alexandros is one of my names," the cowherd said. "I have come to see the king and the queen. I have news that will interest them."

"A cowherd asking to see the king and queen? This is most irregular," Hektor replied. He had reached the other man now and placed an arm on his shoulder, a friendly gesture, or so an onlooker might think. Alexandros squirmed and tried to move away, but Hektor had him pinned. Aeneas moved to Alexandros's other side, and the slighter man slumped in despair.

"Please just take me to them," he said.

"Share the news with the king's son," Aeneas invited, his tone friendly but firm. "Hektor is his father's closest aide and confidante. Your secret is safe with him, and once he has heard it, he can determine whether the king needs to hear it too."

Alexandros's handsome face twisted into an ugly scowl. "I do not wish to share my news with anyone other than the king and queen."

"A night in a cell might make you feel differently," Aeneas suggested, but Hektor held up a hand.

"Peace, Aeneas—we are not in the business of imprisoning cowherds. You understand this is not usual, man. But look, my sister Creusa is here with us. She will go and find my father and ask whether he will have you attend him. If the answer is yes, we will take you to him." Hektor did not say what would happen if the answer were no.

Alexandros nodded. "Please, Your Highness, put my case well."

Creusa did not see that he had much of a case to put. She rose to her feet and walked briskly towards the palace. She was not going to put herself out by running. She understood why Hektor had sent her, but she did not want him to think that she was going to become his errand girl.

She found her parents together, bent over the roses that grew in the little courtyard outside her mother's private chambers. In later years, she would have many chances to reflect on the opportunities they'd had to change the course of history, to avoid their impending fate. She would remember her mother and father, smiling gently at each other, her mother's arm resting on her father's, the low light in the courtyard, the sense of a duty completed. And she would wonder whether she could have changed everything if she had just gone back and told Hektor that their father didn't want to see the cowherd. But instead, she said awkwardly, "Mama? Abba?" and watched them both look up, their faces struggling to hide their disappointment in having their moment ended.

"What is it, Creusa?" her mother asked, straightening up and half turning away from Creusa's father.

"There is a man here to see you. His name is Alexandros. He is a cowherd from Mount Ida. He won't say what he wants except that he wants to tell you he has another name . . ." Creusa trailed off as she saw her parents turn white and grab at each other, as though they were teenage lovers instead of the king and queen of Troy.

"Hekuba, it may not be him," her father murmured.

"No, it is, it is," she replied. "Creusa, you must take us to him at once."

"No," her father said, shaking his head. "We do this properly. Bring him to the throne room."

Her parents turned and walked away, roses and daughter equally discarded. Creusa saw that her mother seemed to be using her father as support, when it was her father who had a bad leg and limped a little.

Slowly she walked back to her brother, Aeneas and the cowherd, mulling over her parents' odd behaviour. She couldn't make any sense of it, so when she reached the three young men, none of whom, she was relieved to see, had yet drawn a sword, although the air crackled with potential for it, all she said was, "Mother and Father will see him in the throne room."

Hektor stumbled back in surprise, and she saw the other man smirk a little, as though he had won the first of many victories.

"Allow us to escort you there," Aeneas said firmly, not removing his hand from the intruder's elbow, and so Hektor, Alexandros and Aeneas made their way to the throne room.

Creusa watched them go.

"Should we follow them?" a quiet voice asked. Creusa spun round to realise that Andromache still sat there, forgotten by everyone. She shrugged, then decided that they might as well. But when they reached the throne room, the doors were already closed, and Aeneas and Hektor had been dismissed and stood scowling outside. And so they had to wait until later that day,

when Priam had the messengers announce that the young cowherd was not Alexandros, but instead, Paris, *Prince* Paris, the boy
who had been exposed on the mountain but had come home to
his own family. Paris who was prophesied to bring ruin to Troy
and all her people. Paris, Creusa's newest and most unwelcome
brother.

☽

Creusa's wedding day was fast approaching, provided that her
new brother Paris returned in time for it, bringing the groom
back with him. Her father was absolutely besotted with the son
that he'd had returned to him in his old age; he would proclaim
loudly to anyone who would listen that the gods had seen fit to
bestow this gift on him as a reward for his years of piety.

Creusa suspected that most, if not all, of his adoration
stemmed from his relief that his necessary but evil deed had been
overturned: he had not murdered his own son, and his hands
were clean once more. No one else, though, had protested too
loudly when Paris had insisted on taking a ship and sailing on a
trade mission to Sparta. Even her mother, she suspected, had had
enough of the constant emotional wails whenever anyone tried
to withhold something from the prince or to impose any bound-
aries on him whatsoever.

He had embraced part of his princely role—the luxuries,
the perks, the clothes, and the attendant women—without any
understanding of the other side, the need to govern the city, to
consider the needs of the people, to take care of the poor.

Paris complained bitterly whenever he thought that Hektor
had received some privilege that was denied him, and yet Hektor spent his days working hard to learn from his father and to
take over the duties his father was struggling to carry out. Paris

attended one session of the law courts and left halfway through the first case, announcing that it was "boring." The plaintiff and defendant, neighbours who were tussling over the ownership of a fertile strip of land between their two estates, sat in stunned silence until Antiphus, one of Creusa's younger brothers who was barely more than a boy, could be persuaded to come and hear the case.

So no one had looked too closely into Paris's reasoning behind this need for a trade delegation. Hektor had been on one recently, and Paris wanted everything that Hektor had. Sparta was some distance from Troy, and Creusa did wonder how he had heard of the place, having lived as an isolated cowherd for most of his life, but she was herself busy, preparing to wed Aeneas and move into a small dwelling on the outskirts of the royal quarters.

The location for their household had been a matter of some debate. Anchises and Aeneas had lived in Troy for over ten years now, and yet Priam was unwilling to let his cousin leave. Creusa wondered what it was that her father was so afraid of, but she also didn't want to leave Troy, and she was relieved that Aeneas, too, was happy to stay in the city, training alongside Hektor and accompanying his father on visits home to ensure their own city was prospering too. But now someone needed to accompany the new prince on his self-imposed task, and as Hektor could not be spared, Aeneas was chosen to go.

Every morning, Creusa woke with a sinking heart as she heard there was still no news as to when Paris—and more importantly, for Creusa at least, Aeneas—might be returning. Finally, the day before her proposed wedding day, she received the news that Paris's ship had been spotted on the horizon, and if he had a fair wind, Aeneas would be home that day.

She dressed and called a servant to escort her down to the harbour to welcome them home. On arrival, she looked about

the waterfront; the atmosphere could not have been more different from that day, only a year earlier, when they had welcomed
Hektor and Andromache home. Today, very few people had
bothered to turn out. Paris had not ingratiated himself with anyone. It didn't seem likely that he would have brought any gifts
for anyone other than himself, whereas Hektor and Andromache
had arranged for servants to distribute sweetmeats to the crowds.
The very skies seemed darker, and rain threatened. Creusa shivered, although it wasn't actually cold.

And then the boat was there, and she had eyes for one man
only. Although he was not at the front of the boat, nor was he to
be allowed to disembark first, there was her Aeneas. She thought
back to the first time she had seen him, the slight, dark-eyed
boy hanging back from the throng. And here he was again, ten
years older, and although he was now coming to a city that he
had made his own, a cousin who loved him like a brother, and
a woman who was soon to be his wife, he still appeared a little
hesitant, a little unsure, and it made her love him all the more
fiercely.

She reached her hand up to wave at him, and seeing her, he
waved back, although he was not smiling. He looked away from
her towards the front of the boat, and following his gaze, she saw
what he was worried about. There was Paris, as beautiful as ever,
and he was holding the arm of a woman as lovely as he as she
stepped over the side of the boat and onto the dock.

Creusa looked back towards Aeneas, puzzled. Paris had gone
on a trade delegation. Who was this woman? Aeneas shook his
head slightly. Paris jumped over the side of the boat and took the
woman's arm again, pulling her close in a gesture that indicated
he was being more than just gentlemanly. Together, they made
a supernaturally handsome couple, both with hair the colour

of honey and bright blue eyes, their limbs slender and supple, standing a little taller than everyone else.

Something was wrong, though. She thought back to Hektor and Andromache, neither as attractive as this pair, even homely looking, and yet on that day she had felt as though she stood in the presence of gods. Today she was not sure what she stood in the presence of.

Paris and the woman strutted over to the waiting chariot, ignoring Creusa completely. It wasn't deliberate, she thought bitterly. He had completely forgotten who she was, her presence on one of the most important days of his life an irrelevance.

Then she found herself enveloped in an embrace, and she could think about her brother no longer. She smelled the salt air on his tunic, felt his warm skin pressed against her arms, and heard the thumping of his heart in his chest, and a little voice in her head, one that she almost never allowed herself to listen to, the voice of hope, said, *Soon he will be your husband, and you can hold each other like this whenever you want.*

They stood clasped together for what seemed like forever, but then Aeneas disengaged and said, "We have to go to the palace. We need to see Hektor."

"Why?" Creusa asked, motioning her servant to bring a chariot, but she thought she already knew the answer. "That woman Paris has brought back? Who is she?"

Aeneas turned white. "She is Helen of Sparta. She's Menelaus's wife."

"What's she doing here?" she asked, but she knew the answer. "Will Menelaus be coming to fetch her?" They climbed into the chariot, and Aeneas took the reins himself, so they thundered up the path, back past the large city gates, towards the palace.

"Not just Menelaus. She's *Helen*. The Greek kings all swore an oath, before she chose one of them to marry, that if anyone tried to take her, they would all band together to bring her back to her husband."

"But Paris didn't swear the oath. He must have been a cowherd at the time."

Aeneas frowned, then continued. "It doesn't matter. They swore the oath that they would protect her husband against usurpers. Paris is a usurper. And that's not even the worst of it."

"How can it possibly be worse than that?" she asked. They had reached the palace now. Aeneas offered her his arm, but she leapt over the side wall without him. Now was not the time for hesitation.

"Menelaus will be returning from his hunting trip any day now to find that not only his wife is missing but also a significant amount of his wealth. Paris and Helen have stolen as much as they could carry."

Creusa felt ill at the thought of the devastation her brother could bring upon them all. Troy could stand against one Greek king, but all of them? "He must send her back. What was he thinking?"

"He wasn't," Aeneas said through gritted teeth. "He was embarrassing. Kept sighing and making eyes at her. Once he knocked over a wine glass, then traced 'I love you, Helen' in the pool of wine with his finger. Goodness knows why she found his behaviour attractive. He must have learned it from his calves."

"I suppose it's obvious why he found her attractive," Creusa said. "She is very beautiful."

"Is she? Seems a bit cold to me," Aeneas said. They had reached the throne room, and they could hear voices within. He took a deep breath. "Come on. I hope we aren't too late." He pushed the door open. A tableau awaited them. In the centre of the room, Helen stood with her hands held to Priam's in a gesture of supplication. Hektor stood to one side, scowling; Paris to the other side, smirking. Her mother, seated on her throne, met Creusa's gaze, her eyes worried. They were too late.

Perhaps it could all still have been saved; perhaps cooler heads might have prevailed if everyone had remained calm and rational. But that was not what in fact happened. For at that moment, Cassandra burst through the room, her robes flapping wildly, her headdress balanced at an impossible angle on her head.

"Death, death, death! She brings death to us all," she cried, her singsong voice a parody of the songs that Creusa had sung to her younger siblings, perhaps even to Cassandra herself, to help them sleep.

"Cassandra," her father said angrily, "what are you doing here? These are matters of state. Do you not have offerings to make?"

"That woman brings death to us all," she said firmly. "She will bring her husband seeking her, and he will bring war, and the war will bring death. Death to *you*"—and she pointed at her father; "and death to *you*"—indicating Hektor; "and death to *you*"—spinning towards Paris; "and death to *you*"—levelling her gaze on Creusa, who shivered, even though she thought that Cassandra was just pointing at each of them in turn for emphasis now. "And death—oh no, not death. Not death to *you*," she said to Aeneas, and smiled, a grim, mirthless look. "No, you have too much to do. You will found the new Troy. You will be king of the new Troy. Your descendants will rule the new Troy—"

Creusa shuddered, her sister's words bringing back a half-remembered image from her childhood. Aeneas had told her, hadn't he, when they first spoke, that his mother had said the same thing? But Cassandra was mad. Everyone knew that.

"Enough," Priam shouted, the very walls seeming to tremble at his rage, the likes of which Creusa had never seen from him before. "Daughter, you overstep! You are not in your right mind, Cassandra, and this is why I will not have you put to death, but what you are saying is treason. This young upstart will not be ruling any new Troy, as you call it. Troy is alive and well, and it will be ruled by me and in turn by my son Hektor, and by his children and his children's children."

Cassandra blinked, but she was used to violent reactions, and she carried on. "Oh, but Father, the new Troy will be ruled by your descendants. Creusa is your daughter, and she will marry Aeneas—"

"Not anymore, not if I have anything to say about it. Anchises's son is nothing to me," Priam thundered. His face had turned a dark, blotchy colour, and Creusa was as worried about her father as she was about her wedding. "Cassandra, if I hear another word from you, I will throw you over the parapets myself."

"Please, Father, I beg of you, send this woman back to Sparta," she said quickly, and then closed her mouth up and shook her head slightly, indicating that she would not say another word.

Priam stared at her coldly, "I swear by the gods that I shall never send this woman back," he said. "Go back to your temple now, Daughter."

Cassandra gathered up her robes and shuffled out of the room. She glanced appealingly at Creusa as she went past, but Creusa looked away. She knew her sister wasn't capable of understanding the damage she had just done, but in that moment Creusa didn't feel like showing her any compassion either. Cassandra thought that all she had to do was shout her prophecies at people, and they would fall instantly in line. She hadn't allowed for her father's rage, his stubbornness, his refusal to listen to any woman, let alone his own daughter.

If Creusa had wanted Priam to banish Helen, she would have spoken to him in private, poured him a drink, appealed to his vanity and his intelligence. Yes, of course, they could defeat the Greeks, but wouldn't it be better not to have to try, for the sake of a foolish woman? But Cassandra couldn't have driven him further towards war if she'd strapped him into a chariot and rode the horses at full speed. Priam was now the protector of poor, maligned Helen, and that was that.

Creusa had hoped her father's rage might be spent when the mad priestess was gone, but instead he turned on Aeneas.

"I suppose you put that idea in her head, that you might take over Troy. Well, think again."

"I am a prince of Dardania, sir," Aeneas said, his tone polite but his face stony. "I have no intention of taking over Troy. My father and I are here because you asked us to be."

"And Cassandra says you want to marry one of my daughters?" Priam asked, disdain dripping from his voice. "Which one would that be? Why is this the first that I'm hearing of this?" He turned to Hekuba, which was a mistake. Her dark eyes flashed with outrage.

"He is marrying Creusa. In two days' time. You have already given your permission, and it is too late to revoke it now. And don't you think it is time that you let go of Helen?"

Priam looked down and saw he still clasped the Greek woman's hands. She opened her eyes very wide and smiled at him as he let her hands go, as if to say that she understood he must listen to his wife, but she had no concern about his closeness to her presence.

She certainly seemed remarkably unperturbed by all that had occurred, Creusa thought bitterly. And Helen, like Aeneas, had been excluded from Cassandra's morbid predictions.

It was clear that nothing more was to be achieved, although nothing had been resolved either. Helen was not leaving, and they would have to wait to see how her Greek husband responded. Awkwardly, they all made their excuses and left the throne room to the king and queen.

Creusa expected that she would leave with Aeneas. She wanted to seek his view on what had just occurred. She also wanted to reassure him that no matter what her father said, she would marry him.

And yet it was Helen who was by her side as they left the room; Helen who tucked her arm into Creusa's as though they had known each other all their lives; Helen who said, "As you are my husband Paris's sister, so shall you be my sister. And we shall be the best of friends."

Creusa managed to prevent herself from ripping her arm away, but it was a task worthy of one of the legends of old.

☽

The day of Creusa's wedding dawned, and for that brief time all thoughts of Helen and the Spartan army were driven from her head. She awoke early and allowed her mother to lead her through to her own royal bathroom, where a slave cut her hair and assisted her to bathe in waters that had been brought from a sacred spring. Then she was dressed in the finest robes, bought just for her, and not for one of her sisters. She breathed a sigh of relief; she had worried that her mother might try to use Andromache's old robes. Her mother motioned the slave to step to one side, and she draped and fastened Creusa's veil herself. She held

Creusa at arm's length to inspect her, and Creusa was horrified to see tears welling up in Hekuba's eyes. Never had she known her mother to cry, at least not in relation to Creusa. She thought her mother might say something, but she held her daughter tight instead, then let her go and stepped away. When Creusa looked at her face again, there was no sign of the tears, and Creusa wondered if she had imagined it.

Creusa was taken down to the banquet hall, where her father was presiding over the feast. Aeneas sat next to him, and it seemed that her father had decided to be civil for the day, or perhaps Hekuba had decided for him.

Hektor sat next to her father on the other side, and Paris was nowhere to be seen. Creusa took her own seat in the corner, still veiled. She found the ritual dinner to be oddly humorous, and she looked around for Aeneas to share the joke, but of course he was still seated at the main table. Servants brought her food and wine, which she could have lifted her veil to eat, but her hands shook and she wasn't hungry. Cassandra had not been invited to the wedding, but little Polyxena had been allowed to attend, and she was torn between running up and down the hall and sitting next to her sister, holding her hand.

At last, it was dark enough for the procession. Creusa and Aeneas were half assisted, half pushed out of the banquet hall into the traditional cart pulled by mules.

Everyone was cheering, and someone started singing a ribald song before remembering whose daughter Creusa was, and stopping abruptly. But they couldn't dampen the general air of merriment. Creusa clutched at Aeneas's hand, within reach for the first time that day. His palm felt warm to the touch, a little sweaty, and she thought perhaps he was nervous too, for all he was laughing and waving at Hektor and Helenus.

The torches were lit, the mules kicked, and they left the palace complex to proceed down the street to the small house that was to become Creusa's new home. Now, not only the palace wedding guests but also other citizens of Troy joined the procession, people that Creusa had never seen before, applauding and singing and wishing the lucky couple well, whomever they might be. Andromache hadn't had this, Creusa thought, because her procession had all been conducted inside the palace. Creusa hadn't been sure she would enjoy it, but now that it was actually happening, she relished it because the well-wishers had no idea they were cheering on Prince Aeneas and Princess Creusa. It was a wedding, and that was enough to make everyone happy. She wriggled a little closer to Aeneas and waved at the crowd with her free hand, anonymous beneath her veil.

As they got closer to the house, Creusa found herself sitting up in her seat. It was customary for the groom's mother to greet them at the house and show the bride around her new domain. Would Aphrodite actually appear? She felt the muscles in her jaw tense; the last thing she wanted was to draw Aeneas's attention to her expectation. She didn't want him to think her disappointed if the goddess did not make an appearance.

Finally, they reached the house, and Creusa could see a figure standing at the door. Taller than most women, she thought, and her heart clenched. But when they disembarked, Aeneas jumping over the side, then gallantly offering her his hand, she saw that it was only old Anchises who had hurried on before them, the worried expression on his face suggesting that he, too, knew that Aeneas would be at a disadvantage if his immortal mother could not be in attendance.

Creusa exchanged a glance with her new father-in-law, then embraced him; they were complicit now. Anchises showed her around her new home, and Creusa enthusiastically expressed her appreciation. The role of the mother-in-law was a women's custom, and it was likely that Aeneas never realised that his father had, for one more time, acted as father and mother both to his beloved son.

Finally, Anchises showed them to their room and firmly closed the door behind them. Creusa removed her veil and instantly felt shy again, even though it was only Aeneas, who had been her best friend for so long now. She didn't know what he would say, but if he made a joke, she didn't think she could bear it. But he just smiled, that beautiful smile of his that transformed his face and made him handsome, and held out his hands to her, and as the last of the twilight gave way to a warm, comforting darkness, she wondered whether the goddess of love had blessed her son on their wedding day after all.

☽

Creusa's moment of peace was short-lived. It didn't take long for the Greek ships to follow Helen. The rumours arrived before the ships did, reports of looting and destruction from coastal cities between Greece and Troy. But the ships weren't far behind. And despite the rumours, the most surprising aspect, the *only* surprising aspect, was just how many ships there were.

"There must be thousands of them," Andromache remarked to Creusa as they stood on the great walls, gazing out to sea. Creusa nodded in agreement, thankful for the sturdy nature of the walls beneath her feet. All they need do was lock the gates and remain inside, and surely the Greeks would admit defeat and go home.

"They made a promise to my husband," a bright voice behind them said, and they turned slightly to see Helen herself looking out across the harbour. She seemed to see no issue with referring to both Paris and Menelaus as her husband, depending on the context.

For one brief, mad moment, it occurred to Creusa that there was another way she could prevent the coming conflict. Helen was slight, barely coming up to Creusa's shoulder. She could bodily hoist her up and over the wall, let the Greeks race to claim their missing queen with her brains dashed out on the rocks below. Her father would probably send her to the Greeks to do with as they would, but at least she was only one person.

Common sense reasserted itself quickly. She had no way of knowing how the Greeks would react, so her sacrifice might all be in vain. And besides, it would be one thing if they were alone, but Andromache was there with them too, and she would never stand for it. Helen and Andromache together would overpower her, and then she would be sent to the Temple of Apollo with the other mad sister.

"A promise, you say?" she heard herself saying instead. "Do tell us more about that, please." And so they listened as Helen explained, as Aeneas had, the vow that the Greek kings had made, that whichever of them married Helen, the others would defend his rights with their lives.

And here they were now prepared to sacrifice their lives, and the lives of all the soldiers they had brought with them, just to take one woman home. Well, one woman and all the treasures of Troy that the Greeks had been eyeing up for years, but it seemed churlish to mention that in front of the woman herself. Just like it seemed rude to ask Helen why, if she set such stock by vows, she hadn't thought to keep the ones she had made to Menelaus, a man she still described as her husband.

So instead, Creusa and Andromache smiled and nodded until it was time for them all to go to lunch. It was a special occasion; Priam had prepared a feast to accompany the granting of special armour to Hektor and Paris, the two Trojan heroes who would be leading them into battle. But more surprises awaited them. Paris admired and stroked the armour that Priam had commissioned specially for him, then airily said, "Of course, as an archer, I do not expect to take the front line, but I'm sure it will come in useful should our defences be breached."

Even Priam had to splutter at that. "Not take the front line? My son, the Trojan army will be expecting it of you."

"It is no matter," Hektor said quickly, tearing his own gaze away from the triumphant plume that adorned his new helmet. "Paris is not the only new brother I have gained recently. No doubt his skills learned defending cattle will serve him well on the archery line, but my brother-in-law Aeneas has trained by my side since we were boys. I would be glad to have him as my second."

Creusa felt herself glowing with pride as Aeneas half lifted himself across the table to meet Hektor's one-armed embrace. Paris scowled.

"That is fitting, indeed," Paris said, spitting his words out at Hektor, "because it is my patron, the goddess Aphrodite, who has decided that I am not to take the front line. Presumably she cannot bear to risk me."

Creusa rose to her feet, although to say what, she couldn't think. Paris's meaning was clear enough, though: that the goddess loved him so much more than her own son, she would sacrifice Aeneas to protect Paris. Out of the corner of her eye, she could see she wasn't the only one upset; her parents, too, looked peeved, as they always did when Anchises's divine lover, and the resulting demigod status that had been bestowed upon his son, and not on the princes and princesses of Troy, was mentioned. But none of them were the first to speak. Instead, that was Aeneas.

"You have spoken to her then? Recently?" He didn't sound angry. He sounded the way Creusa's youngest brother, Polydorus, had sounded when he'd found out he wasn't going to be allowed to join the army. Creusa willed him to stop talking.

"Of course," Paris said, widening his eyes in feigned innocence. "She visits me all the time. As, I'm sure, she does you."

He's lying, Aeneas, Creusa thought as hard as she could, hoping that somehow Aeneas would read her mind and simply ignore Paris. *He wants a reaction from you, the reaction that he can't get from Hektor.* She looked across at her brother and frowned, but he simply looked blank.

Aeneas looked as though he was about to say something, but then his shoulders slumped. "Never often enough, Paris. But you must feel the same way, surely? For we were both raised apart from our mothers. And when that is the case, how can any visits, any communications, as an adult ever be enough?"

He nodded sadly to Priam, pushed back his chair, and walked slowly away, leaving a muted silence behind him. Paris's mouth was slightly open, Creusa noticed meanly before she hurried after Aeneas. She knew that she was not impartial, but she felt sure that everyone there would remember Aeneas had conducted himself with grace.

BOOK NINE

DIDO

The Sidonian Dido, she who was doomed not easily
to endure the loss of her Phrygian husband, received
Aeneas, both in her home and her affection; . . . herself
deceived, she deceived all.
                    —Ovid, *Metamorphoses, Book Fourteen*
                       (trans. by Henry T. Riley, 1851)

Dido was almost blissfully happy. The entire city was talking about Prince Aeneas, the new consort to their queen. As Dido was a popular ruler, Carthage was prepared to accept Aeneas with open arms. The elders, their earlier misgivings forgotten, offered him a seat on the council without Dido's intervention. His belongings were relocated to the royal quarters. Carthage, once merely a host, prepared to become the new home to the Trojans. Starting with an elaborate ceremony to celebrate the marriage that had already been consummated. Even Iarbas grudgingly sent a gift to the man he believed to be the new ruler of Carthage.

And throughout all of this, Aeneas stayed silent. Dido hoped that she had mistaken the look of anger she saw contort his face, because he did not protest his new position. And yet he did not seem to embrace it either. He embraced Dido, certainly, on a nightly basis. And yet when it came to the wedding arrangements and the changes to the government of Carthage, he was passive, like a rock in the water that allows a stream to slip this side and that side of it, doing what it wants, without offering any resistance. But eventually such rocks must either erode or else they are prised out of their resting place and float away downstream.

Dido tried to engage with him. "Aeneas, are there any Trojan customs that you would like to include in the wedding?" she asked one morning as they sat eating their breakfast together. Fully clothed, of course; although it made no difference now,

Aeneas dressed quickly every morning, as though he thought the court would burst into their private bedroom.

A shadow passed over his eyes.

Dido felt a shard of envy pass through her heart. "What are you thinking?" she asked, her tone sharp. She stared at him, daring him to say that he was thinking of his first wife.

"Oh, nothing," he said, looking down at his yogurt.

"I imagine your wife would be happy to see you getting married," she pushed further, like a child who can't resist pulling at a scab. "As you said, she gave you her permission to be happy when you left Troy."

Now there was no mistaking the pain in his eyes. He stood up abruptly. "Excuse me. I agreed to hear the cases in the law courts this morning. I must do my duty."

He kissed her briefly then walked out. It was hard to say which of them the exchange had hurt more, she thought, looking down at her fingers and the blood beside her fingernail, where she had worried the skin away without realising it.

But as the days passed, Aeneas's mood seemed to improve. They no longer cavorted in her private garden by day: Why did they need to when they spent all night together? That gave Aeneas time to fully adopt his new duties. He always seemed to be running from one meeting to another, forming committees to plan the new buildings. The work on the Temple of Juno, which Dido had sadly neglected, resumed, although Dido was surprised to see the plans for the alcove included a statue of Juno accompanied not by her customary peacock, but by a large swan. She meant to speak to Aeneas about it, but she could never catch him during the day, and at night she was too consumed to talk.

Dido allowed herself to become comfortable in her new life, but Aeneas never did. Like the proverbial thief in the night, he did not tell Dido of his intention, but simply packed his bags one night and made his way to the boats. The Trojans followed him as one, although no Carthaginian had ever heard them plotting.

Dido woke in the early hours of the morning and turned over in bed, only to find herself alone. For a moment her hand rested on the space where Aeneas should have been, already cooling.

And then she knew.

She sprang out of bed and pulled on a cloak, then raced to the stables, where she saddled her own horse. Her legs ached; those lazy days drinking wine had taken their toll. But she was still a skilled rider, and she reached the shore before long.

"Aeneas," she called. "Come here, you coward! Weren't you going to say goodbye?"

She half expected the ship to pull away, its captain remaining below deck, but Aeneas presented himself on board. His face was pale. He said nothing.

"Please, Aeneas," Dido said, sliding down from her horse. "You do not have to leave like this. You do not have to leave at all. Come back to bed, and we can discuss it tomorrow."

Aeneas managed a wry half smile. "Ah, Dido, you know that if I come back to your bed, I may never find the resolve to leave again."

"So don't leave," she said. "Why must you leave?" The sun was rising now, and she allowed her cloak to slip, baring her shoulders. Aeneas saw but he made no move towards her.

"It is the will of the gods," he said. "It is the promise I once made. I'm sorry, Dido. I wish you no ill-will, but I must leave."

"And what will happen to me? To Carthage?" Dido asked, her voice rising. The horse reared its head at her panicked tone, and she yanked its bridle closer to her.

"You will go back to ruling as you did before. You are strong—"

"You have been here a year," Dido said, cutting him off. "Everyone believes us to be married. I was able to stave off Iarbas before because he hadn't yet worked up to his proposal. With you gone, I will be a fallen woman, and he will prey on me. And that's if my brother doesn't arrive first." The full horror of her predicament began to dawn on her. She almost lost hold of the horse altogether, her breast heaving as she sobbed out the last words. "How can you leave and call yourself a man? Aeneas, if you ever loved me—"

"I told you, I am not a mere man. I am a demigod, and I must fulfil my destiny," he interrupted her, then turned away from her and began to prepare to lift anchor, his hands shaking as he pulled at the ropes.

Not caring who heard her now, she cried out, 'You have lied to me, Aeneas! You have misled me in the name of love. You are not your mother's son. You do not respect the goddess Venus. I call on all the gods to curse you and to make you repent the day you left me. I call on your own brother, the god Cupid, to show you the error of your ways. Guards! Citizens of Carthage! Why do you not stop that man? He stole your queen's virtue under false pretences! I loved you, Aeneas. I *loved* you.'

Aeneas kept his head down and exhorted his men under his breath to continue their preparations. The gods were on their side, he told them, showing them the favourable winds. They could reach their new home before nightfall.

Dido sobbed herself hoarse, and then she could only stand and stare as the ship sailed away.

She climbed back on her horse, now almost mad with fear, and whipped it soundly to force it to carry her back to the palace. The journey was slow and painful, and Dido had ample time to reflect on her foolish mistake. She no longer cursed Aeneas; her curses were all for herself. How could she have trusted him? How could she have betrayed Acerbas? She had spent so long comparing him, his soft body and his grizzled head, unfavourably with Aeneas, that she had blinded herself to his true value. The thought of her kind, patient husband, whose gold would all now surely be wasted as either Pygmalion or Iarbas took Carthage, was too much to bear. And what would happen to her? Pygmalion would kill her, while Iarbas would force her to marry him. Which was worse?

She could barely see for tears. Better for everyone had foolish Dido never lived.

Continuing to berate herself, she reached the palace. Anna was waiting for her with some of her female attendants, her eyes wide. Dido looked at her tiny frame and wondered how she had ever thought her sister was an adult who could be relied on to provide advice in adult matters.

"We will not stand for this," she told the waiting women. "Prepare a ritual sacrifice. Sprinkle your bodies with river water, bind your hair with ribbons, and gather the animal offerings. Meanwhile I will collect every last item that the Trojans have left behind. Their clothes, their utensils, even the child's cot that Ascanius slept in when he first came to us. I will build a pyre and place all these items on it, and together we will offer to the gods the leavings of the Trojans. In this way, we will banish their memories and cleanse our city of their foul lies."

The pyre was built. Dido inspected it, then kissed her sister. "Go and check the stores," she murmured to her. "Make sure those wretched Trojans have stolen nothing, besides my heart."

When she was sure that Anna had gone, she picked up a lighted torch, climbed to the top of the pyre, and looked out to sea. The Trojan ship had not yet gone far. Aeneas would see the flames, she thought. She dropped the torch. Then she took the sword he had left behind, and drove it deep into her body. The pain was agonising, but as her breath ebbed away, she knew it was only what she deserved. With her last dying breath, she whispered, "Aeneas."

BOOK TEN

LAVINIA

Thereon Allecto, steeped in Gorgonian venom, first seeks Latium and the high house of the Laurentine monarch, and silently sits down before Amata's doors, whom a woman's distress and anger heated to frenzy over the Teucrians' coming and the marriage of Turnus. At her the goddess flings a snake out of her dusky tresses, and slips it into her bosom to her very inmost heart, that she may embroil all her house under its maddening magic.

—Virgil, *Aeneid, Book Seven*

Lavinia woke the next morning, her mind churning with thoughts of Dido and Aeneas. How could he have left her after promising to stay? Anna had even told her that Aeneas and Dido underwent a customary marriage, and he had disregarded it completely. Would he do the same if they had a Latin wedding? she wondered. And if he'd stayed with Dido, she thought selfishly, none of them would be in this predicament. There would be no war between Laurentines and Rutuli. Turnus would not have been infected with madness. Camilla need not have gone to war. It was this last thought she dwelled on most as she made her way to the mess tent, wishing her friend were there to meet her once again.

Feeling a hand on her shoulder, she whipped round, prepared to tell the perpetrator to take his hands off her royal person. But instead, she felt a sack being slipped over her head, pinning her arms to her sides. She scuffled but could get no purchase on the sides. She wriggled further, but burly arms were holding her tight, and she felt herself elevate, to about shoulder height, she would have guessed. At least she could see sunlight streaming through tiny holes pricked through the sack. The person who had kidnapped her did not intend her to die in this sack.

She thought that her legs must be dangling in front, her head hanging over his back—from his size and strength, she deduced he was a man.

She began to feel dizzy, her head banging up and down as he walked. She felt the coarse fabric abrading her skin. At one point he must have walked her into a tree, as she felt the branch and leaves crash into the backs of her thighs. She cried out in pain. The noise of birdsong was getting louder, so they must be going farther into the forest. Twigs crackling underfoot added weight to her theory.

Eventually, they reached their destination. She was dumped on the ground, still in the sack. Rubbing at her arms and legs, she knew she would have some unsightly bruises before long. No one was coming to help her, so she struggled out of the sack by herself, the relief almost overwhelming as she pushed her prison over her head and looked around, blinking.

They were in a small glade in the forest, like the one where Aeneas had conducted his offering to the gods. No altar stood before her, though; instead, a small group of people clustered in front of her. Mostly women, although she did see the odd man, like the one who had brought her here whom she now identified clearly as the commander of her mother's private guard. And finally, standing in front of her, tapping her foot, was her mother.

"What are you wearing?" Lavinia exclaimed. Her mother was draped from head to toe in all manner of leaves, and she had painted stripes of mud on her cheeks.

"I am dressed in the garb of the forest and the goddess."

Lavinia looked at her mother's hair, once pristine and coiffed, now matted with leaves. Fear gripped her once more, but not for herself this time. How could she have agreed with her father to leave her mother unattended for so long?

"Has Turnus put you up to this?" Lavinia asked, looking about, although based on his behaviour when she had last seen him, she did not think he would be much saner.

"We are in the forest worshipping the goddesses, to support Turnus's endeavours in the war. Our goddesses, not the foreign ones that Aeneas worships. They will be of no good to him here."

"Ceres?" Lavinia guessed.

"That's right. We are celebrating the Mysteries."

Lavinia groaned and closed her eyes. It would do no good to tell her mother that the cult of Ceres was considered to be a Greek import. Although her mother had allowed her father to ensure their only child was properly taught, she herself had received very little in the way of education. No one had ever said as much to Lavinia, but it was common knowledge that her mother had been a serving girl in the palace when Latinus was a young man. Lavinia had, on more than one occasion, heard visiting dignitaries gasp in horror that Latinus had seen fit to marry her. That was before her role had been reduced, and Lavinia taken over her main duties as hostess.

"Why have you brought me here, Mother? I thought you were at the palace. This is no place for a queen. Let me talk to Turnus."

"Lavinia, there is no need to be so rude. I have not brought you here to join our rites, although I do wish you would consider it. I have brought you here to keep you away from that camp until Turnus has defeated Aeneas, and your marriage can be resumed."

"I have no wish to be a prisoner. Please let me speak to Turnus," Lavinia exclaimed.

"I am your mother, and I am tired of your father thinking his opinion is the only one that matters." Amata sniffed. She kissed her daughter perfunctorily and moved away, leaving her guard behind. He stared ahead of him. Lavinia eyed him up, noting his strong, muscular arms and legs and humourless face.

"Are you here to make sure I don't escape?" she asked.

"That's right," he said, then quickly added, "Your Highness."

She gazed after her mother, concern rushing through her head. Her mother was not young, and the nights were getting colder. And women were known to die in the Mysteries anyway, even young, healthy ones. Her mother could eat a poisonous plant or be mauled by a wolf. Any grasp on sanity her mother had once was gone. Lavinia wished with all her heart that she had been firmer with her father, so keen on showing Aeneas that he was the commander of the forces that he'd lost sight of the battle within their own family.

"I won't run away," she said. "May I have a drink instead?"

☽

For several days she remained a prisoner in her mother's camp. Her mother and her new followers celebrated their rituals every day, and in the evening her mother sat with her in front of a fire and talked about how wonderful it would be when Lavinia was queen of the whole of Latium, and she, Amata, was the queen mother.

Lavinia was torn between disbelief at the extent of their delusions, and concern for those left behind. Her father must be going out of his mind. Would he and Aeneas think that she, like Camilla, had defected? And who would take care of Anna? In the midst of her worries, her mother would drop in another remark about how handsome Turnus was or how well he would look after them both, and Lavinia wished she could scream with frustration.

"Mother, you do realise that you can't return to Father after this?" Lavinia asked one night. "What will you do if Turnus doesn't win the war? Your position will be untenable."

Her mother looked vacantly at her, her pupils oddly dilated. "But Turnus *will* win the war. Ceres will ensure it."

Lavinia didn't say anything. She wished she could take her mother back to the palace so a physician could examine her.

"Aeneas has his gods, but we have ours," her mother reminded her yet again, her constant refrain. She held her hands out to the fire. "And ours are stronger because they belong here."

Lavinia shuffled. She could see her mother's point—of course she could. Why was Aeneas accepted as the son of a god none of them had ever seen, whereas her mother was considered to be mad? But even so, one only had to speak to Aeneas to see that he was fully in command of his senses. Her mother was even now replacing the dirt on her face that she thought made her part of the forest.

Lavinia looked about the camp, as she had done so often, wishing for help. But she recognised none of these women who had come with her mother. Amata's regular assistants had left her, and this ragtag crew was all she had. *They are all mad,* Lavinia thought. But that was unfair. Several of the women cringed if they were spoken to sharply, as though they were used to a life of beatings. Perhaps this forest existence was preferable to whatever they had left behind. But not her mother. Her mother should be in bed in the palace, not crouched crooning in front of a fire, with cinders in her hair and ashes on her hands and face. Where was Turnus? This was his responsibility. He had always said her mother was like a mother to him. How, then, could he have abandoned her like this?

"Mother," she said in desperation, "would it not make more sense for us to leave this forest and go to Turnus? He could shelter us—both of us—in his palace." And her mother could see his doctors, she thought. And eat his food and drink his wine. The same gods that had inflicted this madness on her mother had caused the rage that had made Turnus unrecognisable to her, but surely, surely if she agreed to what he wanted, he would protect them, if only to secure his advantage over Aeneas.

"We can't risk your father finding us," her mother said. "Don't worry, Lavinia. Turnus will have his victory soon, and then he will elevate you to the throne his mother once sat upon, as his wife. And for me—ah, for me he will build a new throne, a bigger throne, a throne worthy of the mother of the queen. I gave birth to you, you know." And she began singing again, a muddled lullaby this time.

Lavinia pulled her legs up and tucked herself into a little ball. She couldn't think of anything else to do. The noises of the forest were not soothing either: she could hear wolves howling, and she didn't think they were so very far away. She longed for the comparative safety and organisation of Aeneas's camp. There, guards patrolled through the night, and the well-maintained fires were never allowed to go out. Everyone slept in a structured building. Here, they all relied on the single guard who had accompanied her mother. Everyone slept under the stars, although at least she and her mother slept in front of the fire, as befitted their respective statuses as queen and prisoner.

The campfire itself was clumsily put together, and no one bothered to check it, so they often woke up to find that it had gone out during the night. Her mother's lack of concern for heat during the cold nights added to Lavinia's suspicions that her mother was ingesting some sort of plant to aid her in the Mysteries.

Throughout the area of the camp were dotted little mushrooms of a type Lavinia had never seen before. She avoided all stews that were prepared by her mother's maidservants, and wished that she had at least been captured in the summer months, when the weather would be milder. She had felt constantly damp and shivery in Aeneas's camp, but now if she ever returned there, she would consider it a palace fit to rival her father's.

She awoke the next morning, stiff and sore again. Her mother had already left for her rituals, the tell-tale trail of leaves left on the ground behind her. The fire had dwindled, but on this occasion, had not extinguished itself completely. Her mother's guard was stoking it. She turned to him now.

"You, what is your name?"

"Larth, Your Highness."

"Well, Larth"—she stood up, although even had she stood on a table, he would still have towered over her—"do you not think this misadventure has carried on for long enough?"

"Your Highness?" His face was inscrutable. Still, she continued.

"My mother is clearly unwell. We need to get her back to her doctors, not leave her here frolicking in the forest."

"Her orders are that we stay," he said. His voice was slow and ponderous.

"She is in no fit state to give orders!" Lavinia erupted. "She is not a well woman. She has been possessed by the gods."

"Yes, that is what she says too." Lavinia could not tell whether he was being stubborn or stupid. But she tried one more time.

"Despite what my mother may have told you, Larth, I love her, and I have only her best interests at heart. She is not a young woman. Do you wish for her to die of exposure?"

"She will not die unless the gods will it."

She glared at him. He stared back, his dark eyes unreadable.

"But you do work for Turnus, don't you? When will he return?" she asked suddenly.

"No, Your Highness. I work only for your mother."

Lavinia's heart went cold. If the guard did not work for Turnus, perhaps she had misread the situation. Perhaps Turnus had not assisted her mother in her pursuit of the Mysteries and in Lavinia's own kidnapping. Perhaps Turnus, too, was unaware of this camp. In that case, they were truly on their own.

They were interrupted by a rustling in the undergrowth. Larth stood up to see what it was, but he shook his head. "Only a rodent."

Suddenly, though, they were surrounded by soldiers. "We've found her," a voice called. Soldiers surrounded them; Trojans, she saw, by the insignia on their dress. She could hear the singing of the women gathering their mushrooms, still unaware that their camp had been breached. Before she knew it, she was being bundled up and onto a horse. A Trojan soldier climbed up behind her and kicked the horse's flanks.

"Wait," she called, once again struggling to free herself. "My mother! We have to bring my mother back too."

"Don't worry, Your Highness," the Trojan said. "Someone will find your mother and take her back to the camp." He kicked the horse again, and they began to gallop away, flocks of birds soaring out of the trees as they thundered past.

"But . . ." Lavinia was prepared to protest further, yet something made her glance back at the camp. She looked back in time to see Larth slide to the floor, a Trojan spear being pulled out of his torso.

"You killed him," she screamed. "You didn't need to kill him. He was only following orders."

"Stay still," the Trojan warned. "We are going too fast for you to fall." She stopped struggling and began to cry.

☽

When Lavinia returned to camp, she found the atmosphere subdued. Aeneas had not yet returned from his visit to King Evander. As soon as Lavinia's feet touched the ground, she stormed off to see her father.

"Lavinia," he greeted her, but she raised her hand and cut him off.

"You promised Aeneas you would see that Mother was sent back to the palace. You were supposed to take care of her."

"Did she hurt you?" he asked.

Lavinia stared at his familiar face and wondered how it was possible to love and hate someone so much at the same time.

"No, of course not. She's my mother. But she's not well."

"She's never been well," her father said, his tone placatory and his hands raised. Lavinia had seen him deal with supplicants in the same way before. It only incensed her more.

"That's why we were supposed to look after her. Instead of staying in this"—she waved her hands—"this shack, pretending to be an equal to Aeneas. If *I* were the king," she continued, expecting her father to cut her off. But to her surprise, he had taken a step back, as though her rage were tangible, and her words could knock him off his feet. He was too weak, she thought. She had outgrown him.

"It doesn't matter," she said softly, her rage ebbing away. "But I need you to look after her now. She must not be punished. She must be locked up, yes, but for her own good. Will you see to it?"

He nodded, not meeting her eyes. Something had changed between them, and Lavinia knew that their relationship would never be the same again. She smiled sadly at him and watched him leave to carry out her wishes.

She could have threatened him again. She could have said that she would check up on him, or worse, she would have Aeneas do so, but she instinctively knew they needed to preserve the last remaining vestiges of their bond. She wished they had embraced, kissed, even, but they had never been a tactile family.

Was this what it was like to be queen? she wondered. All her life, she had wanted this sort of power, the ability to make others do what she wanted. And now she had tried that power, even if it was by default, and she just felt hollow. *And yet,* she reflected again, *and yet, better to have the power than not to have the power.* Better to be able to direct others than to be directed herself. She did not have to wield a sword, she thought. She just had to ensure she was in a position to direct the person who did wield it. And she thought again of Anna's sister Dido, left powerless and alone. Lavinia did not need to be alone.

Her reflections were interrupted by a sense that someone was watching her. Lavinia looked up to see a Trojan woman, about the same age as her own mother, loitering nearby. When she became aware that Lavinia had seen her, she came to take her hand, tears streaming down her face.

"Please," she said, "you have to come and see." Lavinia reluctantly took the woman's hand and followed her to the edge of the camp, from where they could see the ramparts of Turnus's camp. She followed the woman's pointing finger, and she instantly felt ill. She couldn't be seeing what she thought she was seeing.

"My son," the woman said, her voice cracking. "How could he have done this to my son?"

Lavinia looked at the two long metal pikes jabbing out from the ground. On those pikes were two heads, their size diminished by the lack of a body.

"Who did this?" she asked.

"Prince Turnus himself," the woman said. "Because they were brave. Because they dared challenge him. My son is no older than you, Your Highness."

"This has to stop," Lavinia murmured. "I cannot bear it." The two heads seemed to mock her, gazing down on her as if to say, *"You? What have you to bear? What is there for you to do here?"*

"Please," the woman next to her said, as though reading her thoughts. "Please appeal to Prince Turnus for me. Ask him to return my son and his comrade to me. Let me bury them as is fitting. This is barbaric."

"Why do you think I can do this?" Lavinia asked. Any delusions she might have had about power were as ephemeral as her mother's, she saw.

"Because you are to marry Father Aeneas," the woman said, her tone surprised, as though she had not expected to be asked. "Father Aeneas would not leave Euryalus to be eaten by the birds."

"No," Lavinia murmured. "No, I don't suppose he would. I will see what I can do."

The woman nodded and crept away. Lavinia thought that she would leave, but she had underestimated her maternal nature. Instead, she clambered down the hillside and tucked herself into a natural cranny. From there, Lavinia saw, she could watch her son without being observed.

Lavinia swallowed. She wanted to leave, but it seemed inappropriate, dismissive. She had told the woman she would see what she could do, and she would. She didn't approach her father; her lip curled as she thought of the excuses he would make.

Instead, she called for a messenger, and while she waited for one to arrive, she thought about the prince she had once known. Aeneas seemed convinced that a god or goddess had inflicted madness upon Turnus. She remembered the story of the Greek Herakles, who had been whipped into a frenzy by the gods and killed his own wife and children, whom he loved dearly. But he had not recognised what it was that he was killing. Turnus had known that these were human men, not much older than boys. She remembered the stench of alcohol that had hung about him when he had come to her parents' palace. Were the gods a convenient excuse for a man who had drunk himself into a rage? The woman had said that the boys had challenged him. True, the Turnus she had known had never much liked being challenged. When they were very small, a little slave boy had played with them sometimes until he had beaten Turnus in a running race. She hadn't seen the boy

again. She hadn't thought much of it either until now. At least, she
hoped, Turnus had only had him reassigned.

There was a soft clearing of a throat beside her, and she
turned to see the messenger had arrived.

"I need a message taken to Prince Turnus," she said sharply,
and was horrified to see the man's face pale in response. *Is this
what you have come to, Turnus?* she thought. *A name to frighten
inferiors with?* She had promised the woman she would do her
best, though, so she continued speaking. "You are to tell him the
Princess Lavinia—" *What? Commands? Requests? Begs that you
. . .?*—"is most displeased by your treatment of the young Trojan
warriors and requires that you remove their heads from your wall
and return them to their mothers for burial." She had no idea
whether the other young Trojan's mother was still alive. Too late,
she realised that she had never even asked the other boy's name.
No matter. If Turnus chose to put any other heads on pikes
while her messenger journeyed towards him, he could remove
those as well. "It is barbaric, and not behaviour that befits any
Latin," she added for good measure, although she did not know
whether the messenger would convey those words. As it was, his
white face and trembling hands suggested he might expire of fear
before he even set food outside the camp.

"You will need a token," she added. "Here," she said, and she
pulled a ring from her finger. "Give him this." He took the ring
but didn't move. "Go," she exhorted, and he set off at a trot.

She looked after the messenger, and accordingly after her
ring, with a certain pang. She had been fond of the ring, a small
golden circlet imprinted with a wolf's head, although it hadn't
been especially valuable. But Turnus would know whose ring it
was, if it reached him. She hoped she hadn't sent the messenger to his death. But surely Turnus still obeyed the basic rules

of civility and decorum in battle. She surveyed the two heads again, seeing now how their tongues were lolling out of their mouths. "Turnus obeys nothing," they seemed to jeer at her.

☽

Aeneas returned by sea from visiting Evander, and everyone flocked to see his ship come into the bay. Lavinia gasped when she saw Aeneas, standing at the prow: his hair was aflame, tongues of fire licking about his forehead. The blaze burned high into the sky. Remembering the terror she had felt when her own hair had caught fire, in a time that felt like many years ago now, she started to scream for someone, anyone, to put the fire out. But the crowd cheered, louder and louder, and Aeneas himself smiled and waved, oblivious to the inferno that threatened him.

How could he be so calm? she asked herself through her sobs. She remembered the smell, the acrid feel of the smoke against the back of her throat. How was he not coughing, spluttering, in pain? She put a hand up to her hair and felt that it had regrown completely, not a single jagged edge remaining. And as she realised that, a cloud passed over the sun, and the flames that had threatened to consume Aeneas disappeared from sight. It had been an optical illusion, she understood as she sank to the ground. No flames, no fire. Just the effect of the sun shining on Aeneas's dark curls. She flushed red with embarrassment, although no one had paid her any attention.

When Aeneas disembarked, Lavinia hesitated for a moment before striding with purpose to his strategy tent. Her father had not returned from the palace, and she was the sole representative of her family present in the camp. While her father might have been happy to skulk away, she was sure that she was not going to do so any longer.

Lavinia followed Aeneas and the elders into the strategy tent. Aeneas looked at her in surprise, but something about the look on her face must have warned him, because he simply nodded in greeting.

"Please, do sit down, Your Highness," he said politely. "I am about to receive an update from the front."

Lavinia looked at the soldier in front of them, quaking in his boots.

"Father Aeneas, I bring bad news," he quavered. "Prince Pallas has been killed." He paused, licked his cracking lips, then continued, "By Prince Mezentius—"

He was interrupted by Aeneas's scream of fury, a deafening roar that was heard throughout the camp. Lavinia sat in shock. Pallas, dead? Little Pallas? The soldier went on to update Aeneas about Turnus's treatment of the Trojan soldiers, Euryalus and Nisus, whose heads had been taken down "because of the appeal by the Princess Lavinia," and to give him the names of many more Trojans who had been killed in the battle.

Lavinia barely heard any of it. She registered her own name and realised that the other Trojan soldier had been called Nisus, but her mind was wholly on Pallas. What would King Evander be feeling now? she wondered. What sort of honour could there be in the death of a boy not yet old enough to grow a beard? How proud he had been of his new armour, and how little it had done for him. She sobbed but stopped again when she became aware that people were starting to look at her.

"I promised his father," Aeneas gasped, and although he was speaking to everyone, he was looking at her. "I promised his father that I would take care of him as though he were my own."

Lavinia wished that her parents were there, or Camilla, someone else who remembered Pallas as a boy. But she was surrounded by Trojans, none of whom knew Pallas, and only Aeneas wept for him as she did. Lavinia wished that she felt closer to Aeneas, that they might somehow support each other in this grief.

"The Volsci have withdrawn," the soldier continued, determined to complete his litany of heartbreak and devastating news. "King Metabus says he cannot fight when he might kill his own daughter, although he has not rejoined the battle on Prince Turnus's side. And Prince Turnus . . ." He paused again, this time looking bewildered, as though he could not believe the words he had to say. "Prince Turnus is fighting like a man possessed by the Furies. He leapt into the water fully armed and swam away from the battle."

"He did what?" Aeneas asked. The man repeated his words.

"They think he is mad, Father Aeneas. No one wants to fight against him now. He is not in his right mind, and no one knows what he will do next."

Aeneas walked to the door. He turned back to face them all. "I fought the Greeks at Troy. I faced down the great Achilleus when he mourned the death of Patroklus. I am not afraid of a boy from Rutuli. We have wasted enough time. Now, we fight." He stalked out of the hut, leaving Lavinia and the Trojan elders looking at one another.

"Your Highness," one said (Amicus, she remembered), "we are all most grateful to you for interceding on behalf of our sons." His voice trembled as he spoke, and she shook her head, unable to say anything. Too many boys were being killed, and for what? She allowed him to kiss her hand before she fled the hut. As she left the camp, she heard the thundering of hooves and turned to see Aeneas leading his troops to war, his armour blazing in the sun.

☽

Lavinia looked in her hut, but Anna was not there. Lavinia asked around, but no one could or would give her any answers. She decided to assist in the kitchens. She ignored the gasps of the women as she strode into the kitchen with as much purpose as she had entered the strategy tent, rolled up her sleeves, and began to clean cooking pots. Ruefully, she realised as she worked that one of her main concerns in taking on the work, that it might ruin her nails, was no longer relevant. Life in the camp alone had led her nails to become ragged and torn.

She returned to the kitchen the next day, and this time when she asked about Anna, she was told that a red-headed woman had been seen sitting on the banks of the small stream that led to the river, the Numicus.

"We think she may be a water nymph," one woman told her, her eyes wide. Lavinia thought that was unlikely. She finished her chores, packed some food, and visited the river. It was a beautiful spot, the grass soft and inviting, and she could see why Anna had chosen it. She sat down on the ground and waited. Eventually, Anna joined her.

She smiled at Lavinia, then stared at the river, its verdant waters mirrored in her eyes.

Lavinia trailed her hand in the water, and brought it up, dripping with weeds and frogspawn.

"I used to swim in this river," she confided. "When I was a child, with my friends, Camilla and Turnus. Sometimes Lausus joined us. He is Mezentius's son, you know."

"Ah, the one who doesn't like you," Anna replied, still watching the river. "Those must have been blissful days. What stopped you?"

"My mother," Lavinia said, making a face. "She told me it was inappropriate for a growing young woman to swim naked. After she banned me from swimming, Camilla's mother did the same. And then Turnus and Lausus found somewhere else to swim."

"Your mother was probably right," Anna said. "Reputations can be lost so quickly. And the Greeks believe that their gods are always watchful for naked young women. You wouldn't want to fall foul of one of them."

Lavinia shrugged. She thought of the gods she had grown up believing in; the household gods, so caring of their family; and of course, Venus, the mother goddess. She knew now that these gods were the Greek and Trojan gods bearing other faces, but she still found it difficult sometimes to remember, so different was their behaviour. Like Turnus before the Trojans arrived, she thought. The Trojans corrupt everything.

"It was you, wasn't it?" she asked. "You sent the guards to find me."

"Yes," Anna said. "I was worried about you. I let your father know you hadn't been seen, and he did the rest."

No one else had noticed, Lavinia understood. And Anna hadn't asked to be thanked or rewarded. Most women, on saving the future queen's life, would try to negotiate some sort of courtly position. Anna had not. Lavinia thought with guilt on how little she knew about her, how little she had asked, other than her stories about her sister.

"Anna, what happened to you when your sister died?" she asked. "Why did you come here instead of remaining in Carthage?"

Anna looked surprised. "Why do you ask?"

"I'm just curious," she said. In truth, she was wondering whether Dido's death had been all that had unhinged her sister or if there was more to tell.

"I stayed in Carthage at first," she said. "But my brother, Pygmalion, the one we had flown to Carthage to escape, heard that Dido was dead and Carthage was in a state of disarray. He sent troops, and once again I had to escape in the night. Pygmalion rules Carthage now."

"Where did you go?"

"To Malta, at first. King Battus protected me. It wasn't romantic—I had seen what a mistake that could be. I looked after his children, told them stories. Practised my craft. But then one night he came to me and warned me that I needed to flee again. Pygmalion was demanding my 'release' or else he would declare war. Battus didn't have the resources to fight Pygmalion, so instead he helped me with a boat and supplies. I knew I could live by my wits, and for a while I did. But I was not the best sailor, and my boat washed ashore here. The last place I wanted to be. The rest, you know."

"You can leave, you know," Lavinia said. "I don't want to keep you here against your will."

Anna smiled. "Tell me about this river," she replied, ignoring Lavinia's words.

"I'm not sure there's much to tell," Lavinia said, surprised. "It passes the town of Ardea and flows into the sea. We call it the perennial stream, always flowing."

"Fascinating," Anna said. "Always changing, always beside us. Water flows, and yet water remains. It's beautiful."

Lavinia was not sure how to respond, so she stayed silent. But as she watched the river, she could see, or at least she thought she could see, what Anna meant. From a distance, it was a mass of water held in position by the riverbanks. But as one watched, one could see that the water that passed through was not the same as the water that had been there before. It brought its own debris, sticks, leaves, and twigs that either nestled up to the existing bracken or else, when the water pressure became too great, broke free and pushed down the river to cause a dam elsewhere.

Tadpoles wriggled to the opposite banks, and birds swooped in and out, feeding at will. The leafy canopy overhead produced an ample amount of shade, and even the winter sun was strong enough to cause dappling on the surface of the water.

"It is lovely," she agreed. "And to think I used to desecrate it by swimming."

"Oh, I'm sure any river god would not see it as a desecration, especially when the swimming was done by beautiful young women." Anna smiled. "Which deity keeps this river?"

"Numicus is the river god," Lavinia replied. "But I am not aware of any deity to whom this stream in particular is dedicated."

"A lucky nymph is she who can spend her days here," Anna said. She looked as though she was about to say more, but they were interrupted by shouting. They looked at each other, alarmed.

"Perhaps we should go and see for ourselves what all the commotion might be," Lavinia said. Anna nodded, but her face was ashen.

"Why are you so frightened?" Lavinia asked, although she did not expect Anna to answer her. And she didn't, but her face remained pale. Lavinia placed a hand on Anna's arm sympathetically.

"You stay here. If needed, I will return for you."

☽

As she reached the centre of the camp, the commotion became louder. She realised that the sounds were cheers, but they did not sound joyful. As she grew closer, one after another member of the crowd looked at her face, and their cries grew more subdued. They looked embarrassed. As one by one, people stepped aside for her, she saw the scarecrow at the very centre of the camp, and she felt the blood drain from her face. Was that Mezentius, propped up on a stick? A corpse, like the boys that she had seen outside Turnus's walls?

She remembered how Aeneas told her that the gods inflicted men with madness, and she felt sickened.

Aeneas looked at her, and she saw her mistake. The body of Mezentius lay to one side, abandoned on the ground. It was his armour that was on display.

"Lavinia," Aeneas said, then stopped. He looked at the body helplessly.

"Send him back," she said, her voice sharp and shrill. "Send him to his family."

"His son is dead too," Aeneas said. "He died trying to save his father. It was an honourable death."

She half turned, wanting to run, then realised that she had nowhere to run to. Still, she wouldn't let herself sob, not in front of the entire camp. She pulled herself up high and repeated her previous words, keeping her voice under control this time.

"Send him back. Keep the armour, if you will. It is your spoil. But you are not Achilleus, and this is not Hektor. Send the body back."

Aeneas looked as though he were about to retch, and she saw she had stumbled onto the form of words that would most reach him. Fighting back her own repugnance, she took the last few steps and knelt down by the body. Paying no attention to the armour on display, she picked up a cloth and started to clean blood out of Mezentius's eyes. She felt a small muscle in her jaw twitch, but she was determined. Before she had finished his face, she saw that she was not alone. Aeneas joined her, stretching out the limbs of the body. Together before the eyes of Trojans and Laurentines alike, they prepared the body as best they could, then Aeneas called for a bier. Mezentius was loaded onto it and taken away.

The crowd dispersed when the body left, no one wanting to remain behind when their leader came back to his feet. But for a long time, Aeneas knelt, looking at his hands. Lavinia stayed with him.

"He was my best friend," he said at last. She knew he didn't mean Mezentius. "He was the very best of the Trojans. He should be here now."

"But that was not what the gods wanted," she said, uncomfortable as she always felt when the subject of these warlike gods came up.

"No," he answered. "But not because I am the better man. Because my mother is a goddess. If I were half the man Hektor was, I would not have made nearly so many mistakes."

"I am sure Hektor was not blameless. He would have made his own mistakes."

Aeneas sighed. "Perhaps you are right, Princess. I will hold games to see who can win Mezentius's armour. It will increase morale, although I understand that when the Greeks did the same with Hektor's armour, it nearly destroyed them with in-fighting. Fools. None of them was big enough to wield his spear in any event."

"Could you not send it back?" she suggested tentatively.

Aeneas shook his head. "We strive to be the better men always, Lavinia, but that is a step too far even for the second best of the Trojans. The armour stays. They have the body."

He walked off, back to the fighting. Lavinia thought of the rage that had driven him to mutilate Mezentius's body, and wondered whether Anna was right to fear him.

☽

Every day now, the men went out to fight, and every day they returned fewer in number. With her father back at the palace,

Lavinia had no one to play her kithara for, and she had no desire to practise on her own account. She kept herself busy by assisting in the kitchens regularly and helping tend to the wounded, although she still resisted being listed on Aeneas's roster. But she took no joy in any of her activities. Sometimes she remembered those carefree days when she and Camilla had horsed around in her courtyard at the palace. It felt like a lifetime ago, like something that had happened to another woman. Now everything was dull and dreary, and life was to be tolerated, not enjoyed.

No words were ever spoken about her father returning to the palace, and yet everyone knew that he had gone. The sellswords and other members of the army continued to fight, though, because as long as Lavinia remained in camp, Laurentum was still at war. It made her feel sick to think that this war was being fought in her name. She knew that wasn't true, that she was a means to an end, but she was coming to hate all prophecies and their implications for her life.

With Aeneas away fighting every day, Anna was venturing out of their hut more, and she told stories for the children daily. Sometimes Lavinia listened to those stories. Anna had moved away from those of war and instead told them humorous tales about the gods transforming mortals into various animals. Their favourite story was one about a girl called Io, whom Juno, wife of Jupiter, turned into a cow to protect her from Jupiter's advances. Io went on many adventures in her cow form, travelling far and wide until she reached Egypt, where she was returned to her human form. Lavinia suspected that Anna used some of her own experiences for Io's adventures, but when she asked her, Anna only said that she had never been to Egypt, so it could not have been her.

When it was just the two of them, Anna's stories became more melancholic. They mainly featured her sister, Dido, but they predated even Dido's marriage to her first husband, Acerbas. Anna told Lavinia how she and Dido had grown up together, raiding the palace kitchens for goodies and riding on horseback across the plains together. Lavinia began to worry for Anna, so strong was the hold that the past had on her, but she did not know what else she could do for her.

"Perhaps you should go to my father's palace," she tried. "I am sure if I send a token with you, he will make you welcome."

Anna smiled, but she would not go. "I do not want to become a serving girl or a maid," she said. "If I cannot go as a visiting princess, I will not go at all. And you know I cannot go as a princess. Not only because if Aeneas know where I was, he would want to kill me, but also word would get to my brother, who also wants me dead."

"Why would Aeneas want to kill you?" Lavinia asked. She expected no answer, but Anna was always surprising.

"Because no one else would tell you the truth about Dido," she said, "and that makes me dangerous. Men do not like to have their misdeeds exposed, especially not when the misdeed features their previous wife, and the one hearing the story is the next one."

Lavinia wondered whether what Anna was saying was true. Would Aeneas have her murdered? When he was around her he was courteous and even attentive. But he was the same man who went to war every day, who killed many men every day. He had lied to her about Dido. Perhaps he would have Anna killed to keep her story quiet.

Lavinia tried not to think about the warriors fighting. It all seemed so pointless to her. This time wasted fighting and killing could be spent building, integrating the Trojans into their society. Building a stronger, more caring community. If Aeneas's new Troy was to be founded on bloodshed, what was to prevent it one day meeting the same fate as the old Troy? Men were always going to pillage and destroy one another. Women were always going to be used as prizes, possessions, and casualties.

She could not even admire Camilla, who had taken up a role on the battlefield. The way to make things better was not to follow men. There had to be another way. And when Lavinia did allow herself to daydream, she thought of what she could do if she did not have to be the wife of either Turnus or Aeneas. If she did not have any ties to hold her to one spot. Like Anna, she could travel. She thought of seeing these fantastical places that Anna described. She could really go to Egypt and see the Pyramids. Or the Hanging Gardens of Babylon. There were so many wonders in the world that did not involve being caught up in a war.

But then she would return to her senses, so abruptly it was as though someone had knocked her on the head. She was not destined for these things. The prophecies were clear. She would marry. No doubt after that, she would produce heirs to ensure the family line her father was so proud of, and so certain in the strength of the prophecies that he did not even take action to protect the daughter who was needed to guarantee that family line. She thought of Creusa, killed in war despite never setting foot on a battlefield, and she thought that she would not have been as complacent as her father.

☽

Afterwards, she would wonder when exactly she knew. Sometimes it felt like she had always known, from the moment she heard Camilla's footsteps leaving her. Sometimes she felt certain that the news had come as a complete surprise, that until the words left Aeneas's mouth, she hadn't known, had thought he was there to bring her news about her mother or her father or their impending nuptials. And sometimes she knew that the truth was both of these things, and something else in between as well, because that was what war was, a vicious wolf that swallowed your loved ones whole and only occasionally spat them back out again, alive but mutilated beyond recognition.

Lavinia assisted the Trojan women, whom she now thought of as her people although the term felt too grand for the motley collection of refugees by whom she found herself surrounded. But they were her subjects, she thought defiantly, whether that was because she was to be the bride of their leader or because her father still ruled this land, for now anyway, something both Aeneas and Turnus had chosen to forget.

And so she scrubbed children's faces and told them stories, and prepared food for their exhausted mothers. And every day they would wait for the men to return with news about which of their fathers and husbands had died, and every day another woman would dissolve into quiet tears. This had been their life for so long, they told Lavinia. First Troy, and now Latium. Poor, hated Trojans, killed wherever they went.

She had to admit that Aeneas's system to protect those who could not fight was a good one. Walls had been built around the camp. The women, children, and the elderly had been marshalled into two tents in the centre of the camp, surrounded by guards. The fighting should not reach them, but if it did, they were not left alone. The tents chosen were large and airy. They had sufficient food provisions to last for a couple of weeks. And every woman, with the exception of Lavinia, had been assigned a task or a share of the rotation of chores, which went some way to making sure that no one got bored and started to cause trouble.

The soldiers did not sleep in this tent, but when they did return to camp, they were again allowed to visit with their families briefly, and she saw how their morale lifted when they went back to the fighting. She supposed that ten years living in a city under siege would have made Aeneas an expert in the softer side of managing warfare, but she also thought that not all princes would have learned these lessons, nor would they be so concerned about applying them to all members of their populace, from the most important generals to the lowly foot soldiers' wives.

Lavinia was telling stories to the children when she saw Aeneas approaching the tent, his helmet held between his hands. She knew what that meant and, like all the women, looked about her to see which unfortunate woman was about to be told that her husband would not be returning. But this time, Aeneas crossed the tent to Lavinia herself. She looked at him in horror, her mouth moving, but no words coming out. As she had seen him do so many times, he took her hand in his own and kneeled before her.

"Lavinia, I'm so sorry," he said. "It's Camilla. She fought valiantly, but she won't be returning."

Lavinia felt her world swirl in front of her. Camilla could not possibly be gone. She had known her for her entire life. They had grown up together. They had been inseparable.

"Why did you let her fight?" she asked. That was not what she had intended to ask, she thought now, in a daze. She had intended to ask whether someone had been sent to Camilla's father and mother, who deserved to know what had happened to her. Camilla was a princess, not a mercenary. She should be buried like a princess. But at that moment, all Lavinia wanted to know was why someone hadn't stopped this from happening.

"I couldn't stop her," Aeneas said, and his voice broke as he said it. She looked at him in surprise; she had never seen him cry before. But now there were tears running down his face. "Women

shouldn't be fighting in battles, Lavinia. I saw Penthesilea die outside Troy, and now I've watched Camilla die. But what could I do?
Her heart was set on it, and she didn't answer to me."

"Who killed her?" Lavinia asked. She thought of all the
boys she and Camilla had known, had laughed with and at, had
played with as children and taunted as teenagers. Some fought
alongside Turnus, but others had joined her father and Aeneas.
Surely one of those boys couldn't have killed her.

Aeneas understood what she was asking and shook his head.
"It was an older man, one of the sellswords that your father
employs in his army. He wasn't local. I don't think he even knew
she was a woman until the body flipped . . ." Lavinia felt her
mouth slacken, and Aeneas put his arm around her. "I'm sorry. I
shouldn't have said that. I wasn't thinking, Lavinia. You shouldn't
be here. Let me arrange a guard to take you back to the palace.
You can sleep in a proper bed for a change."

Although the other women had given them space, as they did
every time Aeneas or one of his captains came to deliver awful
news, she felt every one of them freeze on the spot. She could go
home. They none of them had homes, but she could simply slip
out of this battlefield, this nightmare, and go home. But what
was the use? It wouldn't bring Camilla back. And if Aeneas lost
this battle, Turnus would surely turn his wrath on her father and
the palace next.

"I will stay," she said quietly. "I will continue to help where
I can."

Aeneas nodded, satisfied. "Is there someone who can sit with
you?" he asked. She must have looked surprised, because he
quickly added, "I must return to the battle. It isn't helpful to be
away from the troops for so long. Affects their morale."

And what about my morale? she wanted to say, but she didn't.
How could Aeneas make this moment better for her?

She shook her head and managed, "I will be fine." He patted her shoulder, his hand awkward against her skin, and turned and left. She watched him walk away. Was this to be her life now, watching as people walked away to be killed?

☽

Lavinia stumbled back to her own hut and lay down on her bedding. The hut was cool, and she could hear the wind in the trees outside. She didn't think that she cried, but when she put her hand up to her face she could feel the wetness of tears, so she supposed she had done so. She felt no desire to move, or even to speak to anyone ever again. There was no one left who could comfort her now.

As she saw the shadows lengthen outside the hut and perceived that night must be falling, she was aware of someone slipping inside and a cold cloth being pressed against her forehead, then wiping away the dampness from her cheeks.

"Mother," she whispered, before remembering that her mother was imprisoned in her rooms in their palace.

"Shh," a voice murmured, and she recognised Anna's lilting voice, the voice that had told her so many stories.

"Camilla," she began, then started to cry again.

Lavinia felt Anna press her hand into hers, and she gripped onto it; finally, something to cling to. They sat like that for a while; then as the night crickets began chirping, Lavinia sat up. Her head ached, as did her arms and legs as she shook them out, but she took the bread that Anna offered her and ate, and then her head felt a little clearer.

"I just want this war to stop," she said to Anna. Anna nodded, but she said nothing.

Sighing, Lavinia went to the door of her hut and looked out. The soldiers were beginning to return from the day's battle, their numbers diminished once more.

"They say it was like this at Troy," Anna remarked, coming to join her. "The Trojans fought during the day, then retreated behind their walls at night. What must it have been like, I wonder, to lie beside your wife, knowing that you had killed men that day? Knowing you could be killed the next day?"

"Was it not worse for the Greeks?" Lavinia asked. "They didn't even see their wives for years on end."

Anna shrugged. "They made do. At least they could cling to their memories of an ideal woman, untainted by the fear and the bloodshed."

Lavinia shuddered. "Why did the Trojans have to come here?" she asked softly.

Anna took her hand, and Lavinia looked at her, surprised. She saw tears welling up in her eyes. "They bring death everywhere they go," she said sadly. "They don't mean to, but they do. It isn't their fault, but they are still a plague on our world."

"That's a horrible way to talk about people," Lavinia said, but then she looked out again at the camp that had replaced the beautiful groves where she had played as a child, and thought of Anna's sister, burning on her own pyre. "Yet it's true."

They readied themselves for bed in silence, but Lavinia was glad of Anna's presence all the same. She hadn't wanted to be alone that night. "I wish there were some way I could end this war," she remarked at last. "They say they are fighting over me, but I can't tell them to stop."

"Couldn't you?" Anna asked. "What if you told Aeneas you were marrying Turnus?"

Lavinia tried to imagine marrying the Turnus she had last seen, the violent man who had thrown a spear at her as a jest. "I don't want to do that," she said, "and besides, Aeneas will continue to fight. It's only Turnus who has turned this into a contest for my hand in marriage. Aeneas wants the land."

"Then marry Aeneas," Anna's voice came back across the dark. "If you believe Turnus will stop fighting."

"No," Lavinia said slowly. "But there is one way to make them stop fighting. The duel. Turnus said that if he lost, he would leave Latium."

"Aeneas may lose," Anna said.

"Then I will find a way to home the Trojan people. Turnus won't be threatened by them if they have no leader." Lavinia felt her mind sharpening for the first time since Aeneas had told her about Camilla, perhaps even before that. "And besides, I think it is more likely that Aeneas will win."

"Then he will kill Turnus. You know that as well as I do. Only one man will walk away from this fight, no matter what Turnus said about exile. Another death at the hands of Aeneas the butcher. You are sentencing a man to die."

"No," Lavinia said, shaking her head. "They have brought this upon themselves, men, with their fighting and their bloodshed. We women can only sit and wait. We are responsible for nothing."

I will be a queen, she reflected, but not the queen she had once thought to be, wearing beautiful clothes and dining in state. *Here I am a powerless girl, but once the duel is fought and the contender is my husband, I will influence him as best I can. There will be no more mothers' sons killed, no more babies left as orphans. We will build a strong nation, not destroy a dying one.*

But she said none of this to Anna.

BOOK ELEVEN

CREUSA

A CONTROVERSY prevailed among the beasts of the field as to which of the animals deserved the most credit for producing the greatest number of whelps at a birth. They rushed clamorously into the presence of the Lioness and demanded of her the settlement of the dispute. "And you," they said, "how many sons have you at a birth?" The Lioness laughed at them, and said: "Why! I have only one; but that one is altogether a thoroughbred Lion."

—*Aesop's Fables*
(trans. by George Fyler Townsend, 1867)

For two days, Creusa was in labour. She felt the waves of pain pass through her, her body rigid; then as quickly as they had started they would be complete, and she would let go of herself, her mind sky-wheeling into the distance. She drank only water, ate no food, and stopped listening to the conversations of the physicians and midwives surrounding her.

At first, she wished only to see Aeneas, but as time passed, she wished for no one. There were points when she convinced herself that her baby was dead, a stone inside her, not understanding its part in its evacuation from her body. At other times, she believed that it was alive, but clinging to her, desperate not to leave the safety of her womb. Finally, as the second day was drawing to a close, her mind emptied, her body too racked by the spasms that had got her no further towards becoming a mother. She thought she could hear one of the midwives saying to the doctor, "Women cannot survive much longer than this," but then it could have been a trick of her feverish brain.

She was animalistic now, her clothes discarded, her only desire to lie on her back and breathe through the pains. They were coming more frequently, harder and stronger, and like a fish being buffeted about in the ocean, she had no choice but to let the waves take her where they chose. If that were to be to Hades, so be it. She had nothing left now. She was nothing.

But she underestimated her own body. Because just as she thought her mind might drift away completely, she felt the movements in her body bring her back into the room in a rush, and with one last superhuman push, she felt it go, and knew that it was all over.

"It's a boy," she heard one of the midwives coo, and they brought the baby to her so she could see it. "A little boy."

She stared down at him, this little red bundle, his tiny face screwed up tight. She had seen so many of her brothers and sisters born, she had expected to feel very little at this point. Certainly by now her mother had been more interested in having her brow mopped and a glass of wine brought to her. But Creusa was mesmerised. Here he was at last. Her little lion. And she knew that whatever else might ever happen to her, nothing would be more important than this very moment.

"Ascanius," she murmured, the name Aeneas had chosen for a son. "He is our little Ascanius." It was a name with no particular meaning, but he liked the sound.

Now the baby had been delivered, and the midwives completed their messy tasks, leaving mother and baby clean and comfortable, Creusa found her mind returning into her body, and into the present, painfully quickly. Knowing she needed to sleep, she reluctantly ceded the baby to the waiting nurse, but she was only too aware of the noise, the shouts, the clangs, the clashes, coming from outside the city walls.

Ascanius was a baby born into a war, and for all she knew, his own father was lying dead outside those city walls even while she finally sipped on a glass of mead and allowed her shoulders to rest on the pillow. And for the first time since she had met Aeneas, a treacherous thought hit her with the force of a spear clashing onto a shield: it did not matter if Aeneas survived. It did not matter if she, Creusa, survived. The only thing that mattered now was that Ascanius survived, and she was determined to do everything in her power to ensure that was the case.

Idly, she had asked Aeneas several days ago, before she went into labour and he went out to the battlefront, whether he believed his mother might finally come to visit them once the baby had arrived. He had hesitated.

"It is possible, I suppose, but I would not want you to become too hopeful. More likely is that you will have a conversation sometime soon with someone who seems perfectly normal, a nurse, say, or an errand boy, but you will find them discomforting, their eyes a little too bright, their stature a little too tall. You will find it difficult to look directly at them, even though you outrank them and you are used to directing errand boys your entire life. And when they walk away, you will realise that you cannot truly remember the conversation, although you have the sense that it was important."

Creusa saw the sadness that appeared in Aeneas's eyes whenever his mother was mentioned, and quickly changed the course of the conversation, remarking that she hoped her own mother would not attend the birth, because she always made her so nervous. It was not a topic that she liked to discuss, and Aeneas, recognising her purpose, squeezed her hand, then excused himself. Creusa watched him go with sadness, wishing that she were brave enough to curse the immortal mother who had caused him such grief.

But now, looking down at her own small child, she understood Aeneas's mother a little more clearly at last. Because in giving new life, she had seen death. What if the child did not survive? What if he survived birth, only to perish of the Theban plague as an infant? What if he survived his infanthood, only to be killed in battle outside the walls of Troy? Where the world had seemed a reasonably safe place only days before, she now saw that it was filled with monsters and perils. Why, there were entire ships on their doorstep filled with men who would hate him on sight, would kill him even in this fragile, helpless state, simply because he was a Trojan prince. And how much worse would this feeling be for a goddess, used to being immortal and untouchable, but suddenly made vulnerable by the birth of a human son? Knowing that there were not just human men, but entire pantheons of gods who would as soon kill your baby as look at him. And at least she, Creusa, could hope that she would be dead long before her little boy was, and she would be waiting for him in Hades so they could be eternal shades together.

But a goddess would know that even if her son lived to be a hundred, she would have to watch him die, from eyes that were as clear and beautiful as the day she first came into being. Of course such a mother would absent herself from her son. How could she bear to be in the same room as he, knowing all of that?

The nurse placed the sleeping child carefully into his crib. Creusa longed to pick him up and wrap him in her arms again, but she sensed it was not wise. *Let the baby sleep.* However, she did pull herself up to a sitting position, ignoring the pains that still plagued her, and whispered a promise to her son. "I promise," she said through gritted teeth, "I will do everything I can to protect you for as long as I may live."

)

Aeneas came to see them both as soon as he was permitted to do so, although Creusa was pleased that he took the time to bathe first, washing away the horrors of the battlefield. He touched the small, swaddled body of his son with one finger, as though he were a fragile kylix instead of a boy who had already shown he could scream lustily.

"Ascanius," he murmured. "Creusa, you are the most amazing woman."

"Many women have given birth," she said, shifting uncomfortably. It wasn't just the post-birth pains that made her do so. She felt as though she and Ascanius dwelled in a happy soap bubble, away from the perils of the world outside. To mention their good fortune was to invite one of the many gods and goddesses who interfered in human affairs to prick that bubble and set them both adrift in the theatre of war outside her window.

Aeneas placed a kiss on her forehead. "Yes, but not to Ascanius. He is perfect in every way." She smiled wanly.

"We can't protect him," she said, and felt a tear slide down her cheek. "He's so vulnerable, Aeneas. What were we thinking, bringing a small child into the world we live in?"

"We were thinking that the Greeks have made no advances in six years and must run out of resources and go home with their tails between their legs soon. We were thinking that my mother is an immortal goddess, and while she may not be the most affectionate of mothers, she has always protected me and will do so for my son too. We were thinking that you are the most wonderful woman in the world, and you will be the most maternal too. Your son will never starve for lack of love. And," he said, kissing her forehead again, "your mother has already warned me this is most common with all new mothers, to feel weak and unhappy on about the third day after giving birth. It will pass."

"My mother told you that?" she asked disbelievingly. "When did you ever have such a conversation with my mother?"

"Oh, a few months back. She does love you very much too," although I think she does not know how to say it."

She stared at his open and frank face, his trusting countenance. If anyone else had told her this, she would have accused them of lying. She knew her mother, had nursed her through several of those pregnancies, and could never remember her being particularly disheartened on the third day. But then she and her mother had never discussed much of an emotional nature. It would be like Hekuba to note her unhappy feelings and see them as something to be weathered the next time.

"I think she would like to see you," Aeneas added now. "She could demand it, of course—she is the queen—but perhaps you would prefer to invite her."

She nodded. He reached down for her hand and squeezed it tightly. "I must return to the fighting. The sooner we can roust those Greeks, the better. Especially now that I have a son to protect."

He kissed her, then their baby, and strode off down the hallway, his sword bouncing by his side. Creusa closed her eyes. She would summon her mother soon. But now, for the first time since Ascanius had been born, she felt he was safe enough that she might sleep.

☽

When Ascanius was six months old, Creusa attended Andromache at the birth of his cousin. She had witnessed her mother giving birth so many times, she had thought that Andromache's birth would be a simple matter for her, and yet somehow it was not. Giving birth herself had changed her, made her see the process from a different perspective. No longer did she tap her foot through the grunts and cries; instead, she remembered what it felt to be torn inside out. Andromache cried far more than her mother did too, this being her first baby. Again, Creusa remembered that all she had wanted was water, and she kept a steady supply ready for her sister-in-law and mopped her brow with a cool sponge as well from time to time.

As Andromache lay on the bed, her eyes glassy as she recovered from her contractions, Creusa crossed to the window and looked out beyond the walls. She was glad she hadn't had this view when she was in labour; she might have been tempted to cross her legs and not open them again until the war was over.

Nearly seven years they had been besieged now, and still there was no sign of a ceasefire. The Trojans, led by Hektor and Aeneas, drove the Greeks back; the Greeks, led by Achilleus and Ajax, pushed forward again. She was too far away to make out individuals, although she thought she recognised Hektor's plumed helmet. Several years ago, she had asked Helen, her question genuine, why Menelaus was never to be seen at the forefront of the Greek army. It was his wife they were all fighting for, after all. Or alternatively, Agamemnon, Menelaus's brother and the leader of the Greek forces. Surely he wanted his share of the glory.

She never forgot how Helen's lip had curled with scorn. "Them, fight at the front? Ha! The Atreides are cowards, skulking at the back. You can be sure Agamemnon has crafted some elaborate excuse about how a true commander uses his troops to carry out his orders, but the truth is, he's scared for his own skin. I've heard your sister, the mad one, shouting about how only a woman can kill Agamemnon, and it doesn't surprise me. He will turn tail and run before he lets a man get close. Cowards, the pair of them."

Too late, Creusa remembered that Paris, too, held back from the fighting, preferring to sit in safety at the top of the wall and let his arrows fly as he saw fit. *Poor Helen,* she thought, *I don't think she loves either of them.* And now, looking at the soldiers below her, she thought that Helen might be the most beautiful woman in the world, whose face would be immortalised in verse and song, but she had left behind her daughter, Hermione, and no children seemed to be forthcoming with Paris. Much to her mother's disgust, Creusa took Ascanius everywhere with her, wrapped up in her shawl. He had only stayed behind with her maid today because she thought a child's cries might distract Andromache when she needed to focus on her own baby. Creusa missed the warmth of his tiny body pressed against her.

A cry from Andromache brought Creusa back to her side. The baby was coming, she ascertained, and far more quickly than Ascanius had. A few sturdy pushes from Andromache, and Creusa found herself holding a small, red-faced baby in her arms. He opened his mouth and yelled heartily, and Creusa smiled to herself as she thought how much like his father he appeared. But diplomatically, when she placed the newly cleaned child in Andromache's arms, she said, "I think he has your eyes."

"Liar," Andromache said comfortably. "He's Hektor through and through. We are going to call him Scamandrius, after the river. Oh, Creusa, won't it be lovely for Ascanius and Scamandrius to grow up together just like their fathers did? I already know they will be the best of friends."

Creusa glanced out of the window at the beaches below, where Hektor and Aeneas were battling for their lives, for their wives' freedom, and for their sons' safety. And she wanted nothing more than to run downstairs to her own chambers, strap her son onto her back like a peasant, and race as far away from the city as she possibly could. But she already knew that such a flight would be futile. She was one of the least important of the Trojan princesses, but she was still a Trojan princess, and Aeneas was a Dardanian prince. The Greeks would never let them leave, not alive. She resolved to increase her sacrifices to the gods, especially to Aeneas's mother. Surely she would protect her grandson, even if Troy itself were to burn.

☽

Four more years passed. Creusa had stopped watching the battles. She waited by the gates instead, to welcome the Trojan men, and especially Aeneas, back home as they returned from the war. She tried not to count each time how fewer men returned compared to the previous days, but it was impossible. The Trojan numbers were diminishing now that the warrior Achilleus had returned to the battlefield, his gleaming Myrmidons slicing through Trojans like they were nothing more than toy men made of silk. One day, she thought, it would be Aeneas whose body was slung over the shoulders of a couple of these men, or worse, left on the battlefield to be recovered during one of the truces. It would be her job to cleanse the body and prepare it for burial. The idea was unthinkable, and that was why she made herself think it, so she would not falter when the time came. But still, she could not watch the battles.

And so she was not watching when the miracle happened. Polyxena came to fetch her, panting from the exertion. Creusa looked in surprise at her younger sister, face red, struggling to gasp out the words.

"Is he dead?" she demanded, but her sister shook her head, and pulled at her arm, gesturing to her to come up to the vantage point on the walls.

Helen met her there. Ten years had passed, during which Helen had replied to her overtures as seldom as possible, and only addressed her first once, asking her to move some toys Ascanius had left in her path. But now Helen grasped her hands as though she were her sister.

"Creusa, my dear," she said, although before now, Creusa would have said Helen did not know the names of any of her sisters-in-law. "The goddess has seen fit to bless your husband."

Creusa looked out over the battlefield. She thought she saw Aeneas, a small speck on the far side of the fighting. He didn't seem to be moving very fast.

"How so?" she asked, her tone as polite as she could muster.

Helen linked her arm through Creusa's and pointed. "The warrior, Achilleus, made his entry—here—and Aeneas rushed to meet him, so they clashed—here—and they were fighting, but not for long. Because as Achilleus raised his sword to deal the deadly strike, Aeneas suddenly—poof!—disappeared. And then he reappeared—there."

Creusa said nothing. She wished that Helen would take her arm away. She thought of the fate that had almost befallen Aeneas.

"Achilleus is furious," Helen said, her tone sly and confiding, as though she were telling Creusa about the master of a slave who had dropped his favourite vase, rather than about an angry warrior who intended to kill both of their husbands, and would have killed Helen's several times over, were it possible.

Creusa lifted her free arm to shield her eyes from the sun, and looked about for the Greek. It wasn't hard; it never was. He was like a god himself, moving so quickly that no one could pin him down, wielding his sword so fast that no one saw it coming. Look for the bodies falling, and there you will find Achilleus. But at least he was far from Aeneas. For the first time, Creusa realised that he would always be far from Aeneas. Aeneas's mother would see to that. She felt as though a fist that had been holding her heart tight had suddenly let go, and for a moment she wanted to cry from sheer relief. Creusa still had many brothers on the battlefield, though. She couldn't breathe too easily—not yet.

She gazed out over the battle towards the sea, looking at the hazy mist that had spread itself over the horizon. It was better than watching the fighting, but her stomach still surged when she thought of what was going on below. She wanted to leave, but she needed to work out a way to remove Helen's pincer grip from her arm. Did Helen even remember she was there, or had she become a pillar for her to rest upon? No, she realised, looking sideways at the other woman, at the faint glow that had appeared on her cheeks. Helen knew she was there. She had become interesting to Helen, for the first time in almost ten years, because Helen had finally seen proof with her own eyes that Aeneas was the son of Aphrodite.

She fought the urge to wrench her arm away from the other woman, and instead started practising excuses in her mind. My mother will need me. My son will need me. I am needed, anywhere but here. But she was too slow, and soon she became aware of the fight that was happening in the very centre of the battlefield, a fight so significant it seemed as though everyone else had put down their weapons and stopped to watch. Achilleus and Hektor were locked in combat at last.

Achilleus's speed had paid off: he had finally cornered his man. Hektor, taller than any other man below them, bellowed with fury and tried to parry, but Achilleus dodged him. Hektor battled like a raging bull, roaring and trying to attack, but his opponent was everywhere and nowhere at once. Achilleus's blows, on the other hand, landed every time, and it was clear that the bull was tiring. Creusa thought she saw Hektor shake his head and dash his arm against his brow, and she knew he couldn't manage much more.

She tried to call for assistance, although she wasn't sure whether her mouth had made a sound. Helen's fingernails dug more deeply into her arm, and she clung to that pain to stop herself from passing out. Below her, she could see Aeneas, trying to fight his way across the field to come to Hektor's aid, but he was too far away, and the Greeks, realising his intention, blocked him at every turn. He must have killed or maimed half a dozen of them, but they kept coming, and he got no closer to Hektor than he had been before.

Across the ramparts she saw Paris, the Trojans' first archer, take aim with his bow, but he dropped it again after a few minutes, looking across at Helen and Creusa and raising his arms in despair. Creusa saw his problem clearly: Achilleus was moving too fast, and Hektor was too large. Any arrow that Paris shot was more likely to hasten Hektor's end, not spare it. In a fit of pique, Paris picked up his bow again and picked off several Greeks who had strayed too far from the centre of the action, but it was of no use to Hektor.

Achilleus landed the final deadly blow. Hektor toppled to the ground, felled like a giant plane tree. Everyone was still for a moment, waiting to see if the mighty warrior would take to his feet again. He did not. A cheer broke out among the Greeks, unable to believe their luck. Hektor, the great defender of Troy, had finally fallen. The war would turn now. And from behind Creusa, a single cry rang out.

"Aaaiiiieeeee," Andromache wailed, her voice hanging in the breeze for a moment. Creusa closed her eyes, unable to bear the pain in her sister-in-law's voice. When had Andromache even come up to the ramparts? Like Creusa, she hadn't done so in months. Which god or goddess had wanted both of them present to witness this moment? A stinging sensation in her arm recalled Creusa to herself, and she pushed Helen away and turned in time to catch Andromache before she, like her husband, fell.

For a moment they stood together, clinging to each other like the sole survivors of a shipwreck. Then they were surrounded by women, all the wives of Creusa's brothers, her many, many sisters-in-law, holding each other, sharing in Andromache's pain, as they knew they would share in her fate. Some sobbed, some were quiet, but all linked their arms around the woman who should have been their queen, in time.

Finally, Andromache pushed them aside, then ripped off the diadem she wore at all times and tossed it to the ground. Creusa flinched; while she knew the material value of the diadem, she also knew that Andromache valued it for the hands that had placed it on her head, hands that even now were lying lifeless on the ground below.

Andromache crossed to the edge of the rampart, and called out, "Oh, Hektor, Hektor, what I am supposed to do? We were supposed to share one fate, you and I, and now you are journeying to Hades and leaving me here alone. What is going to happen to our son, Hektor? Do you know they call him Astyanax, the little lord of the city? He's not going to have a city to lord it over now, is he, Hektor? What is going to happen to Scamandrius?"

Her words were swallowed up by her sobs. Creusa felt as though she might be ill. Bad enough that Hektor, her oldest and kindest brother, had to die. But what would the Greeks do to his son when they divided Troy between them, as though it were a plaything and they were greedy children? She knew well what would happen to Andromache, and to all of her sisters-in-law, clustered together as they were. Princesses no longer, they would be torn from one another, and forced to obey masters, not husbands. Little girls might be allowed to grow into small slaves. But what role was there for little boys in this diabolical future?

"Excuse me," she muttered, and began to push her way through the throng. "I have to go." As she left, she thought she heard Andromache crying to Hektor about the funeral pyre she would build, and the clothes she would burn on it, but her thoughts were no longer with poor dead Hektor. She needed to hold her son.

☽

She found him playing in the street with some other small boys, Antiphantes and Thymbraeus, the sons of the priest Laocoön, while the slave who was supposed to be teaching him watched on with little interest. The game was of the sort she remembered loving as a child, one with sticks as tokens, and extremely complicated rules that no adult could understand, rules which the children challenged each other on constantly and with passion.

The slave straightened to his feet when he saw her, and began chastising Ascanius, but Creusa waved a hand in dismissal. Great Hektor had died. What use was it now for the slave to pretend he had any interest in teaching her son to count?

She had thought that she would pull her son into her arms and hold him as tightly as she had when he was first born, but she saw now that she would embarrass him in front of his friends, and he would squirm away, leaving her feeling worse than she had done before. So instead she watched him intently, drinking him in with her eyes, memorising every inch of him, every mole and dimple and scratch, as though she didn't already carry around the map of Ascanius in her head.

Aeneas was a good father, but she knew that he could not place the small birthmark at the base of Ascanius's spine, nor did he remember the location of the tiny mole on his head, now covered by hair. She knew all of this, and more besides. She knew that he loved olives but hated apples; that he would run to the ends of the earth for a good story by a bard, but he would fall over himself, spitting, if the bard dared to make the story a romance. She knew that despite his bravado, he still fell asleep best when he curled himself into his mother's side. She had much to teach Aeneas about his son and no time in which to teach it.

A gentle hand on her arm made her blink back the tears that had started to form, and she turned to see Cassandra, surprisingly subdued.

"It's happened, then?" Cassandra asked, her voice small and quiet.

"Achilleus has killed Hektor, if that's what you are referring to," Creusa nodded, then she regretted her haughty words. Cassandra was Hektor's sister too. "Did you . . . did you know it would happen?"

Cassandra nodded. "That doesn't mean I wanted it to happen, though," she said, and a tear ran down her cheek. Creusa put a hand on her shoulder awkwardly, but they didn't move any closer to each other, and Creusa thought how strange it was that with Cassandra, her actual sister, she couldn't break the invisible barriers that separated them and embrace her, although she had been embracing so many of her sisters-in-law not that long ago. But then she supposed Hekuba had never encouraged any intimacy between her children.

Cassandra shifted slightly, and they both looked to the street and watched Ascanius.

"He's riding roughshod over Laocoön's boys," Cassandra said. "He needs other princes to play with. They wouldn't let him get away with so much."

"Like Hektor and Aeneas," Creusa replied. "It never made sense to me how they could be best friends and still try to beat each other senseless. They always united against anyone else, though. That's what Andromache wants for Ascanius and Scamandrius too, but Scamandrius is still too small."

Remembering Andromache's wails, Creusa stopped and swallowed abruptly. While anyone else might have talked brightly of how it was only a matter of time, Cassandra stayed silent, confirming the answer to the question Creusa couldn't bring herself to ask.

"Why do they hate us so much?" Cassandra asked suddenly, and Creusa turned to her sister in shock. In twenty-five years, she could not remember Cassandra ever having asked a question.

"I don't think they hate us," she replied cautiously. "It's just politics, isn't it? We have land and money, and Paris took Helen, so here they are."

But Cassandra shook her head. "I've seen the things they do to us," she said, another tear running down her cheek. "This isn't just politics. It isn't even about Helen. They wouldn't treat their horses as badly as they treat some of us. Nothing is sacred to them. They are going to slit our throats on our own altars. They are going to rape us, all of us—married women, women dedicated to goddesses, women who are barely more than girls. They are going to murder our children."

Creusa took a deep, shuddering breath. "Cassandra, years ago you gave me a prophecy. Do you remember?"

Cassandra nodded gloomily. "I never forget. Not what's happened, not what's coming. I wish I could. And before you ask, no, nothing's changed. But at least you won't be raped or murdered on an altar."

"That's not what I was going to ask," Creusa said, and then added hastily, "and I don't need any more details. Just . . . your prophecy about Aeneas. That hasn't changed either, has it?"

Cassandra shook her head. "His goddess looks after her own. Not like Apollo, my lord and master, oh great one, oh merciful one, oh . . . it doesn't make a difference in the end. He's not going to save me."

Later, Creusa would tell Aeneas that this, and not the death of her brother, was the worst moment of the war so far for her. To hear Cassandra criticise Apollo, who gave her the gift of prophecy. To see her so low. Creusa had known the end was in sight; they had all seen it as Hektor's great body toppled. But now she realised just how close it was.

"I need one more prophecy," she interrupted her sister, before she could hear any more of her litany of woe. Cassandra followed Creusa's gaze to Ascanius, his small body crouched intently over a broken piece of bark, his grey eyes thoughtful as he listened to his friend's petition. Cassandra nodded and closed her eyes.

☽

As she had expected, Aeneas was home late from the battlefield. He had gone first to visit Andromache, to pay his respects to his best friend's widow. Creusa took one look at his face as he sank down into a chair, and didn't ask how the visit had gone. Instead, she served him his favourite fish, prepared in the Dardanian way, and sat quietly as he continued to mull over the devastation of the day. She had sent Ascanius to bed early, much against her own instincts as every sinew, muscle, and bone in her body was screaming to her to wrap him in her arms and to shield him with her body, if necessary. But she knew that was not what she needed to do.

Finally, when Aeneas sighed, and she saw some of the tension lift from his shoulders, she knelt before him, placing her hands on his knees in supplication. Alarmed, Aeneas tried to raise her to her feet, but she stayed where she was.

"Aeneas," she said, her voice soft but firm, "you are my love. I have never desired another man since I met you. You are the father of my child. You have given me everything that is good in my life, without my ever needing to ask. But now, Aeneas, I need to ask something of you."

)

And then, as suddenly as they had arrived, the Greeks left. Overnight, every man, every slave girl, every ship just sailed away. They took everything they had: their arms, their clothing, their cooking utensils. They stripped their makeshift huts that had served as their homes for ten years, and even the wood disappeared.

The Trojans stared, confused. At first, as they had done for so many years, only the warriors had left the safety of the Trojan walls, fully armed, ready to start the day's battles. But they searched in vain for enemies to fight, staring at one another, bewildered. Eventually Helenus returned to the gates and banged on them loudly. "Send out Priam," he called. "Send my father. The Greeks are gone. We need our king."

Priam went down to the shore for the first time in daylight since the war had begun, but he did not go alone. Hearing that their enemy was missing, the women and children saw their opportunity to pass beyond the walls that had been their security and their prison for so long. Only Andromache remained behind, still weeping in her bed. Creusa looked in on her, but decided to leave her. Andromache's sunshine was gone. What good would it do her to splash in the sea?

Instead, Creusa pulled Ascanius away from his street game, and laughing, they ran down to and out of the gates. They stared at the sea and then each other, blinded by the dazzling lights the sunshine cast upon the water.

Creusa saw Aeneas, deep in discussion with Helenus and Priam. She waved at him and he frowned at her. She shrugged in apology; she knew that he would have preferred her to be cautious, especially after their conversation the night before, but some opportunities had to be seized in the moment.

Casting off her sandals, she pulled her skirts up to her knees and gathered them in one hand. With the other, she grabbed Ascanius's hand, and pulled him into the sea. She heard a little gasp of breath as his feet hit the cold water, and she realised that despite living in a coastal city all his life, this was the first time Ascanius had felt the sand between his toes and the water lapping at his feet. Forsaking all hope of keeping her dress dry, she picked him up with both hands and swung him into the waves, drinking in the joyous sounds of his giggles. Over and over again, they leaped over sea froth, and when they had tired of that game, splashed each other with sea water. Ascanius put his tongue into the water and then drew back. "Salty!" he cried, and she laughed at his surprise and disgust.

Finally, exhausted, they collapsed against each other, stretching out their legs so the water could buffet their toes. Creusa hugged Ascanius's warm little body to her and thought that she had never had a more perfect morning in her entire life.

Eventually, Aeneas came to join them. Although he'd removed his helmet, he was still in full armour, so he stayed back from the water. Seeing his scowling face, Creusa stood up, keeping one hand on Ascanius's shoulder. It would be dreadful if, after all Aeneas's fighting to keep them safe, Ascanius was washed out to sea on the first day of peace.

"What's wrong?" she murmured quietly.

"Your father. Refuses to see the danger." Aeneas looked round and glowered. Priam was looking away.

"What danger? The Greeks have gone."

"There's danger. Why have they gone? We have been struggling since they killed Hektor. Yes, Paris killed Achilleus before meeting his own death, but there are still many strong Greeks. The two Ajaxes, Odysseus, Diomede—the list goes on. They had the upper hand, and they've just given up?"

Creusa opened her mouth to say something and then closed it again. Aeneas was right. Why would the Greeks leave now? "They don't have Helen," she said slowly.

"Exactly, and more than that, they don't have any of the riches Troy promised them. Oh, I know they've done their looting up and down the coast, but the bounty is in here."

He turned from her and gestured at her father. "Priam just believes what he wants to believe. He's had no heart for this war, not since Hektor died."

"None of us has," Creusa said, compelled to defend her father. Aeneas put his hand on her arm.

"Creusa, I know—believe me, I know. I miss him too. I know he was your brother, but he was also like a brother to me. My cousin. My brother-in-law."

Creusa put her finger to his lips to stop his stumbling. "He was your best friend, Aeneas. I do not deny your grief."

"Thank you." He bowed his head, and she saw the glistening tears. But then he lifted it again. "But you, of all people, know that we cannot give up just because Hektor died. That would be the last thing he would want. We have the children to think of—Ascanius, Scamandrius, and so many more. I do not trust the Greeks. I do not think we are right to let our guard down."

Before Creusa could say anything, they were interrupted by a loud shout. A young soldier, one whose name she didn't know but whose face suggested he might be her half brother, was calling everyone over to the rocks. Despite his heavy armour, Aeneas sprinted towards him. Creusa lingered for a moment; then, seeing that everyone else was moving towards the soldier's find, took Ascanius's hand and led him to the rocks. She felt the weight of him pulling on her arm, and she knew she would have to take him inside soon to sleep, but she wasn't ready to go yet.

She stopped short when she saw what the soldier had found. A giant wooden horse, the height of at least three men.

"When did the Greeks build this?" she asked no one in particular. This was where the wood from their huts had gone, she realised. But why?

"Perhaps it is a gift," her father said, his voice cracking. "Perhaps the gods instructed them to leave it to us as recompense for what we have suffered."

It was all Creusa could do to keep herself from throwing herself at her father. A gift? Recompense? Would a wooden horse bring back her brother or any of the other Trojans who had died? Would a wooden horse compensate Khryseis, the daughter of the priest of Apollo, who had been held captive by the Greeks until the gods demanded her release? Or Andromache, unable to sleep without an herbal tincture? Would it compensate Ascanius, living with the shadow of war over his head, never knowing if his father would return home at night, unable to play on the beaches as she had done as a child? A caged lion cub, not free to grow as tall and fierce as he should.

But she said none of this. She knew her father would never listen to her. And besides, she didn't have to. Laocoön, the priest, had begun to berate her father.

"A gift from an enemy? Priam, did you lose your mind with your boy?"

"Who are you to talk to me like that?" her father shouted back.

"Destroy it, Priam. Burn it to the ground before it destroys us. Here, let me spark a flame!" He began to rub two sticks together furiously, although he must have known, as they all did, that any driftwood would be too wet to burn. As he did so, a cry was heard from the waters. To her horror, Creusa saw that the priest's sons had strayed too close to the sea. A sea serpent of some form had risen from the waves and was grappling with the boys. Barely bigger than Ascanius, they stood no chance. She pulled Ascanius close to her and closed her eyes, unable to watch as the warriors on the beach ran to the water. She heard rather than saw them slash at the serpent with their swords, and the monstrous splash of water as the beast disappeared under the waves with its prey.

Laocoön collapsed. Still holding Ascanius's hand, she crept over to him, gingerly stepping over the seaweed and shells that littered the shore. She stroked his hand and helped him to his feet.

"I will take you back to the palace," she said, keeping her voice gentle. "We will need to tell your wife." She didn't know his wife's name, although they were on nodding terms as mothers of boys about the same age. She swallowed guiltily, remembering those same boys playing with Ascanius in the street. She should have been keeping a closer eye on all the children. She would have expected another mother to make sure Ascanius did not wander too close to the water.

Laocoön nodded, his eyes wide and unseeing. As they made their way back to the palace, stumbling over every step, the priest on her right arm as slow as the small boy clutching her left, they passed Helen, sashaying in the opposite direction. She did not acknowledge Creusa, her eyes fixed on the scene ahead. Creusa paused and turned to watch as Helen and another figure converged on the horse at the same time. She thought the man on the beach might be a Greek, and her heart felt cold. Aeneas was down there, she reminded herself. *Aeneas will see sense. He won't listen to Helen, he has never done so before. But my father does,* a small voice said. *Aeneas is sensible, but Priam does not listen to reason, not when a pretty woman is telling him what he wants to hear.*

Creusa turned back and continued towards the palace. For a brief, shimmering moment, she had thought she could escape her fate and Troy's, the destiny Priam had never accepted. But she knew better. Aeneas would do his best, and she would hold that moment of happiness close in her heart for as long as she could.

☽

The horse was wheeled in to the city. She didn't see it again. Although others went to visit it, to slap its flanks and admire the craftsmanship, she kept Ascanius inside and stayed there herself. He paced about like a trapped beast and repaid her by pulling out every toy he had, and all her cooking utensils too, but she remained firm.

Later, Anchises came to the house, and they exchanged worried looks, although he pretended he was just dropping by, and she professed that the bed she had just made up was a coincidence, as she was airing the blankets. Anchises at least was able to entertain Ascanius, telling him stories of his immortal grandmother and the other gods so Creusa could tidy her home and prepare their dinner. She felt as though she were trapped in a story herself, going through the motions of such everyday activities while her head and her heart told her that danger was approaching.

Could they leave, she wondered? But Aeneas was not yet home, and in any event, she also felt that it would be futile. Her lot was determined, and she would see it through to the end.

☽

Danger, when it arrived, came in the middle of the night. They heard the shouts and cries of the Greeks rampaging through the city first. The room flickered red, and Creusa wondered what it was, before the smell of smoke led her to the realisation that the curtains that covered the windows were not thick enough to block out the infernos outside. A party of Greeks must have passed by outside, as their shadows were cast onto the bedroom wall just as she sometimes made hand puppets of butterflies and hares for Ascanius. This was no light entertainment, though, but a deadly theatre of raised spears and swords imposed directly onto her own chamber wall. Aeneas, who had been sleeping beside her, sprang to his feet. Creusa hadn't slept. She remained where she was for a moment, sitting in bed.

"It was the horse, wasn't it?" she asked. "They were inside the horse."

"I think so," Aeneas sighed. "You know after you left, Helen walked around the horse and called each of the Greeks by name? She mimicked their wives' voices, or so she said. I've never heard any of those women speak. And nothing happened. So Priam decided it was safe."

"There's at least one Greek wife's voice she wouldn't have had to imitate," Creusa said bitterly.

Aeneas nodded. "Yes, I suppose she will be going home now. How could two people bring so much misery to so many?" He was pulling his clothes on as he spoke, and Creusa, remembering Ascanius sleeping in the room next door, began to do the same.

"You would think that beautiful people would be nicer," she said.

Aeneas laughed hollowly. "Beautiful people only care about themselves. They don't need to be kind to make others love them."

So many things she wanted to say. She wanted to tell him, just as he had done for her, that she didn't care that he hadn't inherited his mother's legendary beauty. That from the moment she had seen him until the moment Ascanius had been born, he had been the centre of her world, the only star in her sky. She knew their time had run out, and she wanted to go back and live it all again, but better. Leave Troy as soon as Paris and Helen arrived. If her father wished to sacrifice his legacy for the sake of a son he'd never known and a daughter-in-law who was already married, let him. Why did Aeneas and Creusa need to try and save him from himself, save all the Trojans from themselves?

But that was not her story. And if they had left, perhaps she would not have given birth to Ascanius. Ascanius who had inherited his grandparents' beauty. Ascanius, her little cub, who needed to reach safety so he could become the lion he was fated to be. Another party of Greeks bellowed below the window, and when she peeked through the curtain, she saw the house opposite catch alight, a blaze that lit up the entire sky. She heard the pained shrieks of the inhabitants, their neighbours and friends, beneath the crackling of the fires. If she didn't get her family out to safety soon, she would be too late.

She allowed herself one more moment, pulling Aeneas to her, smelling his familiar scent, inhaling his very essence. Then she let him go.

"We need to wake Ascanius and your father," she said.

BOOK TWELVE

LAVINIA

Venus thus answer'd; . . . Aeneas . . .
My son, of all mankind my most beloved . . .
                    —Homer, *Iliad, Book Five*
                    (trans. by Cowper, 1791)

The next morning, Lavinia resolved to seek Aeneas out. But as she was walking to his hut, she was interrupted by a shout. A messenger from the palace had arrived and immediately doubled over, trying to catch his breath. She put a hand out instinctively, to steady him, and they were immediately joined by her father and Aeneas. Latinus's face paled when he saw the colours that the man was wearing.

"What is it?" he asked sharply. "Spit it out, man." Later Lavinia was to reflect on her father's impatience, so unlike him. Was it the stress of the situation, the runner's twisted torso betraying his need to speed beyond what would normally be required? Or had he left the palace that morning knowing what was burning on the metaphorical pyre? She would never ask.

"Your Majesty, the queen is dead by her own hand," the messenger said. He stumbled, his legs giving way beneath him.

It was customary now to encourage him to rest and drink a little, but her father did none of this. "What do you mean?"

"She was watching the battle from her window. She thought she saw Aeneas—the Prince Aeneas—defeat the Prince Turnus in combat. She said that she was the cause of all this misery." He looked at Lavinia in anguish but carried on. "She tied a noose around a high beam and jumped to her death. I think she was not in her sound mind, sire."

Lavinia and her father exchanged confused glances.

"Could she have seen the battle from her window?" Lavinia asked first. "I did not think we were near enough to the palace."

Her father shook his head. "In any event, her window faces to the sea. The message may have been a bit confused, but . . ." he tailed off and sighed. "As this man says, she was not in her sound mind."

Lavinia wanted to say something, but it seemed as though her father had doubled into two men, and she didn't know which one to address. The ground under her feet seemed to be moving up and down. She reached out her arms, and found herself being taken into an embrace.

"Lavinia, are you all right?" she heard Aeneas ask. "I have you, Lavinia. I won't let you fall."

Falling? Was that what I was doing? she wondered. She allowed Aeneas to support her, to hold her upright while she regained control of her limbs and her mind. Her vision returned to normal, and she looked up to hear her father say, "I wonder if a god possessed her, or perhaps she had a vision of the future. It will not be so long until Aeneas slays Turnus, after all. This may be a positive sign."

Her mouth dropped in horror, but it was Aeneas who spoke, not she. "By the gods, Latinus, are you so unfeeling? Your wife has died. Your daughter has lost her mother. Do you think that people are mere signs, blank backdrops on which the gods may paint their will?"

Latinus scowled at Aeneas, who ignored him. Aeneas looked instead at Lavinia, holding her a little way from his body so he could study her face.

"Lavinia, I am so sorry for your loss," he said. "Please, if there is anything I can do, you need only say it."

Latinus turned and walked away. Lavinia let him go.

"She was never well," she said to Aeneas, ignoring years of instructions never to mention her mother's health except to say she suffered from headaches. "She was not like other mothers."

"I understand," Aeneas said. "She cared for you, though. I could see that."

He pulled her close again and allowed her to cry, not caring that they were in the middle of the camp, where anyone could see them.

"I will need to lead the mourning," she said, her voice muffled from being pressed against Aeneas's chest. "Will you allow me to return to the palace to ensure that the ceremony is carried out correctly?"

She felt Aeneas stiffen, and she wondered if she had asked too much, but he replied, "You have never been my prisoner, Lavinia."

He shifted position so his arm was around her shoulder, and led her to her hut, saying, "You will need to sit down." Together, they entered the room. Too late, Lavinia remembered that she had left Anna in the hut, but she saw no sign of her. She allowed Aeneas to help her onto the bed and to sit down, all the while stroking her hand.

"You don't know what it's like," she said, feeling the sobs well up once more. "Your mother is immortal."

"True," he said, "but my wife was not, nor were many people I cared for in Troy."

"It's different when it's your mother," Lavinia replied sadly.

She expected Aeneas to disagree with her, so she was surprised when instead he dropped his gaze instantly, flushed a little, and replied, "I am sure there is no relationship as special as that between mother and child. I should not deprive you of that."

"I have been deprived," she reminded him. "My mother is dead."

For a moment they sat in silence. Lavinia could not tell what Aeneas might be thinking; she could only picture Amata. *I let her down,* she thought. *I was ashamed of her, and I should have helped her. What sort of daughter am I?*

"I'm sorry," she said at last. "I've been holding you responsible for so much that has gone wrong since you arrived, creating a phantom Aeneas to blame for our woes. It isn't all your fault."

He laughed a little when she said *all,* and she smiled. "I'm sure some of it is," he said. "I would be the last to argue that I've conducted my life without error."

"Would you change it if you could?" Lavinia asked with interest.

He frowned and was quiet, then said, "The day I married my wife, I would have taken her far from Troy. Perhaps even before I married her. I would have done anything to save her; I still would. I'm sorry, Princess—that's not a romantic thing for you to hear."

"I'm not a romantic person," Lavinia replied drily. But Dido was, she thought. Did Dido know that Aeneas was still in love with his wife, even when he was marrying her? And yet the more she knew Aeneas, the more difficult she found it to reconcile the man sitting beside her with the cold-hearted one who had made love to, then abandoned a beautiful princess.

With a jolt of surprise, she thought, *I am actually becoming quite fond of him. Not a passionate love, not a romantic one, but he is steady, at least. He is kind, to his friends.* She did not feel her anger dissipating, so much as that she looked into the pool of anger in her mind, and realised that it was not there anymore.

"Too many people are dying," she said at last. "This is supposed to be your war, but now my people are dying too. Camilla, Pallas, my mother—all are dead."

He studied her face for a moment. "That is war," he said gently. "I am sorry, Lavinia, but war is cruel and unnecessary, and people will die. The Trojans cannot leave," Aeneas continued, his voice still gentle, but firm. "I have made promises. I have a duty. There is room in this land for all of us to live side by side, but Turnus chooses not to see it that way."

"Then more people will die," Lavinia said wretchedly.

Aeneas nodded. "Yes." He let go of her hand and stood up.

"Why won't you fight the duel?" Lavinia asked, the words bursting out of her.

Aeneas sat down heavily again on the bed. "He is just a boy."

"Are you frightened? Because that is what everyone thinks. Aeneas, the great Trojan hero, too scared to fight in a simple duel." Lavinia leaned forward, trying to meet his eyes.

"You do not understand. You and Turnus—children, both of you." He turned away from her, although she could have sworn she saw tears in his eyes.

"If he is such a child, fight him then. What are you so afraid of?"

"I do not want to kill a child," Aeneas thundered, turning back towards her. "He is barely more than a boy, barely older than my own son. I am not frightened of losing, Lavinia. I am frightened for Turnus because I know that I will win."

Lavinia shrank back. Aeneas seemed larger than before, his broad shoulders filling the room. She didn't feel afraid of him, exactly; she knew he meant her no ill-will. But rather, like an unpredictable horse, she didn't know whether he intended to bolt or rear up, and although he might not mean to hurt her, she didn't want to be trodden underfoot either.

"How can you be so sure?" she asked. "He's younger than you. He's a good fighter. I've seen him train. It would be a fair fight. And it's a fight he's asking for."

Seeing her cringe, Aeneas slumped back again. "If I fight Turnus, one to one, man to man, I will win. The gods have foretold it. And that means that I will kill Turnus as surely as if I crept up behind him in the night and stabbed him in his bed. It's not heroic, Lavinia. It's just bloody murder."

Lavinia was silent for a moment before she continued. "But why are you so sure that you will win this battle?" she asked. "What have the gods foretold?"

He frowned. "I cannot tell you that. Only know that I am certain I will win. The gods will protect me. Whenever I have come close to death, they have spirited me away, leaving my opponent looking about him in confusion. This time, they will deal the winning blow, and I will kill Turnus. And I do not wish to do that to someone you love."

"But I do not love Turnus," she exclaimed before she could stop herself.

"It is no matter," Aeneas said. "I still do not wish to kill him. There is too much blood on my hands already."

"Like your wife? And Queen Dido?" She studied his face intently. The pain that flashed across his eyes when she mentioned his wife. And the mix of emotions, ending in surprise, when she spoke of Anna's sister.

"This is not the first time you have alluded to Dido. What do you know of her?" he asked.

"She was your lover—your wife—and she killed herself."

Neither of them said anything. They could hear rustling sounds from outside the hut: birds settling down for the night, a small animal hunting its even smaller prey.

"Who told you?" Aeneas said at last. "No one was supposed to tell you. Does your father know?"

"I don't know," Lavinia said. "Why are we not supposed to know?"

Aeneas flushed. "It is foolish. It is all foolish. Lavinia. Dido was not my wife. You are correct—she was my lover, and she killed herself. But she was not my wife. We thought it best—the Trojan elders and I—not to tell your father because it may dissuade him from allowing you to marry me, and we thought that marriage was the best way to lay our claim to this land, without bloodshed. But look where we are now. There is always bloodshed. Someone always wants to fight a war."

"When you returned from Pallantium," she said slowly, "I saw you on the prow of the ship. You looked out towards us all, smiling and waving. Everyone was so happy to see you return. And it appeared as though your hair was on fire. But then the sun went behind a cloud, and the fire disappeared. It was an illusion."

Aeneas shook his head. "It was not an illusion. It was an effect, one created for me by my mother. It made me appear stronger, braver: a leader to follow, the man who can tolerate the fire. The man who can touch the fire and not get burned."

She nodded. "Yes. And yet, it was an illusion. No one can touch fire and not burn."

She saw he understood her meaning, as he sighed, his expression forlorn.

"None of us can change our parents," he said. "My mother, the immortal goddess, questing for dreams that I, a mere mortal, cannot understand. And your parents, your father, so keen to marry you to a man he'd only just met."

Lavinia frowned. "You heard the prophecy. No heirs for him unless I marry you."

Aeneas smiled, a cold smile without any mirth. "Your father hasn't listened properly to the prophecy."

"What do you mean?" Lavinia asked, puzzled, and then it dawned on her. "The prophecy doesn't say he will have any heirs if I marry you. It just says that he won't have any heirs if I marry Turnus."

Aeneas nodded. "Ascanius has already been prophesied to inherit this land, and his son Silvius after him. It is my mother's prophecy, and those have a way of coming true. I couldn't tell you before. But now you know."

Lavinia rocked back onto her heels. She felt the world suddenly opening up to her in a way she could not have anticipated.

"You were going to marry me, knowing that we would not have children."

Aeneas nodded again, mistaking her wonder for outrage. "I'm sorry, Lavinia. It was unfair of me, but it seemed the best way to guarantee Ascanius's legacy. I have no interest in gaining this land for myself. But I need to protect Ascanius. I made a promise."

"You will still benefit, though," Lavinia said. "Ascanius is only a boy. You will have many years to govern before he inherits your title."

To her surprise, she saw that Aeneas was blushing, a dull red colour beneath his tanned skin. "Oh, Lavinia. When I said we had lied to you, this lie of omission was the worst of all. According to the prophecy, I will only live for three more years."

"Only three more years! And if we do marry, what would happen to me?" Lavinia's voice was small. She thought of Queen

Dido, governing alone. She thought of the problems that could beset a woman by herself. There were many Iarbases nearby. Evander was an ally, but he wouldn't live for much longer. And Pallas was already dead.

"Perhaps you could assist Ascanius to govern. Act as regent until he comes of age. I will ensure that he takes care of you," Aeneas offered hopefully, holding his hands out.

"But there is a risk," Lavinia said, and she knew that she was about to make her choice, and the thought both thrilled and terrified her. "Ascanius may not want a stepmother watching over him soon, and certainly not one as young as I. I will watch over him until he comes of age, but I need protection too. You need to settle money on me, to make me independent in my own right. Give me the ability to choose what I do, be it stay in Latium or travel the world." Her voice caught on the last three words. Could such a fate truly be within reach? There was so much that could go wrong, she knew. But at the same time, the Fates had prophesied that she was to marry. She was not aware of any prophecy that said what she had to do after that.

Aeneas looked scandalised. "It would not be right for a young woman to have such freedom," he muttered. But then he looked again at Lavinia.

"I will agree to your request. I have lived my life according to prophecies. The only time I chose my own path, I chose so badly that someone I cared for died. But does this mean that you will marry me, even knowing the truth?"

"On one condition," Lavinia said. "You must fight Turnus in the duel."

Aeneas shook his head. "I'm sorry, Lavinia, but I won't do it. You have no idea how desperate my mother is for her line to inherit and take over this land. She will ensure that I annihilate Turnus. It would be tantamount to murder."

Lavinia was silent. She thought of Camilla. Had her death not been tantamount to murder, fighting for the cause that she believed in? Aeneas could have prevented her death. He could prevent many more. She said quietly, "I just want this war to stop."

"I understand," Aeneas said, and he laid a gentle hand on her shoulder. "But I believe that we have the power to stop the war without fighting the duel. Our numbers are stronger than Turnus's, and the men who came with me from Troy are better trained. Let me win the war my way, Lavinia. With honour."

Lavinia tried to think of another objection, but before she could say anything, Aeneas jerked his head up sharply.

"Someone is listening to us," he said. He crossed the room swiftly and pulled aside the bundle of bedding on the floor. Anna was crouched there.

"Don't hurt me," she cried.

"Anna," Lavinia exclaimed. She saw Aeneas's mouth go slack with shock.

"You!" he said. He looked to Lavinia. "And you see her too. I thought I was seeing ghosts. I thought you were—never mind. What are you doing here? And why do you think I would hurt you?"

"My sister is dead because of you," Anna replied. She cowered away from Aeneas, still standing over her. Lavinia leapt up, ready to come between them, if necessary.

Aeneas took a step back, then sat down heavily on a chair. "I know. I'm so sorry, Anna. I suppose it was Anna, then, who told you about Dido, Lavinia?"

"You killed my sister," Anna said. She began to cry. Aeneas shook his head, dazed, then crouched down to try and aid her to stand. She batted him away and continued sobbing.

"How did she die, Anna?" he asked, running a hand through his matted hair. "I saw the flames, but she couldn't have done that, could she?"

Anna looked up, her face red from tears and twisted with hate. "She stabbed herself first, then threw herself upon her own funeral pyre. I tried to pull her from the flames, but I was too late. She died for you, Aeneas. She was worth ten of you, but she died because of you, and you are still here."

"No," Aeneas replied. "Dido understood that I had to leave. My mother willed it to be so. I cannot argue against my fate."

"Your fate?" Anna cried. Lavinia watched on, mesmerised. Neither of them seemed to be aware of her presence any longer. "What has your fate to do with anything? You tricked my sister."

Aeneas looked away. "I did not trick her," he said, although his voice wobbled a little. "I never told her that I would stay. I never told her I would marry her. She believed those for herself. She tricked me, not the other way around."

The two were on their feet now, facing each other from opposite sides of the room. Aeneas had not wanted a duel with Turnus, but he perhaps wanted this duel with Anna even less. At least Anna had no weapon, other than her voice and the tears that coursed down her face.

"Anna, believe me," Aeneas tried again. "I did not want Dido to die. But I had made a promise. I told Dido that. She knew that I would have to leave.'

"All I hear from you is excuses," Anna snarled. "'*My mother willed this; I had to promise that.*' You say my sister should have taken responsibility. Where is your responsibility, Aeneas? Why are you not owning up to your part, great Trojan prince?"

"Enough!" Aeneas bellowed. Lavinia cringed. "I never intended to stay in Carthage. Your sister was beautiful and cultured, and I admired her very much, but I did not wish to marry her. I had a divine mission, and I intended to carry it out. She tricked me."

"You sought glory." Anna nodded. "You wanted the renown that came with founding the new Troy."

"I wanted to look after my son. How can you not understand this? You left Tyre for the same reason, to keep yourselves safe. Do you know what they did to the son of Hektor? He was barely more than an infant, and the vile Odysseus threw him over the walls of Troy. He was dashed to death on the rocks below. A child not old enough to say his own name. You call me a murderer? That monster murdered a child, and yet the bards sing his praises. And then we lived in Carthage, and it was fine. It was more than fine; your sister had a beautiful palace imbued with every luxury that money can buy. Would I rather have lived my years out there than spend my days sleeping on the ground and washing in a cold stream? Of course I would. But what happens to Ascanius then, when I am gone? Would the children that Dido bore live in harmony with their half brother and rule alongside him? Or would they, too, try to annihilate the competitor, as the Greeks did to the Trojans, as your own uncle tried to do to your family?"

"You are just as bad," Anna hissed. "Here you are, stealing land from the Laurentines."

"We were prepared to share the land," Aeneas said. He began to pace up and down. "But the gods will have a battle. I have seen those gods. During the war of Troy, my mother let the scales slip from my eyes, and for a brief moment I was permitted to see gods. They loomed over all of us, and they were destroying

Troy. The achievements of the Greeks, even the monstrous deeds of the one they call godlike Achilleus, were nothing compared to those gods. You think a tremor caused the walls to fall? I saw Apollo and Poseidon pushing at it with their mighty arms. You think the Greeks were more skilled with their arrows? I saw Ares grabbing those arrows and plunging them into the hearts of their targets. You think the Greeks were fiercer with their swords? I saw Athene and Artemis wielding those swords with them, carving up their victims like they were lambs, and I saw them laughing as they did so. Believe me, you never forget a scene like that. Every time I step out onto a battlefield, I look around me, wondering which gods are fighting against me and where they might be. When I close my eyes at night, I picture those gargantuan forms, obliterating one of the greatest cities in the world, and smiling as they do so. If the gods want me to found a new Troy, I will not stand against them."

Anna looked as though she wanted to say something, but Aeneas continued, smacking his fist into his open hand as he did so.

"And besides, King Latinus does not want war. It's his land and he accepts me as his heir. It is Prince Turnus who is causing the war, no doubt enraged by one of those same gods. I can guess which one, but I don't like to say.

"You want honesty from me, Anna? The truth is, I did not love your sister as much as I love my son. I did not love your sister at all. I admired her, and I liked her, and I did not want her to die. But she had her duty, the same as I had mine, and she chose not to carry it out. What has happened to Carthage, tell me that? She left it vulnerable to the very monsters she wished to protect it from."

Anna said nothing, her breast heaving. Eventually, she turned to Lavinia and said, "You see what sort of a man he is.

You know how wretched he has made me. How can you possibly marry him?"

Lavinia looked at Anna, at the emotion writ large on her face. Lavinia understood her pain, and yet, as she turned Aeneas's words over in her mind, she felt something inside herself harden. She couldn't shoulder everyone else's pain alongside her own. It was too heavy a load. "You say he told your sister he loved her; he says he did not. What is it to me? Aeneas is right. Your sister had a duty, and she neglected it. As long as women stand accused of being subject to their emotions, we will never be allowed to be rulers, like men."

Anna dropped her head. Lavinia wished she could take her words back; she did not wish to cause Anna pain when Anna had only ever been kind to her. She remembered Anna comforting her when her hair had been lopped off. Had it just been a ruse so Anna could poison her mind against Aeneas? She didn't think so.

Lavinia stepped forward to comfort Anna, to apologise. But before she could speak, Anna said, "My sister cursed you before she died, Aeneas. I reiterate that curse. You have killed both of us, and many more besides."

She turned and fled from the room. Aeneas and Lavinia were alone once more. Aeneas sank back onto his chair.

"My father only accepted you as his heir because he thought we would carry on his bloodline," Lavinia said quietly. Aeneas looked up, surprised; she thought he had forgotten she was there. "You lied to him."

"The gods lied to him," Aeneas said, but then he sagged back again. "And yes, I let him believe the lie. Why did you not say that to Anna and thus give her more rocks to throw at me?"

"I will, and to my father besides," she said, "Unless you fight Turnus," she said. "It is time to end this war."

He didn't reply, so she stood up and left with as much dignity as she could summon. Aeneas followed her out, but she walked quickly, and he did not try to catch up to her. When she returned to her hut later, Anna's belongings were gone.

☽

For the next couple of days, the war continued, and Lavinia's life settled into a new, dreary routine. Aeneas was leading the fight from the front, so she didn't see him. Anna didn't return.

At night, she struggled to sleep as her mind constantly went over the argument between Aeneas and Anna. Uncomfortably, she realised that while her heart sided with Anna, her head saw the logic in what Aeneas said. She had spent many years with her father, listening to his strategizing, plotting, and arranging, all in aid of ensuring that their kingdom remained safe.

Turnus, too, kept her awake. It was easy to blame the gods for his sudden rage and his need to defeat Aeneas. But had he really always been so lackadaisical before Aeneas arrived? Or had there been a latent aggressive streak in his character? She found herself reliving memories that were over ten years old, memories of Turnus playing at swordfights or building a dam or storming a fort. Had he needed to win, even then? Had he had a tendency to drink? She no longer knew, and she thought the constant re-examination would drive her mad. And after all, what difference did it make why he was behaving this way? Whatever his motivation, he needed to be stopped.

The war was changing. More casualties were being brought home every day. The mood among the soldiers had darkened. Women had started stealing away from the camp when they could. From what Lavinia could tell, the tide had turned, and they were now the losing side. She thought of what Aeneas had said, those gods on the battlefield, laughing at their victims. Greek gods, she thought with horror. Trojan gods. Not our gods. Gods brought here in Trojan ships to destroy us.

When she was walking about the campsite, she saw again Euryalus's mother, sitting on a low stool, clutching a doll. Lavinia wondered if she could ever understand what the woman was feeling, especially now she had been told she would have no children. The woman looked up and saw her and waved her over. Lavinia crossed to kneel by her side.

"Was this Euryalus's doll?" she asked tenderly. The woman started laughing.

"Oh no, Your Highness. Did you think I had lost my mind? It belongs to one of the little girls in the camp. The arm has come loose, and I said I would mend it."

Lavinia looked down at the toy, made out of rough clay. She thought it might be holding a shield, surely an inappropriate accessory for a little girl's plaything.

"It is hard for children, growing up in a place of war," she said.

"That it is," the woman agreed. "But Father Aeneas says this is the place we must be. The war cannot last much longer."

Lavinia looked at the woman and felt a new sort of anger surge up inside her. After all the deaths that had occurred, how could Aeneas still remain so stubborn? How could he cling to a code that had never applied on Latin soil?

"It will not," she said firmly. The woman looked questioningly at her. "Trust Mother Lavinia," she said, and rose to her feet and strode off.

☽

Aeneas quickly dismissed everyone from the strategy room when she asked him to, and he looked upon her with concern in his dark brown eyes. Lavinia remembered with a wrench how her father had tried and failed to dismiss these same warriors. But daughters could be strong when fathers were weak.

"I'm glad to see you, Lavinia." He coughed and looked away. "You haven't spoken to your father yet,"

"I have not," she said. "I'm not sure I need to. If I leave the camp, any Laurentine still fighting for you will leave your side immediately. You cannot defeat the Rutuli with Trojans alone."

"There aren't that many Laurentines still fighting," he replied bitterly. "But why do you care anyway? A loss for Troy is not a loss for your father."

"I think it will be," she said. "I do not see that Turnus will now stop at evicting the Trojans. He won't stop until he has conquered this entire realm, and more besides. You need to fight that duel."

Aeneas scowled. "We have been over this."

"You want to be the greatest Trojan hero," she replied. "You are sacrificing your people on the altar of your own vanity."

He looked surprised, but she continued, choosing the barb she knew would go deepest. "You can't keep Ascanius out of this war forever. What happens when Turnus decides to kill the great Aeneas's beloved son?"

"My mother will protect him," he said. "She wants to be the mother of a great nation."

"Perhaps she has more in common with my mother than I thought," Lavinia said drily, remembering her mother's inane ramblings about a throne for the mother of the queen. "Very well, Ascanius is protected. But do you think that every other parent cares less for their children than you do? Why should they all die just because the great Aeneas and his son have a different destiny?"

"I promised my wife," he said, his face pained. "I said I would take care of Ascanius."

"That doesn't mean you can't take care of everyone else," she said sharply. "How dare you criticise Anna's sister for leaving her own nation, when you are sending out mere boys to fight for you? They call you Father Aeneas. You are the commander of this force. Act like their father and end this war."

"Every man is responsible for his own kills on the battlefield," he protested. "Every man can earn glory through honest kills."

"That worked in Troy, but this is Latium," Lavinia said firmly. "In Latium, every kill is the commander's kill, and every death, one of the commander's children. The commander has a duty to his people. You are shirking your duty unless you end this war."

He was still for a long time. Neither of them moved. Then he looked at her and slowly nodded his head. "You speak to me as my wife once spoke to me. Very well. I will fight, and I will win."

"It is time to send word to Turnus," she said. She hoped he was right. She didn't know what would happen if he was wrong.

Aeneas nodded. He sent for a messenger and gave the necessary instructions. Together, Aeneas and Lavinia walked to Aeneas's hut. He would need to prepare for the battle ahead. He kissed her hand, then strode into the hut. Almost immediately he returned, his face glowing.

"Lavinia, I have a sign from the goddess. My mother has bestowed a gift on me."

"A gift?" she repeated, confused. But he pulled her into the room, and she gazed down at the most majestic suit of armour she had ever seen. The burnished copper gleamed seductively. The fierce sword was sharpened to a point, ready to penetrate the most unwilling flesh. And most magnificent of all, the shield.

Lavinia did not understand armour. She had never worn any, never cared to. But she could see that this shield, with its accomplished carvings, was a work of art.

"Where did it come from?" she whispered, awed.

"My mother will have appealed to her husband, the god of the furnace," Aeneas said proudly, and he stood a little taller. "She intends for me to win this fight, just as she intended for me to survive Troy."

Lavinia looked at the carvings on the shield. "These are beautiful," she said, pulling a finger across one delicately. "Look: here is a wolf nursing two babies. Is this a man being executed? He looks to be in agony, poor fellow. And so many scenes of fighting and war. Is this a naval battle?"

Aeneas nodded. "I do not recognise these scenes. Perhaps they are a sign of what is to come."

War and bloodshed, Lavinia thought. That is what the Trojans have brought to us. We have always been a peaceful kingdom. And now we are to be changed into something else, something I do not recognise.

Aeneas smiled at her. "Perhaps I need to distract you a little. You are always so ready to prevent me from going too deep into myself, but now it is you who looks morose."

Recollecting herself, she forced herself to smile at him.

"Not at all. I was just thinking that only a god could have carved something so beautiful. You must wear it with pride."

He nodded. "Of course, I will. Thank you, Lavinia."

☽

The response from Turnus came quickly; he was ready and willing to duel, the next day if possible. The duel was to take place on the battlefield.

The sun rose in the morning, and Aeneas was ready, dressed in his beautiful armour. Lavinia came to wish him well.

"It's a shame you won't be able to watch," Aeneas said. "Or perhaps you are relieved?"

Lavinia nodded and didn't answer him. She had no intention of missing the duel, and relying on messengers from the battlefield to tell her of progress. She had already arranged with Euryalus's mother that she would sit in the little crevice in the cliff overlooking the battle. Although Aeneas was certain that he would win, she disliked relying on the capriciousness of the gods, and she would need to act quickly if he lost.

Before he walked out onto the battlefield, Lavinia took Aeneas's face in her hands and kissed him. Surprised, he kissed her back. They clung together like two dying people, and thoughts passed through Lavinia's mind of the woman Aeneas had loved in Troy and the description that Anna had given her of Aeneas, bare-chested, waking up with Dido in a cave. It made no difference. As she pulled away, she felt nothing, and she could see Aeneas felt the same. Theirs was not to be a long marriage, nor was it to be a passionate one. No matter. She had all the rest of her life to discover passion.

She made her way to the cliff and tucked herself into her vantage point. No one knew she was there, but it still felt perilous to be this close to so many weapons and so many armoured men wielding those swords, and she wondered how Camilla had felt, taking her place among them. She had been told that she would be safe, that no matter who won, she would be queen, but now that she was actually beside the thick of fighting, she remembered how Aeneas had said that in battle there was no time to have consideration for the enemy, to look under the visor and see the person that you are fighting, and she shivered.

In the songs, she thought, the bards always told how nobles killed other nobles. Hektor was slain by Achilleus; Achilleus was slain by Paris. But some warriors must just get unlucky, and who was to say that a young soldier, Trojan or Latin, might not recognise her, and might kill her in error? Or that one of those cruel Trojan gods might decide to pull her from the cliff and dash her brains out on the rocks below. She shivered again.

The army moved aside to allow Aeneas to pass, and Lavinia could see Turnus's army doing the same from the other side. As Aeneas walked, he seemed to grow taller, stronger, more muscular. His skin and eyes began to glow. Had she ever doubted his divine parentage, she did not now. Turnus was younger than Aeneas by almost twenty years, and yet he seemed to pale and wither in comparison.

"Aeneas," Turnus called, seemingly intent on a battle of words beforehand. But Aeneas just raised his hand.

"I come to fight you, Turnus, as you asked. Let us begin."

The two men fought. First, they threw spears as they approached each other across the plain. Then, as they came closer, they switched to swords. Was Aeneas being aided by a goddess? Lavinia could not have said for sure. Certainly he seemed to be tireless where Turnus was wearying. Aeneas was strong where Turnus was weak; consistent where Turnus was erratic. But could that not be explained by his experience? Even his age, seemingly a weakness in the heat of battle, seemed an advantage now, as Turnus waved his sword but missed, danced around and wore himself out, and made mistakes that the elder swordsman would not. Finally, Turnus's sword hit Aeneas's new armour, and disaster struck. The sword shattered on impact, leaving Turnus brandishing only a sword hilt.

"Lavinia!" Turnus cried, and Lavinia cringed. "Lavinia, I am fighting for you! It has all been for you!" He took his eyes away from Aeneas, who promptly dealt him a blow that wounded his sword arm. Lavinia shook her head. She had never asked for Turnus's devotion.

Turnus began to run, chasing across the battlefield. He looked about wildly for her. "Is it so bad to die, Lavinia? Is it?"

Why was he calling to her? He didn't even know she was there, she thought with anguish, and clutched her stomach as though winded. To die . . . Camilla, Pallas, and now her mother, all dead. All dead because of their own choices. Was it so bad? She didn't know. All she knew was that in choosing Aeneas, she had chosen life for herself but death for Turnus.

Turnus tried to escape, but the Trojans blocked his way at every turn. Finally, a Rutulian ran towards Turnus and gave him a new sword. But it was too late. Aeneas hurled his great spear at him, and Turnus sank to the ground.

Lavinia closed her eyes and muttered a short prayer to the gods, that his be the last death, but she didn't know to whom she was praying anymore. To her own household gods? To Venus, that tubby local goddess who cared for romance and babies? Or to the gods that Aeneas had brought with him, the gods of fire, who seemed to hate and love mortals in equal measure and let them dance with swords for entertainment?

For a moment it seemed as though Aeneas was going to grant mercy to Turnus.

"Please," Turnus gasped. "Please, give me back to my people. Send me back to my home. I will not fight any further."

Aeneas wavered, but the sun moved from behind a cloud, and Turnus's armour, bedecked with the spoils of Trojan warriors and of the young Pallas, glinted as though it were on fire. With a wordless cry, Aeneas lifted his sword into the air and plunged it into Turnus's body. There was silence. Lavinia held her breath.

Aeneas had won. He stood over Turnus's body and raised his sword aloft, then stepped back and allowed his men to strip Turnus's body of its armour.

Lavinia let out a long, ragged breath. The battle was over, and now she wanted to cry. She looked down on the field at Turnus and saw that death had softened his features once more. He was no longer the angry drunkard, but the young boy who had composed songs for her and had never been brave enough to sing them.

Pallas, Camilla, Lausus, Turnus, and Lavinia. Once an inseparable quintet, but now only Lavinia survived. It was almost too much for her to bear. Pallas and Camilla she wished she had acted sooner in order to save. But Turnus—was she not as responsible for his death as Aeneas? Aeneas had known that his mother could and would protect him from anything, no matter the cost to others. But Aeneas was little more than the sword that Lavinia had wielded. She had used her intellect, her words, her powers of persuasion, and she had ensured that Aeneas had fought and won the duel.

It was an intoxicating thought.

She turned her attention back to Aeneas, resplendent in victory. *At least Turnus put up a fight,* she thought. Who was to say whether the goddess had assisted Aeneas or if it was one of the honest victories he was so proud of? She leaned forward and listened intently, seeing that Aeneas was about to make a speech.

"Rutulians," Aeneas called. "Laurentines. All those of you who fought for Turnus. You know the grounds of this duel. We agreed, Turnus and I, that the winner would take Latium, and the winner would marry the princess Lavinia. Lavinia has already agreed to be my bride. But now I say to you, no man will be judged for deciding to fight on Turnus's side. I intend to build a new, magnificent city, named for the fair princess Lavinia, and I will need all your help to build it. I will not ask whether you fought for Trojans or for Rutulians. All will be united in Lavinium."

Lavinia listened to the sounds of the cheering crowd. Lavinium. The city of Lavinia. She would have no children, and yet every Latin would be her child. And what would her place be in that city? The wife, then the widow of Aeneas. The stepmother of Ascanius, a boy who would need guidance when his father died. Something opened up inside her, a world of possibilities she hadn't dared believe in until now.

☽

Messengers were dispatched to the palace to let Latinus know that Aeneas had won and that Aeneas and Lavinia would be returning home. There was no longer any talk of maintaining a separate camp. In defeating Turnus, Aeneas had asserted his leadership over the entirety of Latium. Laurentum, too, would be his, and so would the palace. If Latinus objected, he would need to raise his own army, but Lavinia knew her father would never dare.

She walked through the war camp already being dismantled, and smiled to see that her own hut had been taken down. She felt a strange nostalgia for it, her feelings of hatred dissipating even as the wooden slats were being packed away for use elsewhere. She decided to take one last trip to the river, to hold her hand in the cool water, before she returned to the palace and a world of servants drawing her hot baths.

As she strolled down, she had to jump aside to avoid crashing into a Laurentine man running towards the camp, shouting and waving his arms.

"The river," he gasped as he ran past her. "The river has been polluted."

Lavinia raced towards the river. Longer legs thundered past her, and she saw it was Aeneas who threw his arm back as they reached the banks, as though to block her vision, but it was a futile gesture. In one glance, she saw everything: the small group of Trojans and Laurentines clustered besides the water, and floating amidst the sea grass, long strands of reddish-brown hair. Again, Aeneas tried to thrust himself in front of Lavinia, but she pushed him aside and ran to kneel down in the shallow, muddy water. Everyone else moved back from her as she placed her hand under the chilly water to draw out a blanched hand. The only sound anyone could hear was the shrill calls of birds as Lavinia sat with Anna's hand in her lap, gazing into the distance and seeing nothing.

☽

Hours passed. Lavinia did not move. Food and drink were brought to her, both of which she refused. A blanket was draped around her shoulders, and she didn't resist. The sound of lapping water made her aware that she was sitting in the clammy river, but she couldn't feel it. Aeneas himself approached her and asked her to return to the camp, but his voice was little more than a mosquito buzzing in her ear, and she ignored him.

It was impossible to shake the idea that somehow this was her fault. If she had done something—anything—differently, Anna might still be alive today. She remembered her sitting bolt upright, calling on the gods to help her tell her stories. Would stories now be told about Anna? She had been a princess, just like Creusa and Dido and Camilla. Just like Lavinia.

As though from a great distance, she heard the elders of the camp agreeing that Anna must have tripped and fallen, perhaps knocked her head on a branch, and drowned accidentally in the murky waters. Almost certainly this had happened farther up, where the waters were deeper, and this was why it had taken several days for the body to wash up near the camp. Lavinia felt a strange desire to laugh. What difference did it make to Anna now whether she had tripped accidentally or, as was more likely to be the case, she had killed herself? But then she realised that their concern was not for Anna, but the river, which would be polluted by a suicide.

Her eyes adjusted as the light dimmed around her. Now Anna looked more as Lavinia remembered her, green eyes glinting in the half dark of their cabin. If Lavinia squinted, she could imagine that Anna was only sleeping, even though her skin had taken on an unnatural pallor, and her limbs had begun to harden.

She felt herself being raised to her feet, and once again strong arms wrapped around her.

"Would you like me to fetch your father?" Aeneas asked.

She shook her head. "No. Aeneas, please take me back to the palace now. And make sure she has a proper burial."

She felt his chin move against her forehead, and realised he was nodding.

"Yes, of course."

"Goodbye, Anna," Lavinia whispered as she left, leaning on Aeneas as she was becoming accustomed to do. "May your spirit find peace in this river, as you did not find peace in life."

She thought she heard the river murmur in response.

Epilogue

In Elysium, Creusa watched as Turnus made his way across the river Styx, escorted by the grim ferryman. Turnus had the slightly dazed look that all new shades had. Soon, she was sure, he would drink from the waters of the river Lethe, and his earthly life would become a distant memory. Drinking was supposed to be mandatory, but there was no time limit within which consumption needed to take place, and some shades kept their memories, their earthly ties and their joys and grievances, for several generations. Young men always drank quickly, unable to bear the immediate recollection of their strong, taut bodies compared to the mere wisps they now found themselves to be. Paris, for instance, shot by Philoctetes before the Greeks had withdrawn from Troy, had had no idea who Creusa was when she joined him in Elysium. But then, he hadn't always remembered who she was in life either.

She had not drunk. She wanted to remember. She wanted to know. She knew this desire wouldn't last forever, but the horror that she felt whenever she remembered that last night, her feet pounding and her throat burning as she darted through the streets of Troy, desperate to catch up to Aeneas, even as she knew she never would, faded away in comparison to her joy when she thought of the fate she had secured for Ascanius.

Aeneas had cried when she had told him what needed to be done. She'd felt pity for him then, but he had to be made to understand. So she told him what Cassandra had seen. The city on fire, and Creusa lost in the smoke. But she would not suffer. He must not go back for her. No matter what, he needed to take his father and their son and lead them out of Troy. If he could do this, Ascanius's future was secured. But if not, Ascanius would be at the mercy of the Greeks, and the Greeks had not shown any mercy so far.

She held her husband and forced him to look into her eyes, the eyes their son had inherited from her, and swear on all he held dear that he would rescue Ascanius. And she had been right to do so; soon after she had arrived in Hades, she had seen Andromache's son, little Scamandrius, so small that he didn't even need to drink from Lethe to forget. Odysseus, she later discovered, had thrown his tiny body over the walls of Troy with little more regard than if he had been a ragdoll. She remembered what Cassandra had said about the Greeks being driven by more than politics—by an innate hatred—and she had to agree with her. She avoided Greek warriors, even those who had drank of the waters and knew nothing of the Trojan War to which they had given their lives.

She sometimes regretted missing Aeneas when he'd visited the Underworld. He had seemed so virile and dynamic, and she was nothing more than a shadow, so she thought it best to see him when they were both shades. What seemed like a long time, like a lifetime in the mortal world, passed so quickly here anyway. She had watched with amusement, though, as Dido, her supposed rival, had allowed Aeneas to see herself, but then floated away again, her nose in the air. She never came near Creusa, preferring to pretend she didn't exist. Dido and Aeneas, a love story for the generations. If only it weren't for his first wife, ruining the narrative.

Old Anchises had not been especially happy about Aeneas's time with Dido either, which amused her. Anchises, of whom she had always been fond, spent a lot of time with her these days. Her father-in-law had also refused to drink, as, like many of the older shades, he preferred to look back on his memories. But he had rather piously recast himself as an elder statesman and adviser to his beloved son, and it was hard to see in him the beautiful youth who had once fathered a child on the promiscuous goddess Aphrodite.

Perhaps an even greater irony was the fact that the war had ensured that even in death, Creusa was still surrounded by her siblings. So many of her brothers had preceded her, including Polydorus, who had never been allowed on the battlefield but had been slain by the Greek king who had promised to take care of him. Polydorus's fate had alarmed her; they had all thought he was safe. Despite Cassandra's reassurance of Ascanius's destiny once he left Troy, Creusa often drifted as close as possible to the river Styx, to see the hazy outlines of the living and to gather information from the newly dead. So far, Aeneas seemed to have chosen only trustworthy men to protect her own child. Polyxena had arrived soon after Creusa, sacrificed to the Greek fighter Achilleus, as much a monster in death as he had been in life.

After those two had arrived, their mother, Hekuba, joined them, having gained vengeance on Polydorus's killer, aided by Odysseus the merciless, of all people. Now she was usually to be found sitting with her two youngest children, one on either side of her, clutching them in her arms as though she thought that even in the land of death, death could somehow take them from her once more.

Neither Helen nor Andromache, Creusa's most renowned sisters-in-law, had joined her yet. Helen's absence did not surprise her; she was a survivor to her very core, and Creusa did not expect to see her until she died of old age in her bed. But that Andromache continued to live did shock Creusa, and when she saw Hektor playing with the small shade that had once been Scamandrius, she wondered how his mother could bear to go on living.

But now Creusa had reason to rejoice because she had seen in the Styx that Aeneas had defeated Turnus, and she knew that meant that in three short years, the gift her mother-in-law had promised to bestow would finally be hers. Aeneas was not to be taken up to Olympus to live with the gods, but would come and join her in Elysium. In time, their son would join them. The other promises that were made for Ascanius in the meantime were of little consequence to her. Let his divine grandmother bask in the reflected glory of the founding of an empire that would last over a thousand years. Let Ascanius complete his great deeds and pass the torch on, in his turn, to the next heir of Venus, and onwards through so many generations of formidable men. She was his mother, and she cared only that he was safe. Ascanius, her little lion.

And then, with her beloved family by her side, she would drink of the waters of forgetfulness. Together they would dismiss all their earthly worries, and as shades, enjoy for all time the quiet existence that had been denied them in life.

Author's Note

I first learned about Aeneas in my sixth form Classical Studies class, on reading Virgil's *Aeneid* (in translation) for the first time. It was something of a shift, as we had just been learning about ancient philosophy, and it took the class a little while to understand we didn't have to question absolutely everything; not all ancient literature takes the form of a Socratic dialogue. Then, like many a student, I was enthralled by the story of Dido and Aeneas, less interested in the almost invisible Lavinia, and perhaps glossed over some of the battle scenes. The received wisdom was that Virgil, like other Roman authors, had taken a minor character from Homer's *Iliad* and given him leading man status, transforming him from Homeric Hero to Roman Hero, and cementing Rome's status as the successor to Troy.

When I began to research this book, though, and reread the *Iliad*, with a focus on Aeneas, I questioned the received wisdom. Aeneas is second only to great Hektor as a defender of Troy. He is the first to charge Achilleus when Achilleus, insane with grief, returns to the battlefield to avenge Patroklus. How different might the battle have been had Aeneas's mother, the goddess Aphrodite, not spirited him away to safety? Far from being a minor character, Aeneas is the son of a goddess, a mighty hero, and has already been prophesied to found the new Troy. (He was also already disliked by Priam, no doubt for exactly those reasons).

The Heir of Venus is not a retelling of the *Aeneid*. Rather, it is a retelling of the story of Aeneas, whose story can be found in

Ovid actually used his story
three times: in the *Metamorphoses*; in the *Heroides*, a letter pur-
porting to be from the wronged Dido to Aeneas; and in the *Fasti*,
which contains the lesser known myth that Anna, Dido's sister,
was a reluctant visitor to the Trojan camp in Latium. Anna's end,
which is only hinted at in *The Heir of Venus*, is perhaps more
positive than her story thus far: she was transformed into a water
goddess of the stream she loves so much in *The Heir of Venus*.
In one version of the myth, Aeneas himself is transformed after
death into a god of the same river, but I preferred to think of him
being reunited with his first wife, Creusa. Lavinia's fate is rather
more open-ended; while the line of the kings of Latium, ances-
tors of the emperors of Rome, passes from Aeneas to Ascanius,
one version of the myth provides that he was succeeded by his
brother Silvius, Lavinia and Aeneas's son, while another version
has Lavinia married to Ascanius in order to be the mother of
his children, including his son, Silvius, and take her part in the
lineage that way.

As always, the conflicting stories means that a modern nov-
elist's job is not to present all possible options, but instead to
find a narrative. Among the modern sources I read, I credit
Venus and Aphrodite (Hughes, 2020) with the idea that the Latin
Venus may have been more of a fertility goddess than a beautiful
icon. *Women in Ancient Greece* (Blundell, 1995) added a lot of
the colour around weddings and childbirth, although I do note
that the myths take place in prehistoric Greece, not fifth-century
Greece. Any errors, as always, are mine.

I would always encourage anyone who wants to know more
about the myths themselves to read further and, in particular, to
read the ancient sources themselves. We are living in a golden age
of female translators, which can mean a fresh look at the texts.

One perhaps more unusual source for *The Heir of Venus* was the poetry of Sappho, translated by Anne Carson. In the poem fragment numbered 44, she describes the homecoming of Hektor and Andromache. It is delightful to read of a Trojan celebration, instead of the more usual focus on Troy's downfall, and I hope I have infused some of that joy into the scene in *The Heir of Venus*, where it is seen from Creusa's perspective. I will confess, though, that when it came to the *Aeneid*, I continued to read and reread the David West translation I first studied in sixth form all those years ago, coming full circle on my own journey with Aeneas.

Acknowledgments

Even more so than a first book, a second book is a team effort, and I couldn't have asked for a better team.

As always, my lifelong gratitude to my agent Nelle Andrew, who is with me on every step of my writing journey and always knows when to step in and assist, sometimes even before I realise I'm floundering. The support of the team at Rachel Mills Literary Ltd., and in particular Charlotte Bowerman and Alexandra Cliff, is also much appreciated.

Thank you to the team at Alcove Books. Tara Gavin, my editor, has supported, encouraged, and guided me through the process, from brief synopsis to finished novel. Katie Ponder designed the exquisite cover. Mikaela Bender, Dulce Botello, Mia Bertrand, Stephanie Manova, Megan Matti, Rebecca Nelson, Thaisheemarie Fantauzzi Pérez, Doug White, and Matthew Martz all contributed their expertise, skills, and talent to the book you hold in your hands today.

Thank you also to the team at Sphere, my UK publisher. Rosanna Forte has worked tirelessly and patiently to draw out the very best possible work. The team, consisting of Brionee Fenlon (marketing); Gabriella Drinkald (publicity); Hannah Wood (cover design); Frances Rooney (managing editorial); Tom Webster (production); and Hannah Methuen, Caitriona Row, and Ginny Mašinović (sales), have again worked seamlessly and professionally to give *The Heir of Venus* the best possible opportunity in the UK market.

Ms. Heath of Mt. Roskill Grammar School first introduced me to Virgil's *Aeneid* and instilled the passion that led to this book over twenty years later. My thanks again to Doctor Sarah Burton and Professor Jem Poster, both great teachers from whom I learn more every time we meet. Thank you to Helen McVeigh, who patiently teaches me Classical Greek over the internet each week—I have absorbed so much in the short time we have been working together. Thank you to her colleague, Lynn Gordon, who fielded my questions about Greek language and nationality in Italy in the time of Aeneas, and saved me from making some horrendous mistakes (it goes without saying that any mistakes remaining are my own.) Thank you to Clare Worley, who is now not just my friend, but my children's honorary aunt and godmother.

Thank you to everyone whose support for *Phaedra* paved the way for *The Heir of Venus*. Thanks to the 2023 Debuts group, who understand the perils and pleasures of launching that first novel. I'm not sure whether we stayed sane together or went insane together, but I know I couldn't have navigated that first year nearly so well without you, and I am immensely proud to be part of the group and to continue to celebrate our successes (and commiserate our frustrations) together. Huge, huge thanks to the booksellers who supported *Phaedra*, especially James from Canterbury; Dan from Clifton; Sorcha from Cambridge; David Headley and team from Goldsboro, who also created the beautiful special edition and hosted my wonderful launch party; and the team at David's in Letchworth, my own local independent bookshop, which we are so lucky to have. Thank you to the members of the Hitchin Book Club, who have been so hugely supportive of my literary endeavours. I always enjoy our discussions, and you may even recognise that one of our conversations indirectly led to one of the themes of this book. And thank you to everyone who read and shared your enjoyment of *Phaedra,* from the generous established authors who shared their blurbs, to the reviewers and book bloggers, and finally to the readers. Without readers, there is no need for writers, so I thank you from the bottom of my heart.

Thank you always to my family, my mum, my dad, and my sister Emily and her family, whose support from the other side of the world keeps me strong. Thank you to my best-loved husband, Steven, whose own unfailing dedication to his family, his work, and his faith inspires and motivates me. He also provided the copious amounts of chocolate and tea that went into this novel. And finally, my own cherished little lion cubs, Amelia Joan and Lucian John, who astonish and amaze me daily. I love you all.

Discussion Group Questions

1. Aeneas makes no secret of the fact that his mother, Venus, is a goddess, but does he see it as a blessing or a burden? What do you think?

2. Lavinia, Creusa, and Dido are all princesses, but their position and power in their respective kingdoms are very different. How does their level of power affect their choices?

3. One of the themes of the novel is the need for sacrifice in order to be an effective ruler—or parent. What sacrifices must each of the characters make to achieve their needs?

4. With which of Aeneas's three wives did you empathise the most? With which did you empathise the least?

5. Perhaps the most famous of Aeneas's wives is the woman he didn't consider to be a wife, Dido. What do you think about the decisions that she made? If you knew in advance about Dido's fate, did you have more or less understanding about her choices having read her sections in *The Heir of Venus*?

6. Dido's sister, Anna, encourages her in the decisions she makes. Do you think she bears any of the responsibility for Dido's choices? Does this affect your view of her dealings with Lavinia?

7. Each of the three wives, as well as Dido's sister, Anna, has her own opinion on Aeneas himself. Did you feel that one woman came closest to the truth?

8. Aeneas is famed for being a character in both the *Iliad* and the *Aeneid*, a Trojan hero, renowned for individual valour and glory, who becomes a Roman hero, renowned for patriotism, order, and loyalty. Can you see characteristics of each kind of hero in Aeneas?

9. Lavinia is offered a choice: marry Turnus or marry Aeneas. What do her two suitors represent? Do you agree with her choice?

10. What does Creusa take from the story about the fox cubs and the lion cubs (an Aesop's fable)? Why do you think storytellers were banned from telling her that story? How does it affect her relationship with her own son, Ascanius?